I0847423

Hey girl, hey!

Let's have a kiki.

This is a work of extreme horror.

It's bloody.

It's violent.

It's gross.

It's offensive.

Like your mother's haircut in her twenties. You've seen the pictures.

Ask her if THAT was a phase and see how she likes it.

Anyhoo, if you enjoy extreme horror, you picked a winner, baby.

If you don't . . . consider this your WARNING. A full trigger list is located at the back.

If you've made it this far . . . prepare your undercarriage and let's start the show.

We're about to have a gay old time!

Passive-aggressively Yours,

Phrique

Halloween 2022

"Coming to the stage, everyone, *Miss* Gamble Donna Phart!"

The audience cheered. A few feeble boos wafted from the "ugly section."

"Ohhhh, be nice!" a lone, shrill voice rang out above the turmoil.

It was the fishy drag queen's time to shine, but the recalled screams ricocheted through her pulsating skull. A flash of the pools of gore she sloshed through to get onstage shook her reserve. The bottoms of her platform heels were still slick with blood, leaving a ruby red procession behind her. Reliving the final body landing in the pile disoriented her, causing her to stumble into the spotlight.

Like a newborn fawn, her green eyes seemed equally lost in the proverbial headlights. Stage lights gleamed off the ornate details of her bronze headdress and chest piece, creating galaxies in her vision. The lighting, combined with camera phone flashes, blinded her to anything beyond the bright, elevated stage.

Gamble's fractured mind begged the up-and-coming drag queen to peer behind her to make sure no one had followed her onstage. She willed the ruminating thoughts away, instead tightening her smile, lifting her chin, and pulling her shoulders back. She steeled her nerves and sashayed down the catwalk. The flowy white fabric from her dress and sleeves undulating around her as if she hired wind fans to blow on her at all times.

"Miss Thang is giving us Akasha realness tonight, y'all!" piped the MC. "Queen of the Daaaamned!" Gamble could feel the echo and reverb ripple around the auditorium and through her blindingly white teeth.

The MC hyped, "Shots fired!"

The bronze and white on her gown looked stunning against the skin of the golden goddess. The doll babies gushed when they noticed the intricate red beaded embellishment that resembled an arterial spray on the otherwise immaculately white fabric. Those lucky enough to be nearest to the stage noticed the "beads" on her skirt began to trickle farther down the impeccably styled garment. Gamble eyed her mark at the end of the catwalk. She twirled into position, propelling specks of blood and brain matter flecking onto the stage.

She somehow maintains her smile. The little focus she has left is dissipating. She fights the urge to scan the crowd for the active threat. Try as she might, she can no longer mask the trepidation bleeding onto her captivating face. She turns to face the crowd once more and her eyes align with those of the killer. The plague behind it all, smiling back at her with that sharp, devilish grin. The scourge intent on ruining her big chance, shattering her life, sabotaging her entire drag career. Everything Gamble worked so hard for dashed away by the one true Queen. Her entombed fury exhumed, her visage cracking into mirrored shards. Gamble's vision blurred as her neurons flickered like the stage lights above her. Her knees felt like melted wax held them in place. She crumbled, staring incredulously as the killer's grin dissolved into hysterical laughter, their hands dripping blood and impunity.

All her good Judies[1] were dead. Gamble, forsaken, as the Queen willed it so. She watched her world dissolve as her vision skewed and her weary body crumpled to the floor. The blood collected on her heels skidded onto the stage. Her final thought was, *You can't return scuffed shoes.* The spectators-turned-witnesses gay-gasped in horror at the realization that this wasn't part of the show. A shriek resonated backstage. The stage lights all unceremoniously flickered into darkness. The show was over. That's all, folks.

The last words Gamble heard was the MC howling, "Hes, Shes, and Theys! We've got a death drop! Death Drop!"

---

1. good friends

GIG OF THE DAMNED

Copyright © 2024 Phrique

Edited by Danielle Yeager, Hack & Slash Editing

Cover by Jeremy Lopez @neonclownart

Formatted by Phrique

ASIN : B0D13K7J2Z

Contents

The Breeders Glossary

WHETHER YOU ARE NEW to drag or just need a refresher. Drag culture has its own rules, customs, and lingo. So check yourself, Loretta.

- Good Judy: (noun) good friend

- Trade: (noun) casual sex partner of a gay/bisexual man, usually "straight"

- Pay Dust: (verb) deliberately ignoring someone

- Lewk: (noun) a bold/creative style or aesthetic

- Shook, shookness: (verb, noun) shock

- Beat: (verb, noun) perfectly done makeup, "beat" with a makeup sponge

- Twink: (noun) a young-looking gay man with a slender build

- Kaikai: (noun, verb) sex between drag queens, usually in drag

- Give Cheekbone: (verb) a passive-aggressive air kiss on the cheek with an eye roll

- Drag Mother: (noun) drag queen mentor

- Bake: (noun, verb) applying concealer/loose powder and letting it sit or "bake" so it sets better

- Eat It: (verb) eat their hearts out, especially when feeling confident

- Tea: (noun) the truth/news/info

- Bone Collector: (noun) gossip/secrets to hold on to for later use

- Gooped: (verb) amazed, stunned, shocked

- Shout the House Down Boots: (verb) enthusiastic approval and excitement

- Mopping: (verb) stealing

Dedication

Dedicated to the LGBTQIA+ community, but especially the drag community. To all the queens who blow kisses in the faces of those who wish to subdue them. They hate what they don't understand, yet it entices them. You will conquer and defeat your foes effortlessly, looking gorgeous while doing so.

tongue pop

Gamble Donna Phart
Chapter 1

OCTOBER 21, 2022, **THURSDAY**

"Fake blood is so played," quipped Roger zestfully. "Just slice up some poor innocent trade[1] and use the real shit."

"You are fucked in the head, you know that, right?" said Antonio as he and his pasty roommate were perusing the Halloween pop-up store aisles. "I thought that one girl you went to school with did beadwork. Didn't she do a piece for Mulva Vagenstein last year?"

Roger clicked his tongue in reply while looking at the hanging masks. "She isn't cheap, sweetie, and you are barely making rent as it is. Miss Mulva Vagenstein might could afford her, but not Miss Gamble Donna Phart."

Antonio mockingly pushed his longtime fair-weather friend and roommate into a rack of costumes. "Not this month, at least." A look of defeat came across his emerald green eyes. "We have expensive tastes on a Top Ramen budget. There's nothing wrong with aiming higher for ourselves."

"There is something wrong with referring to *yourselves* in the third person, though," Roger retorted, putting a hockey mask to his face. It blended seamlessly with his alabaster skin and its shiny, pockmarked texture. His face reminded Antonio of dimpled focaccia before it went into the oven. "It's bad enough most of y'all are crazy as it is. At least try and hide it better." He pulled the mask away from his disgusted face. "That smells like balls."

"You'd know," spat Antonio as they made their way to the props section. "Dribblin' Dicks never got back to me for another interview. They made it sound like I was overqualified for having my pharmacy tech certification. Heaven forbid a

---

1. casual sex partner of a gay man, usually "straight"

bartender have anything else going for them."

Roger was placing a diamond necklace close to Antonio's neck. The stage jewelry shimmered just like the real thing against his tanned skin. Roger scrunched his nose, made eye contact with Antonio, and mouthed the words "Too classy" before grabbing another piece of fake jewelry. "Wasn't that the job interview that you also showed up late to, after not getting home from the gig till an hour beforehand?"

"It was worth it to see the look on Yanita's face when she found out I was filling her slot that night. You should have heard the crowd."

Roger and his 2002 frosted tips snickered. "Who hasn't filled that slot?"

"YOU BITCH!" cackled Antonio, caught off guard by the comment. An outraged soccer mom with an inverted bob hissed and quickly moved her child to the next aisle.

Roger hissed back, "Oh, calm down, Karen. It's fucking Halloween." The mood now soured, they only had a few minutes before Karen inevitably called the police.

"I'm not seeing anything good. Not like I have any money anyway."

Roger whispered loud enough for the whole store to hear, "Sweetie, you know I can spot you if you really need it. Maybe if I didn't know it was going toward lace fronts and breastplates, at least."

"No spank you, I won't be needing your white savior powers too soon. Not until after Halloween, at least." Antonio raised his arm and gave his best pageant wave as he walked down the store aisle. "When I *win* the Miss Trick'd and Treated Pageant, with the prize money and the tips alone, I will be set for life . . . or at least the next month or so."

Roger didn't hide his doubt well, but he still responded in a cheery tone, "That's my girl, stay positive and delusional." He took a last look at the costumes on an endcap. "Are you sure you will be okay without me for two weeks? Who will you get to schlep all your shit to the gig the night of? My hamstring still hurts from the last time." He rubbed the back of his Express jeans, just below where his buttocks should have been.

"Oh, don't worry, honey, I'll find another sucker to help me." Antonio started heading to the front of the store before sassily flashing his manicure in Roger's face." Maybe I'll have an entourage by then who realizes that these hands aren't meant for manual labor."

"Well, Mom said she'll miss you." Roger sounded sincere *for once*, eyeing the Halloween candy display. "You know she still just thinks you like to dress up as Barbie for Halloween? I don't have the strength to tell her why her honorary-adopted son buys rolls of duct tape by the dozen."

"Bless Mama Trudy's heart. She's the mother I never had," Antonio said, his eyes downcast. "The only one who'd ever have me, anyway." The front door opened and closed. The cardboard witch cutout crudely taped to it danced in the breeze. Antonio's eyes began to water as the malevolent creature seemed to come to life, glaring in his direction. Her form seemed to balloon off the flat door, her head and shoulders propelling her body forward. Her severe stare was filled with hate. Looking disapprovingly at him, his lifestyle, him wasting his life playing dress-up as a career. Her mesmerizing green eyes, the eyes she passed on to him, turned black and sinister before they flickered into flames. They threatened to burn a hole in his head if he didn't look away.

His lip quivered and his bladder threatened to empty right then and there, when he caught his breath and rationalized the situation. Roger was still speaking but Antonio couldn't recognize any of the words coming out of his mouth. The blurred edges of the enchantress in the doorway reverted back into cardboard as his body fought his spellbound state. Through tears and gritted teeth, he croaked out, "I'm glad you're dead," before snapping back to the real world, back to the dusty Halloween shop.

"Ugh, bitch, let's go!" piped Roger as he thrust his middle finger toward Inverted Bob, interrupting her heated conversation with the manager, and pulled Antonio into the sunlight.

Antonio stumbled out of the darkened store, blinded by the sun. He rubbed his eyes as he ran into an angry skeleton in Old Navy sandals. "Hey, watch where you're fucki—" He paused.

"Hey, wait," Old Navy Sandals said. "Aren't you . . . Gamble Fart something?"

Antonio's vision cleared as he noticed he and a total stranger nearly embraced on a street corner. He couldn't help but turn and beam in his shady friend's direction. "Gamble Donna Phart, in the flesh."

"Ay, Papi," the little Puerto Rican scarecrow said coquettishly. "God bless your eyes!"

Antonio wiped the last of his tears away, still smiling. "Thank you, honey. I love to meet a fan."

"I'm a fan of you, but not your name. Why a name about caca? I think you are better than that," chided this stranger he'd never met in his life.

"She isn't," Roger interjected. "I said the same thing. Anyway, we have to get going. You said you would help me pack, bitch."

Not one to miss an opportunity, Antonio turned on the charm and asked, "Will you come see me perform on Halloween at the Trick'd and Treated Pageant? Tickets are still on sale, Daddy."

The spicy little man took the bait, baring his jack-o'-lantern smile and said, "I promise, Mama, as long as you promise to murder the competition."

Annoyed at this public display of attention, Roger pulled his roommate away from the odd stranger.

Antonio gave in but looked back at his new number one fan, blew him a kiss, and yelled back, "They're as good as dead!"

Dyna Fyre
Chapter 2

O**CTOBER 21, 2022, THURSDAY**

"Dyna Fyre?" clucked the patron. "That's horrible!"

A suspiciously large woman pushed her way through the crowd. With her red and black ombre wig teased to the rafters and a billowing red-sequined chiffon dress, she made her way to the dressing rooms from the bar and chuckled, "I *am* horrible, sweetie." The large lass raised her voice. "Move it or lose it, sisters. Make way for the talent! Dyna Fyre coming through!" The patrons parted like the *Read* Sea, hoping their toes didn't get trampled by the Amazon's clomping black cha-cha heels or swallowed whole by her layers of red ruffles.

"Wow, that's so rude," said the lone cherubic face of a twentysomething with a bridal headpiece and mini veil among a group of bridesmaids seated next to the stage. The crowd oohed as Dyna's heels did an about-face and headed their way. She snatched the mic off the DJ stand, tapped it to see if it was on, then barked, "Well what do we have here? A bridal party? On a Thirsty Thursday at Flamin' Mo's? Well, that was certainly a choice now, wasn't it?" She strutted in front of the stage. The spotlight fired up and centered on her stunning mug.

"Don't we love it when straight girls invade our safe space, get drunk off two drinks, and then barely tip the talent when the time comes?" She held the mic out so the oohs of the crowd echoed off the poster-covered brick walls of the scene's most popular drag bar.

"Hello, sweetie. I'm Dyna Fyre. I'm rude, I'm horrible, and I'm the headliner for Thirsty Thursdays . . . Little Miss Bride-to-Be. So just remember that you are a guest here and be on your best behavior, 'cause I'm not afraid to check a bridezilla if she needs it." Dyna downed the last of her drink and grinned.

"But I don't think we are going to have ANY problems from that corner tonight, so let's get back to the celebration. The ATM is down in front, girlies, and I just *know* the tips are going to be flowing tonight," she smirked. "Now, if you'll excuse me, I need to freshen up. But I'll be back and we are READY to set this mutha on fire tonight! Can I get a HOT DAMN?" The crowd yelled back "HOT DAMN" in adoration and excitement as Dyna bowed.

She made her way backstage, passing a few other queens on their way out. The wafting sweet pea body spray almost choked her. She stopped to hug Elektra Komplex but paid the rest of them dust.[1] She entered the main dressing room, seeing only two other girls, to her relief. "Hey girl," Dyna said as she walked past. "Damn, these boots were *not* made for walkin'."

Edema Kanklez stifled her laughter. "I heard that. These wedges are cutting off my circulation." Miss Kanklez checked herself in the mirror, puckered her plum lips, capped her lipstick, and shuffled toward the door. She left a Snickers wrapper and her phone charger on her station. "But as the ringleader said to the clowns, the show must go on! I'll see y'all out there." With that, she and her velvet jumpsuit sauntered to the main stage.

Dyna didn't have enough time to give her dogs any air to breathe, just a quick makeup touch-up before her big number. It was hard being the headliner, but it was a role she was born to play. Her back ached daily from having to carry all this talent around. There were a lot of girls who wanted to be in her place, but she earned it through hard work, determination, and a *lot* of duct tape. She powdered a few shiny spots on her face and uncapped the aerosol can next to her. The figure in the last makeup station stood and made her way toward "the talent," her heels tapping the linoleum.

While Dyna was applying a final layer of setting spray, she couldn't take her eyes off the pink rhinestone-studded ski mask coming her way. The silent trench coat-donned drag queen came closer, making Dyna question this queen's identity as she side-eye studied her features. She finally turned to face her. "Damn, girl, that's quite a lewk[2] you got going on tonight." She gazed into her familiar eyes and gave her the up-and-down inspection.

"Somebody got a BeDazzler for Christmas, huh?" Before she could chuckle at

---

1. deliberately ignoring someone

2. a bold/creative style or aesthetic

her own joke, a flash of steel zipped across her neck. Dyna Fyre turned back to the mirror as her eyes bulged to a ridiculous level. Blood began pouring down her chest, her eyes not leaving the masked assailant. The pink pantheress slinked across the room to lock the door.

Dyna attempted to stand, but the disbelief that her life force was draining out of her derailed all rational thought. She felt no pain, only adrenaline, as the woman came back with the straight razor still in hand. Unable to speak, unable to ask why her good Judy had done this to her, she took a swing at her hot pink face. The punch was weak and barely connected, but it was enough to throw her attacker off. Dyna turned to face her, knocking a slew of detritus from her station onto the pooling blood below her.

The identity of the attacker finally surfaced to the top of her haze of shookosity.[3] She threw her shoulder into her old friend, knocking the weapon out of her attacker's hand before the momentum caused her to topple to the floor. With Dyna's hand around her gaping neck, her vision started going blurry. Her face contorted in pain. She was only able to utter a forced whisper, "Why?"

Reality was escaping her as time felt like a trippy fever dream. With a grin that froze the dying queen on the spot, the pink attacker picked up Dyna's setting spray as well as her lighter. *This shit synthetic* was Dyna's last coherent thought as the makeshift flamethrower doused her in puffs of orange. Before Dyna had time to react or crawl out of the line of fire, her chiffon shoulders and wig were already a conflagration.

She released muffled whimpers as disbelief struck her dumbfounded yet again. Coated in her blood, melting sequins began to caramelize, napalming to her flaking skin. The flames licked her lips as her scalp sizzled, the clangs and movement in the background unbeknownst to her. The unbearable heat began to roast the contents of her skull as her skin popped and fizzed. She lost vision in her left eye as she saw the dark figure coming toward her with a fire extinguisher.

Was she going to put the fire out? She must have changed her mind. Dyna Fyre would not go out as her moniker declared, she thought as the butt of the extinguisher collided with her nose and lip. Barely able to breathe in the intensely-heated air as it was, her collapsed nose and top lip curled into her concaved

---

3. shock

skull before the cool spray of the extinguisher doused her charred flesh.

The Queen cursed under her breath as she dug through the contents on the floor. The flames had reached Dyna's *slaystation*, engulfing her glamour shots as they ignited, one by one. Having found her straight razor, The Queen stood over her still-sizzling fajita platter of a friend. Dyna gurgled her final breaths as the Queen stood above her. She placed her knee on Dyna's chest and looked into her only working eye.

The quickness of the razor opening confused Dyna as it flew up toward her hairline. The blade steadily traced the circumference of her once beat,[4] now beaten and charred, face with a shiny red, thickening line. The Queen brought her razor-turned-scalpel in her hands back up to its point of origin at Dyna's forehead. The killer's hot pink lips pulled tight under the mask, exposing a venomous smile with perfectly white teeth.

Just before Dyna faded away forever, the veiled sadist whispered into her ear, "There can only be one Queen."

The killer's gloved hands gripped the bottom of Dyna's neck, winced, and pulled. The flesh tore from Dyna's yelping skull like carpet tacks ripped from floorboards. The flap of skin now only anchored to her chin and face made puckering noises amidst the ripping of sinew. With one final forceful uppercut motion, The Queen had her trophy as the last of the perished queen's face released in one jiggling sheet of seared flesh. By now, the Queen noticed fire sweeping the room and smoke was filling the space quickly. She glanced down at the mangled skeletal remains of a once-talented beauty and mentally said her farewell as she made her way to the door.

After locking it behind her, she headed to the exit only a few feet down the hall. The music thumping through the walls and the rowdy crowd was cut short by the screeching smoke alarm. The Queen smugly puckered her pink lips as the sprinklers went off just as she pushed through the fire exit. The melting of wicked witches and the panic of the crowd should keep the fire department busy while she made her escape. The Queen reveled in her first victory, with the still dripping trophy in her hand. One girl down, eleven more to go.

---

4. perfectly done makeup, "beat" with a makeup sponge

Gamble Donna Phart

Chapter 3

OCTOBER 21, 2022, **T**HURSDAY

"Now I have to grow my hair out because Geoff cut his short and everyone keeps thinking we're twins," whined Antonio's roommate. "How creepy is that? As if all 5'8" blond twinks[1] with blue eyes look alike," Roger said with folded arms.

Antonio raised his eyebrows, shrugged his shoulders, and compressed his lips: the official face for *welp*.

Geoff was looking through Antonio's bookcase, barely listening, but added, "Well you *have* been using my gym membership and no one's said anything." He pulled a book with a screaming skull on it. "How is this one?"

Antonio snapped out of his disassociation. "I loved that one. It was so fucked-up, horribly bleak ending. I just didn't like how the author wrote people of color."

Geoff scoffed, "What do you mean?"

Antonio sighed and prepared himself for his soliloquy. "You know how when you're reading a book and it's just *implied* that characters are white? Like it's just a given? Then they introduce a character and all of a sudden they have 'beautiful chocolate skin' or 'delicate cinnamon elbow wrinkles.' Like, just say Black or Hispanic. You don't have to fetishize us for the sake of inclusion."

Geoff's porcelain face scrunched in confusion, the fine lines around his eyes like ripples in a bowl of skim milk. "Huh. I've never noticed that before."

Antonio did his best to hide his shock and awe. "I would just like for *someone*

---

1. a young-looking gay man with a slender build

to reverse the roles and see how that reads. That's all."

Roger walked up to his disoriented boyfriend, lost in thought. "It's too deep for you, babe. Don't hurt yourself. I'm just glad you can read in the first place." Roger kissed his doppelgänger on the mouth, their thin lips pulled back as their teeth clicked. Their faces pooled together like paint primer on a garage floor. Antonio recoiled at the gross display of affection in their common area.

Roger pulled away from their ivory embrace. "Hey, can I borrow your suitcase? I talked Geoff into coming home with me, so he's using mine."

"Sure, it still has the tags on it." Antonio got up sullenly. "I thought I would be landing gigs all over the country by now, but not so much." Antonio headed to his room to retrieve the suitcase.

"Aww, don't be like that. It just takes time, sweetie. You're still a baby drag queen." Roger was trying to be helpful. "You'll find your stride soon. I promise."

Antonio plopped back down on the couch and picked up his book. "I left it in your room for you."

Roger was already making his way back. "Thanks, beehhhtch." Down the hall, he yelled back, "You were supposed to help me, whore!"

Antonio rolled his eyes and shouted, "Just let me finish this chapter, then I'll be right there. I promise." Roger continued his bitchy soliloquy to deaf ears, so Antonio went back to reading.

Geoff was still looking at Antonio's books. He ruffled his newly cut blond hair before reflecting, "Dude, this is all horror. Like, that's all you read?

"Pretty much. It's the only thing that keeps my attention. The bloodier and more fucked-up, the better."

Geoff strained to see the cover of what Antonio was reading. "*Rearranged Guts*? What's that one about?"

Antonio slammed the book shut, grinned, and raised an eyebrow. "It's about this guy who uses Grindr to find his victims, and then when they meet to hook up, he kills them all with sex toys turned into torture devices. All the while, his pure little boyfriend has no idea that he's dating a serial killer. This one guy just got split in half like he was being fucked with the jaws of life. I needed a break after that one."

Geoff's face somehow went a few shades lighter, almost translucent. "That's disgusting! Who the fuck would come up with that?"

Antonio made the *welp* face again and left the book on the armrest of the couch.

Geoff was still thinking about what it must feel like to be split in half . . . but not the fun way. He shook off the thought and asked, "Are you going home for the holidays, at least?"

Annoying rap with the cadence of a nursery rhyme on top of a cheesy beat started playing in Roger's room. He shrilly yelled, "Stop flirting with my man and get your asses in here, sluts!"

They both sighed and made their way back, no longer able to put off the inevitable. Roger was "dancing" to the "music" as best he could. The poor thing seemed to be dancing to the words, not the beat. The noise that was coming out of Roger's Bluetooth speaker was vibrating the framed Taylor Swift posters on his wall. Antonio then remembered the music could have been much worse.

Geoff started folding the women's petite T-shirts that were Roger's trademark go-to, which sat crumpled on his bed. Antonio plopped on the floor near Roger's closet after unzipping the suitcase.

"Turn this shit down." Geoff tapped Roger's phone until the noise became mere mumbles. "I was trying to see if Antonio had plans for the holidays or not."

"None whatsoever. Hopefully by then, I will have some bookings out of state. Then I can be a jet-setting bitch too." Antonio was eyeing Roger's dirty shoes in his closet as he spoke.

"Don't you go home to see your parents ever?" Geoff innocently asked. Roger immediately chopped at his neck and mouthed the word "No" with *zero* tact whatsoever.

Antonio, staring dead at Roger and wondering why they were still friends, replied, "My parents are dead." He paused. "Well . . . dead to me anyway. My dad left when I was younger and my mom . . . we never saw eye to eye. She never accepted me for who I was. You know, the usual. Didn't like to see her little boy being a sissy and all that." Antonio paused to see if the two of them were listening or clicking teeth again.

Roger was playing on his phone but Geoff was staring at Antonio with shock. "Wow, that's so fucked-up. I'm glad my parents were cool with it. Not like they had a choice. Not like *we* had a choice. At least they understood that part."

Antonio sighed. "Yeah, I thought my mom would be cool, too, but after my dad left she just became this other person. She was just somewhere else. A lot of mental shit that she never got help for."

"Wow, I'm sorry you had to go through that. No wonder you cut her off." At least Geoff feigned interest; Roger must have heard this story one too many times.

"She cut herself off," Antonio said, collecting himself again. "She was a piece of work . . . I'll put it that way." Antonio fought back tears. "Now she's just a reminder of what I don't want to be. I might be a sissy in a dress, but I'm okay with myself and I'm happy. She can't take that away from me." Antonio fanned his eyes. "Anyhoo, she's dead now and I'm not, and that concludes story time today, kids."

Crickets. Geoff finally said, "Wow."

"Yeah, I tried to warn you," Roger chimed in. "She's pretty in drag but she can really suck the air out of the room."

Geoff tried to lighten the mood. "So where did your drag name come from?"

Antonio nonchalantly said, "I got drunk one night, drank a whole bottle of peach schnapps, shit myself right there in the club. Booboo running down my leg and everything. Worst night of my life."

Geoff finally put two and two together. "Oh! I get it now! Gross. Gambled on a fart!"

Bless his heart. Antonio chuckled and nodded his head. "And lost."

Reba Durchy
Chapter 4

OCTOBER 21, 2022, **T**HURSDAY

"Move, bitch, get out the way!" yelled Reba Durchy while she attempted to get past the crowd gathering around the stage. Her height combined with the wispy hairstyle (she *borrowed* from a certain McEntire) helped keep the cobwebs out of the corners at Kuntry Kitchin's Buttered Biscuits "drag eatery." A few steps ahead of her, Suzee Ho Maker tried to clear the hall, knowing that Reba notoriously had a tiny bladder and was no doubt dying to relieve herself. Reba finally made it to her old, but not *old,* friend. They locked hands and gave a good squeeze.

"You killed it, babygirl!" exclaimed Suzee, excited for her good Judy's successful performance. Suzee picked a speck of glitter off Reba's tied flannel shirt. The houselights started to dim.

"Thank you, thank you, but girl, I need to PISS!" Reba clomped down the long hallway toward the dressing rooms, already unfastening her Daisy Dukes, leaving behind her a trail of blue suede shoes. Suzee followed and held the back of her own *ho-down* overalls dress so she wouldn't flash any poor onlookers as she collected Reba's scattered objects. The high-gloss black door that simply said *Outhouse* slammed and locked. It almost closed on a piece of gnarled couch padding that was once shaping Reba's rotund derriere. After an hour-long meet and greet and sweaty performance under stage lights, the polyurethane foam smelled like a hootenanny in Hell. The sounds of a faucet followed by a toilet flush, then Reba emerged a new woman.

Suzee was already in back packing up Reba's station when she moseyed in. Reba exhaled. "Thank you, babygirl. You're an angel." She plunked down in her seat, peeling a centipede of eyelashes from her lid. "Remind me to never buy this brand again, the right one kept fluttering in my eye. I thought I was having a stroke right onstage."

"Wait, don't dedrag just yet, girl! They have an after-hours party downtown and I don't wanna go alone!" begged Suzee. She had just got new cowboy boots and wanted to get more life out of them. Besides, the night was still young.

"Girrrl." Reba sighed heavily. "You know I've been on my feet all night! My shit is achin'!" She pulled up her foot and attempted to rub it, to her friend's disgust.

"Girrrl, but everyone's going to be there. Even the Lady Mayonessa." Suzee sat back and let that marinate while she filed her nails, her blonde pigtails bobbing to a nonexistent melody.

"The recently single Miss Xtra?" Reba asked enticingly. "Mmmmm, you know I've wanted to get my fist in that jar of mayo for *some* time."

Suzee heaved and almost filed her yellow pinkie nail off, "There is something *very* the matter with you. I'm not one to kaikai[1] but if I did, it wouldn't be with that one."

Reba Derchy had already put her pantyhose back on and was snapping her heels. "That's funny because I'm pretty sure it was . . . last happy hour where I saw you getting awfully close to li'l Miss Phart with your drunk ass."

Fastening her earrings, Suzee Ho Maker grabbed her cowboy hat and Reba's belongings from the makeup tables before responding, "That's my little baby drag queen. So innocent and naive, a little dead behind the eyes but who could blame her in this day and age?" The click-clack of heels could be heard as Suzee shut Reba's station lights off. "Maybe we'll both get lucky tonight." She joined her friend, who was packing her cigarettes and making her way toward the back door. They hooked arms and walked out together.

"Maybe I'll get me a Mayonessa mustache!" Reba cackled as her friend did her best not to throw up near their parking spot.

---

1. sex between drag queens, in drag usually

The cherry from Reba's cigarette flew by Suzee's face as an ambulance zoomed past Reba's car at the red light. Suzee gasped and sunk into her seat. "Bitch, you catch my hair on fire and I'll haunt your ass for life, you hear me?!" Reba, laughing and coughing at the same time, pulled down her visor mirror. Suzee checked her wig in the rearview, no singed pieces, luckily. Behind her reflection, the red lights flashing caught her eye as a fire engine whizzed past them.

"Hot time in the city tonight, baby," oozed out of Reba's smoggy mouth as she reapplied her lipstick.

"Has anyone ever told you that you are classier than a crystal ashtray on a bedside table?" zinged her friend. "People could be hurt."

Reba lit another cigarette. "I'll have you know, I have *two* crystal ashtrays, one on each side of my bed. I am *one* classy broad." The extra-long red light finally turned green as Reba teased her hair helmet back into place. They whizzed down the boulevard, Suzee looking for a parking spot as they got closer. Reba looked skyward toward the gleaming high-rise tower. The bumping music could be heard from four flights above them. Marcus/Yanita Shower's condo was the after-party spot for Friday "ho hours" mornings in the gay part of WeHo. Good luck finding parking. One block over, the two "women of the night" texted Yanita to let them up as they headed toward her place.

A group of belligerently drunk guys were walking toward the pair as they turned the corner. Suzee grabbed Reba's arm, motioning her toward the street so they could cross without any confrontation. Reba threw her cigarette butt down. "Nah, fuck that, keep walking." The closer they got, the wider the sleepy eyes of the men got. A concoction of carnal desire, confusion, and cheap bottled-piss beer was unflinchingly approaching a few feet from them. Suzee tensed as the drunkards parted, leaving the tiniest sliver of space for the two queens to squeeze through. The split second of silent tension soon erupted when Reba Derchy, almost a full head taller than all, plowed through them like stupid, drunk saloon doors. "Learn how to use a fucking sidewalk, assholes," Reba yelled back over her shoulder as they made their way past the catcalls mixed with angry slurs and empty threats.

"My shero!" cried Suzee as they approached Yanita's building. Reba rang the apartment buzzer. They entered the lobby just as two familiar harpies with matching brown wigs were threatening to claw the other's eyes out.

"Prepare for trouble," said Reba as she flicked the cigarette butt out the door, "and make it double." She choked as she exhaled her last puff of smoke.

"Sheera, be nice to your little sister for once," said Suzee as they slid past them to the elevator and hit the call button.

"You always take her side!" said Sheera, pouting as Thea hugged them both.

"That's only 'cuz she's the one who got all the brains," shot Reba. "But don't worry, honey, neither of you got the looks."

The elevator dinged as the seasoned queens stepped in. Thea yelled through the lobby, "Your muzzle hair is coming in already, Homer Simpson. Remind me to give you my wax lady's card!" The sisters cackled. Their annoyingly cute plaid skirts swished as they pushed past the door and made it outside. On the street, Thea spotted drunk frat boys—her favorite. Sheera buttoned her cardigan and adjusted her glasses, fairly certain this night was going to end in disaster.

"The youth today . . . so fucking rude," Reba remarked, her hand grating on her prickly chin in disdain.

The elevator doors dinged open, and the two were greeted with laughter and a million conversations. Wigs, eyelashes, and inebriation seemed to have spilled out onto the entire fourth floor. They passed faces that barely seemed recognizable amongst the dimly lit hallway. The only thing that shone brightly was a figure wearing a hot pink, jeweled ski mask they couldn't take their eyes off as they passed a group of particularly ghastly ghouls.

"Whew, I know she's hot in that," Reba snapped. "Take that shit off, it's hot in the club, gworl!" she yelled back to the masked figure, who only sent back a steely stare.

"Tough crowd tonight," Suzee said, as they pushed through to Yanita's humble abode.

Yanita's door was wide open so guests could come and go. They both peered inside at what once was a fancy new condo. Reba entered first, sneering as she accidentally kicked an empty beer bottle a few feet ahead of her. It rolled on the laminate floor, past the hostess with the mostest's line of sight. There she was, sitting on one of the leather couches between a set of boys who looked to be out past their curfew.

"Now, Miss Durchy, don't you be coming up in my house making a mess," Marcus, out of drag, yelled over the music. "I know your mama raised you better than that!" He stood up and smoothed his tank top, motioning for the jailbait to stay put.

Reba chuckled. "Young man, my mother raised me to close my front door because *trash* is known to *steal!*" She yelled the last part loud enough so everyone could hear her, met with a few laughs and a boo-hiss from the shady party squatters. Marcus gave Reba a slice of cheekbone[2] and hugged Suzee. "I love what you've done with the place, sweetie. Is Daddy Warbucks still paying your rent?" Miss Durchy jabbed as she looked for the nearest bathroom.

A few oohs cut the steely silence as Marcus pulled away from Suzee with a disgusted look. "Girl, nobody under thirty would even get that reference. Why did you bring ol' Auntie Busted and Dusted with you again? For her senior citizen's discounT?" zinged Marcus. "If you need to change your diaper, the bathroom is down that hall and to the right." He pointed a bony, polished pinkie in the direction and made his way to the kitchen to get him and his prey some liquid refreshments.

Before she even finished her sentence, Reba was heading back. She learned a long time ago not to pay that man any mind, especially when *she* had a few drinks in her. *Her sugar daddy must be out of the country again*, she thought before screaming at the common gutter trash to get out of her way. Suzee stayed up front, ever the social butterfly, having a kiki with the doll babies.

Suzee was definitely the Rose Nylund of the drag community. Loved by all, wouldn't harm a fly, shame about that uncle face, though. What she didn't have in looks, she made up for by being Miss Congeniality (crowned three times). However, at this moment, the last thing on her mind was being congenial. Antonio, a.k.a. Miss Gamble Donna Phart, was in her sights and she was aiming for a bullseye. She knew that Snow White apple shoulder tattoo anywhere, peeking out from between the tresses of an unfortunate Party City wig. She could help this little Latin boy in drag, though. She could be the drag mother[3] she never knew she wanted or needed. Then Antonio could be all hers.

She snapped out of her *Little Shop of Horrors* dream montage to make her way to her soon-to-be drag daughter. Before she could seductively glide across the

---

2. a passive-aggressive air kiss on the cheek with an eye roll

3. drag queen mentor

floor to him, Reba emerged from the hallway with a cigarette tucked between her glossy lips. "Shitter's clogged." Caught off guard by her demure friend, her face froze in a shocked exhale. Reba shrugged her shoulders. "I'm going to go smoke." She grabbed a wine cooler out of Marcus's hand and stomped toward the balcony. "You still making me smoke outside, Miss Shower?" she belted while feeling around in her bra for her lighter.

Marcus glared in her direction and snapped back angrily, "Don't ask questions you already know the answer to, old woman. Not in *my* house." Reba was already on the way out, her lighter in hand. "And girl, it's 2022. Ain't nobody smoke anym—" Her words were cut off as Reba slammed the sliding glass door shut and lit up.

Marcus pouted, closed the fridge door with his hip and sashayed back to his boy toys. "Trash."

Suzee still seemed to be suspended in her own little world before Marcus jostled her brain back to Earth.

"Don't bring that hobgoblin with you next time. She always got something rude to say when ain't no one even shook her cage."

Suzee explained, "She's just tired after her gig, honey, you know how she gets."

Marcus kissed his teeth, handed wine coolers to Mary Kate and Ashley, and excused himself to powder his nose.

Suzee seized the opportunity to sidle up to Gamble, mindlessly scrolling on her phone. "Hey, babygirl!" She said, laying an actual kiss on her cheek a smidgen longer than she should have. Gamble smiled her movie star smile, with Suzee's pink lip gloss emblazoned on her dimpled cheek. "I haven't talked to you in so long, my little working girl."

Gamble seemed to deflate a little. "I've been taking every gig I can get. I need the money for the pageant."

"You don't need money to win, hon. Just let the world see your beauty and charm and the rest is fate. Trust me, I know. I've got a closet full of gowns I paid too much for and will never wear again." Suzee paused. "Besides, there's girls with lots of *cough* Daddy's *cough* money that have nothing to show for it but a condo their sugar daddy bought them just to hold all their tacky gowns!" The two did their best to stifle their laughter as Marcus shot out of the hallway.

"Which one of y'all NASTY ASSES left a grown-man-sized shit in my bathroom and clogged the damn toilet?!" Marcus was squeaking lividly as he slipped and slid, the bottoms of his sneakers slick with doo-doo water. "Who raised y'all?! Y'all need Jesus and some fiber in your life, I swearrrrrrrr."

Marcus angrily galloped back to the couch, past Gamble hugging Suzee good-bye. Marcus practically threw one of the small boys off the couch cushion looking for his phone. Maybe his super would be able to unclog it before Big Daddy found out. He unlocked his phone to text him when he noticed a string of messages from Elektra Komplex plus a TikTok Live notification from the Dacity Twins that read *OMG FLAMIN MO'S IN FLAMES! WE COULD HAVE DIED GIRL.*

Reba sat smoking on the balcony, wondering why she left her phone in the car. The red-headed Italian was tall enough so that one ass cheek could sit on the railing while she looked out at the city lights. The gentle wind carried her smoke away as she took in the view. The sliding glass door opened, and the cacophony of music and what sounded like panicked histrionics invaded her peace. She turned her head to see the pink ski-masked woman had joined her. Reba took a long drag off her cigarette, sizing up this mystery queen as she slinked to the corner opposite her.

"I thought I was the only smoker left in LA." She laughed, expecting the same from the silent Amazon, but got nothing. The intense stare of her green eyes made Reba uncomfortable, even though most girls knew they didn't want any smoke with this old battle axe. The silence was a growing monster between the two, a malicious energy that was hard to pinpoint. The city lights hit the jewels on the stranger's ski mask, creating a halo of disco ball twinkles around The Queen.

Reba said, "Somebody got a BeDazzler for Christmas, I see." She smirked and turned to take her final drag, the ash sprinkling the dumpsters five stories below with delicate gray snowflakes. The sound of heels cut through the silence temporarily, but Reba didn't notice them. Her attention was instead on the black smoke billowing from the strip. What looked like *Flamin' Mo's . . . but that couldn't be.* She strained to turn her upper body more, so she could verify it when a familiar perfume wafted toward her. Her mind didn't have time to recognize the smell before she felt the enraged push against her shoulder and upper arm.

Her body teeter-tottered over the railing in half a flash. The feeling of weightlessness felt so alien to Reba, but it was cut short by the wall of an open dumpster her lumbar spine cracked onto at the velocity of about forty-five miles per second. The Queen had no time to revel in knowing that in less than a second, the loudmouth Reba Durchy had made her final farewell and ended up where she belonged.

The Queen picked up the lone (not so) crystal slipper the "Cinderfella" left behind and tossed it over the balcony to rest with its owner. Happy endings were only reserved for the true Queen.

The Queen stealthily slid the glass door open again, only to be greeted by a frantic crowd in a full panic.

Shouts of "Ohmygawd" and "Is that my chiffon?" rang out as the music stopped and lights flickered on in the party house. Marcus was in tears watching the twins give their best news report of a story they hadn't even witnessed. A line was filing out the door, many on their way to see the wreckage with their own eyes.

Suzee was swept up in her emotions as she hugged a crying friend before saying goodbye. She screamed for Reba as she grabbed her purse from Marcus's bedroom. The Queen in the mask stomped past her as the smell of cigarettes wafted behind her. Suzee stared intently in The Queen's direction as she watched her make a speedy exit from the condo. She turned toward the balcony but was puzzled to see it empty. She even slid the door open to be sure. "Reba??" The smell of cigarette smoke still lingered, but her friend was long gone. Suzee even called her but didn't hear her friend's signature country ringtone anywhere.

Suzee went back in to check the rooms, even the backed-up bathroom from hell, before calling it quits. "Did Reba leave already?" Suzee asked Marcus, still watching the fake news on his screen.

"Ain't nobody care about no fuckin' Reba, girl." Marcus was attempting to hold back tears. "They're saying something like eight people might be dead. I've been texting Dyna and getting no response. I don't know what's going on or what to do."

Suzee wasn't sure either, to be honest. She hugged her whimpering friend and decided she had to go see if she could help in any way. They were only a few minutes away. She had a bad feeling about everything but chose to ignore her gut this one time.

Four flights of stairs later, The Queen pushed the back door of the complex open. The unsavory smell of the alley was luckily muted by the lack of a nose hole in her mask. That detail would prove to be helpful considering she still had a trophy to recover.

The Queen walked up to the glistening dumpster, the one thing that seemed out of place was the tattered comforter in the shape of a person draped over the edge. The only noise she heard besides the gravelly slide beneath her heels was a sickeningly wet sucking sound coming from the trash receptacle.

To the Queen's shock, Reba was somehow squeezing out a few shallow, stunted breaths. The light from the street caught what appeared to be a navel protruding from a shaggy, dimpled inner tube of wilting flesh. The fall had not only fractured Reba's spine but forced it and several ribs to protrude from her taut skin, spilling over the edge of the dumpster. Like the stamens of a blooming lily, her upper body petalled in a wash of trickling crimson.

Reba's inanimate arms were carelessly dangling next to her bleeding facial orifices like jellyfish tentacles. The wheezing was now in short spurts, her suffering wouldn't last much longer. The Queen produced her trusty straight razor in her gloved hand. She attempted to hold still the mangled mess of blood and heavily salivated vomit that was Reba's face, to make her necessary incisions.

She made a mental note to herself, face *before* we push next time. She had no choice now. After she wiped off and closed her blade, she had to place her heel on the expired queen's neck in order to get the traction to *deface* her. After a deep inhale through the filtered nose fabric, she stepped on the neck with a crunching celery *snap* and grabbed for the flap of skin next to her shoe.

The back of Reba's skull was crushed in from the impact, which kept it still as The Queen pulled at the stubbornly slippery skin. It finally gave way, dropping to the alley floor. The Queen used her shoulder to nudge the busted firecracker, who was once competition to her, fully into the trash. Where she belonged. "Good riddance," escaped the Queen's pink lips as she slammed the lid shut and bent down to fetch her second trophy. Dawn was on the horizon, and as luck would have it . . . it was garbage day.

Gamble Donna Phart

Chapter 5

October 22, 2022, Friday

"Oh, so just fuck my drag, huh?" Gamble laughed, bookended by the deafening doubles, Thea and Sheera Dacity. The twins were interviewing Gamble for their YouTube channel.

"Not at all, sweetie!" piped Sheera.

"We love a horror queen!" Thea exclaimed.

"It's just, sometimes they have a habit of looking a bit . . . " said Sheera.

"Party City," they said in unison.

Gamble gasped in mock offense and hopped off the barstool.

"Are you implying that Tiffany, a.k.a. the *Bride of Chucky*, is cheap?!"

Gamble did a full spin for the camera. The wedding dress she got for forty bucks at Goodwill looked damn good on her. Luckily, they couldn't see that the back didn't actually close, the leather jacket hid that. Her spiderweb hose were brand-new and the combat boots she borrowed from Evayda looked like pure movie magic. Her blonde ombre wig was a shake-n-go, but she only went blonde for her Halloween looks anyways.

"Not at all, Mama," Thea said assuredly.

"Not to your face, at least," Sheera said assertively.

Gamble threw her head back theatrically. "And now we know who the evil twin is."

The twins laughed in unison and in the same pitch. The same way they did everything which creeped out most and annoyed everyone else.

"Well thanks for being on the vlog, Gamble!" chimed Sheera.

"The next time we see you and the next time you guys see us . . ." chimed Thea.

"Will be at the Trick'd and Treated Pageant!" they said unanimously.

"Where there will surely be the first ever tie for number one," proclaimed Thea confidently.

"With both of us being crowned!" declared Sheera confidently.

"Or you both can tie for second place. I plan on wiping the floor with all of you," said Gamble in a sinister tone that made both girls recoil a little.

"We can edit that out later," Thea said matter-of-factly, grabbing the camera.

"Don't forget to like and subscribe!" Sheera interjected, just before Thea stopped the recording.

"Hey! I think you cut me off, ho!" Sheera barked at her sister.

"We can just do a voice-over later, calm down. Geez. I just need to get out of this corset, there's a needle or something stabbing me," Thea said, grabbing her pained side.

Gamble needed to hit the ladies' room and was more than enthused to get away from this twin tantrum preparing to erupt.

"Bitch, I'm bleeding!" shrieked one of them.

"Oops? LOL." Laughed the other, getting quieter as she walked through the hall to the restroom.

Gamble entered the restroom while reflecting on how glad she was to be an only child growing up. She couldn't imagine having a sister, let alone having to stare at a complete copy of herself every day.

Ever the lady, Gamble lifted her Goodwill wedding gown at the urinal. Washing her hands, she checked the mirror to see her complete copy staring back at her. The low lighting, the wedding dress, and the ombre wig rocketed her back to pictures of her mother on her wedding day. Bad dye job and all.

Even at her worst, that woman was stunning. She used to beam with pride when she showed little Antonio pictures from her pageant days and all her crowns that she kept dust-free and on display. Then it all came crashing down. Gamble tried her best not to smudge her makeup, but the tears wouldn't stop. She rested her hands on the edge of the sink and let her sobs rock her shoulders. One of the last *good* things his mother said to li'l Antonio before the accident was how beautiful he was. One of the last *good* things li'l Antonio said to his mother before the fire was where do you think he got it from? So many things left unsaid, so many questions left unanswered.

The ugly Kardashian crying face caught Gamble off guard in her reflection, bringing her back to now. She sniffled and dotted her tear ducts with a tissue point. She inhaled, shook her body, and exhaled back to being *that bitch,* reapplied her black lipstick, and exited stage left.

The wonder twins seemed to still be bickering so Gamble decided to make a detour before rejoining them. She was going to need a drink if she had to break up that sibling rivalry. Plus, she needed something to calm her nerves before her performance later.

"Vodka Red Bull, please and stank you," she said to the back of Evangeline, the best bartender in town, who called Stiffies her home.

Evangeline spun around enthusiastically. "Gamble," —she looked Gamble up and down—"or should I say Tiffany? I thought I saw you come in earlier. How you been, sweet thang?"

They pecked each other on the cheek before Evangeline started to make her drink. Gamble pulled up a seat. "Working like a ho on payday and the rent is due." They both laughed and Gamble continued. "I miss sleep, though, girl. I think I'm burning myself out."

Evangeline set her drink on the bar, "I'm sure you are darlin'. You have to take it easy. You know the gigs aren't going anywhere."

Gamble frowned. "I know, I just spent too much on my dress for the pageant and I'm trying to make up for it."

"Oh! That's next week, right?" Evangeline paused to check her phone. "Damn, I'll be out of town for that."

Gamble frowned a little deeper now.

"We both know you're going to kill it. I'll be there in spirit." Evangeline said as her boss and the owner walked up to the bar.

The owner, a nervous little tit of a man, beckoned to Gamble to come closer. "Wanna come back and do Monday too?"

Gamble responded back instantly, "Of course! But could I get an advance?"

The little man's cell started ringing as he pulled out a wad of twenty-dollar bills and handed several to her, saying, "See you Monday." Then, "Hey, Evangeline, give me a stone sour," before he answered it.

"You got it," Evangeline said as he stepped away. She turned back to Gamble and mouthed, "On the house. Good luck next week, babygirl." She winked and got back to work.

Gamble nodded, blew her a kiss, and headed back to the girls.

"OMG, why are they hyping her up? They know they aren't doing her any favors," Thea said, looking at her phone screen when Gamble walked up.

"Who?" Gamble asked.

Sheera replied, "Ugh, Xtra's extra ass. Have you seen the one of her twerking on the bar that she posted last week?"

Thea handed her phone to Gamble and clicked play, "She barely makes it thirty seconds before she falls off the damned thing. Then her halter top rips and we get flashed a titty . . . or an elbow or I don't even wanna know. It was hairy and had a nipple, I'm pretty sure."

All three of them dry heaved as the Mayo hit the ground.

Thea glanced at Gamble's slightly smudged mascara. "OMG, bitch, were you crying?

Sheera dizzily glanced at Gamble's embarrassed face as well.

Gamble fake laughed. "No no no, I think I'm just allergic to you guys' sweet pea body spray. That's all."

The two mental dynamos looked quizzically at each other. Sheera's eyes shifted, still assessing the statement, and said, "Ohhh, okay."

"Are you guys ready for the pageant?" Gamble asked apathetically.

"This one is still working on our gowns, but they'll be ready in time," Thea said.

"And our wigs still haven't even arrived in the country last time I checked. I leave you to ONE task and you forget," barked Sheera angrily at her sister.

"Hey, they said they'll be here in time. Get off my back, ashy," Thea fired back.

"Your hairy back," said Sheera with an eye roll. "Always last minute with this one."

"Sisters! Sisters!" Gamble interrupted. "I don't have the strength to sit through another fight. Y'all are blood. You're supposed to look out for one another."

Thea sneered at Sheera and continued to doomscroll. "What did you think of Yanita's last post?"

"Gowns. Beautiful gowns," Gamble intoned.

Sheera squealed with glee. "Finally a reference we understand, something from this millennium!"

Gamble yelled, "Bitch! I'm only twenty-six!" before she rolled her eyes and sucked back the last of her drink.

"Well anyhoo, if you two don't mind. I need to touch up and listen to my song one more time."

Thea chirped, "Oh! What song are you performing?"

"'Dressed to Kill' . . . by Cher." Gamble smiled and winked. "We love an easter egg around here, don't we?"

Thea and Sheera Dacity

Chapter 6

October 22, 2022, Friday

"Hurry up, bitch, we were supposed to be LIVE twenty minutes ago!" yelled Sheera to her twin sister, Thea.

"I wouldn't have to let out your bodice if you would eat something other than Panda Express every day, you know." Thea huffed, attempting to find any light source possible in the dim costume storage room. Her fingers were sore and swollen trying to sew in the dark. Meanwhile, her bratty clone stared daggers at her before she applied mascara with her mouth agape like a taxidermied fish. Thea had to admit, their makeup looked flawless, as always. Even when Sheera didn't have a top on and the juxtaposition between her fishy face and her boy chest made the sixteen-seconds-older twin giggle.

"Bitch, what are you trying to say?" Sheera turned to watch her sister chew her lip and begrudgingly stitch, the pregnant pause thickening the air in the already dank back room. Thea did the sewing and Sheera did the makeup, that was the agreement. Even when they were little, their Nani made saris for their Barbies. Thea quickly learned and was soon working alongside the rest of the family in their online sari shop. Sheera never had the patience for sewing, instead, an eye for design. In the drag scene, the wonder twins were rising up the ranks, working off the other's strengths and minimizing any weaknesses.

"Ugh, all done." The glint of steel flashed Thea's eye as she snipped the final string with her oversized sewing shears. "Put this on." She passive-aggressively threw the shimmering orange ball of fabric in the brat's direction. "Meanwhile, I haven't even finished my fucking hair yet." The heavy shears lobbed a knock-knock joke at the work table that had no punchline. Thea stood up and brushed off her matching shimmering bodice, hers in hot pink. Her black pants hugged the curves that she had sculpted and padded an hour before, needing a readjustment after sitting for so long. She didn't have to pad Sheera, thanks to Panda Express.

Sheera slid the top over her head, careful not to smudge her makeup. It was a little snug, but beauty was pain, right? Thea appeared behind her and started pulling the laces, tightening around her carbon copy's rib cage loop by loop. Her hands ached but she made it to the top, her favorite part. Thea held back her enjoyment and asked, "Ready?"

Sheera hunched over the table and sucked in as much air as she could. Thea planted her foot on the small of Sheera's back and pulled as if her life depended on it. Hearing her sibling wheeze in pain brought her more joy than she cared to admit. She stifled her smile as she secured and tied the laces taut. With the deed finally done, she grabbed her wig off her station and disappeared behind the rippling walls of costumes suspended from the ceiling racks.

Sheera hobbled over to her seat and tried to ignore her bruising ribs by focusing on just not dying. She plugged in her ring light, popped her Valium, and glued her last strands of blonde hair down. She yelled back to her sister, "It's 9:40! I'm starting, don't come out here looking crazy. Make sure all your shit is glued down!" She got her phone angle just so, took a drink of her water, and fired up TikTok LIVE.

Thea heard her sister yelling obnoxiously, like always, making her way to the only room left with enough light to tame her unruly wig. The building was older than the twins combined and stored some of the most detailed costumes she'd ever seen. It was any girl's dream come true to be allowed back here . . . during the day. At night, it was an entirely different story. The poor lighting and hanging garments contorted into demonic shapes, the darkness concealing her worst living nightmares. She tried not to think about it, knowing it was just her and her bitch sister . . . and the cleaning lady. Who apparently worked on Sundays?

"Heyyyy, twinners! Sorry I'm running late, you know how *sisters* can be." Sheera rolled her eyes, more so in pain than aggravation. She had to update their fans on where their upcoming appearances would be and what new merch they were dropping. "OMG, I'm so excited for our new *If You're Not Twinning, You're Losing* shirts that go on sale tomorrow! Send me a twin emoji if you're going to buy one in the morning!"

She paused to feign interest and let her minions flood her screen with emojis.

Going LIVE was great and all, but trying to look skinny and read all these comments amidst the barrage of emojis made her head swim.

> *GlamourPu$$: left eyebrow looks wonky AF girl.*

> *AgreesWeverything77: periodT. ^^*

Sheera took a vexed look at her screen and compared her brows. "Fuck," she mumbled as she grabbed her makeup bag from behind her. She gritted her teeth before exclaiming happily, "Thanks for the help! Where would we be without our twinners?" She tensely attempted to fix her crooked brow as the rack of costumes behind her swung in place.

> *Shauna Cuntery: Yaash honey, shlay that pusshy!*

> *TeleportUs2Marz: I can't wait for GOTD season 2!*

> *Phrique69: All these Easter Eggs, I sweatergawd.*

> *TheaDacityFanNo1: is that Thea?*

"The doll babies have been waiting on you, sis!" She painted a fake smile on her face and waited for her sister to join her on camera. After waiting a few beats, she was met with a still, albeit menacing quiet. She produced a nervous laugh as she turned in her chair. Just an empty sewing room, racks of costumes, and the deafening silence. Turning to her adoring fans, she heard a shuffling of plastic. She sighed in relief, forcing a grin. "It's just the cleaning lady. Haha. Thea needs to hurry the fuck up. This place gives me the creeps at night."

> *ThickeryDickeryDoc: Oooh so scary, stunt queens*
> *gunna stunt*

> *DebbieDoesWindows: *hot shingles in your area**

Sheera turned back around, regaining her composure as she smoothed out the edge of her brow. Her half-focused eye caught a flash of shimmering pink entering the room. She continued to smooth and let her facsimile have her entrance. She heard plastic and the thump of the sheers on the work table. *Now what?* She had to stall once more (the Twinners couldn't see how unprepared they seemed). "It's about fucking time!"

The pink ski mask caught her off guard, mainly because she wanted one too. "Apparently Thea is changing things up on us tonight." Under her breath, "And not telling me shit about it." Never breaking character, she beamed for the camera and their hundreds of fans watching. She stared hard at her screen, waiting for her companion to do something besides harshly staring at her through the rhinestones of her mask. The ring light glared off each one, drilling the seeds of a headache into her skull. "Thea is mad at me, guys," Sheera said, padding for time, hearing the blood throbbing in her temples. "Bitch, did you change your outfit th—"

> *Nita_Cockatoo: somebody got a BeDazzler for Christmas lol*

> Maya.Dixshun: ooo shade! *fan thorp*

Sheera's eyes widened as she realized this queen was much too tall to be her sister. The shock showing on her face quickly turned to fear, just as the contractor-grade garbage bag slipped over her head. The Queen pulled on the plastic so hard that Sheera's head snapped back. A burning pain bloomed from her neck down to her shoulders. The sensation made her inhale deeply, pulling the plastic to tightly seal around her mouth and nose.

> *MyPhoneSucks1991: look out behind you! (Sorry my phone lagged)*

> GretaGarbage: y'all play too much lmao

The Queen twisted the bag tighter. Sheera kicked and thrashed as her face smudged inside the collapsing dark bubble. Her lungs ached as the realization that this wasn't some prank set in. She reached for her neck, attempting to slide her slender hands under the plastic before it was too late.

> *GlamourPu$$: and the award goes to . . . lol*

> *Optika.Lussion: ugh girls we can see the air holes*

> ScreamQueen666: just kill her already, damn

Sheera maneuvered one hand under the plastic as she felt her consciousness start to drift, trying to pull in any air she could. The bag was being pulled down further as the vertebrae in her neck crunched against one another. Her face was now pointing toward the heavens. If only she could see, she would have seen the shears stab into the shiny black mask fixed in a permanent scream. The steel pierced through the thick plastic and into her cheek, slamming against her teeth, dislodging three molars as the weapon scraped back out.

> Dee.Dee.Moniq: bitch wtf

Cool air entered the bag, temporarily promising Sheera false hope. It wasn't until the twin blades jammed into her encapsulated skull again that the blood started to splatter and drip from the two gashes. The second stab took a momentary pause, scraping through the thin bone of her temple as it shattered in pieces. The sharpened point impaled her eye socket as the bludgeoning pressure extracted the assorted viscera from inside the disconnected eye.

> *Specific_O.Shaun: That blood is faker than my Louboutins!*

> WellGuessWhatMimi: you in danger gworl

> *DaddysLilDeathDrop: Y'all ate this kill scene, left no crumbs. Okurrrr*

The Queen was getting frustrated with Sheera's aggravating will to live. She released the bag, letting splashes of blood and bits of teeth drip out. Then in one solid move, the Queen drove the scissors into her nasal cavity with all of her weight behind both hands. The sounds of wet cracking wood and scraping concrete were joined by a quiet bubbling gurgle. The handles stuck straight out of the plastic like wrapped roadkill tied with a shiny silver bow.

The Queen grunted and stared irritatedly at the ring light and camera.

GlamourPu$$: yass bitch slayyyyy

Porcelana.del.Commode: we have to stab.

*Porcelana.del.Commode: stan**

The Queen thrashed out at the phone, wiping the entire surface of the station onto the floor. The ring light crashed, plunging the workroom into dim darkness once again. The Queen exhaled after her accomplishment, collecting her thoughts. She crossed the room and walked through the parted clothing racks. The flamboyant regalia swallowed her whole as the increasingly louder sound of heels came from the back.

"Girl, my notifications are blowing up! I didn't even hear you say you were starting. You know I can't hear shit back here." Thea emerged from the tiny bathroom and entered the hallway. She clomped toward the workroom, pushing through the hanging costumes swaying in the doorway. "Throw me your lip gloss, though, I can't find my—"

She paused, attempting to process what she was seeing. The room was still incredibly dark, besides the few dull bulbs clinging to life. Sitting in her sister's chair looked like a large rotten piece of fruit, fetid juices dripping on the floor beneath it. Thea's eyes began to water as she stumbled closer, her mind piecing together what she was really seeing. The body of her once annoyingly lively twin was slumped in the chair, her head pulled back at an unnatural angle. Black plastic cascaded off her face, glistening in the weak light. The toe of Thea's heel stopped instinctively just before reaching the dark pool of syrupy liquid.

The shape of her sister's head wasn't registering to her due to the side of it appearing to be dented in and a huge empty hole that was filling with spurts of blood. Her mind went blank, seeing her reflection dying right before her. *Does that mean I die too? If one twin dies, doesn't the other?* The sound of click-clacks coming toward her cut her thoughts short. Makeup and shock dripped off her face as she began to turn while blubbering, "He-lp me, my sist—"

The blood-caked sewing shears jammed into Thea's thin neck, tearing through muscles and breaking through the side of her trachea. The stunned queen turned toward her masked assailant. *Pretty in Pink.* An embarrassing final thought to have as the Queen pulled the shears back out, leaving behind a gaping hole of gored flesh that instantly gushed gurgling blood. Her knees started to give way. She was perplexed that she could not fully catch her breath, air exiting her improvised stoma. Her knees cracked as they hit the floor, then slid akimbo, having landed in Sheera's bloody leftovers. The Queen calmly tossed the shears onto the table, peering around at the materials surrounding her.

Thea started to choke and gag as blood spilled out of her mouth. The more she coughed, the easier it was to breathe but the more blood and pain came. This was all a nightmare, this couldn't be happening to her or her sister. She could not be bleeding out as her own sister's blood was dribbling onto her trembling body. The Queen grabbed at the tufts of fabric left in the corners until she found a strong swath of silk. Wrapped around one fist, the crocodile tail of fabric flowed and swayed behind her.

Thea continued to choke on her own blood as the Queen pulled the fabric around her spitting neck. Powerless to thwart another attack, the Queen maneuvered behind her. The fabric pulled taut around the wound. The pressure was enough to seemingly stop the bleeding, until the Queen placed one sharp spiked heel against the small of her back and yanked. All at once, the lustrous noose crushed her windpipe and blood pumped into Thea's aching throat. Weakness flooded her body and stars filled her eyes. Every attempt she made to fight or flee was obstructed by the slick crimson floor beneath her.

The Queen left Thea with the end of the fabric in her hand. She grasped the pipe of the makeshift clothing rack nearest to them, satisfied it would do. With her other hand she threaded the fabric up and around. The silk tightened, pulling Thea across the slippery floor for one last indignity. The Queen continued to pull in short, strong tugs as Thea was hoisted to her feet.

At this point, Thea was a soulless marionette being pulled by a lone string. Blood continued to seep out of her neck, but it paled in comparison to what was pouring out of her mouth and nose. Her feet started to dangle as the Queen took one final pull, looping the fabric around the leg of the heavy worktable and tying it off.

The Queen rested her palms on the table's surface, catching her breath as the last bit of Thea's soul was leaving her mortal husk. She faced the last twin as a final burbled whimper left her gaping gullet. Her body hung and went slack. Bulging red eyes boasted road maps of busted capillaries upon her downcast face. The hardened steel gaze of the killer faltered momentarily, indicating a glint of remorse. The twins *were* gorgeous, and talented, to boot. They could have easily taken the crown right out of the hands of who it truly belonged to. This had to be done. *There could only be one Queen, after all.*

The flicker of humanity blinked away as soon as it appeared. The possessed sneer returned as she unfolded the straight razor. She followed the path of blood swirls and smears back to Sheera. The Queen ripped the garbage bag from her mangled head. The damage was more grisly than expected as her skull folded in like a bloody crushed eggshell. The swollen apple of her cheek wasn't hiding the fractured bones beneath it. With the speedy blade, the Queen traced her once angelic face with adoration. The pulverized underlayment made for an easy pull from her ear and across, breaking free of the already coagulating blood-jellied strings. With Sheera done, it was Thea's turn to *give face* one last time. She turned to look at the girl eye to eye, making her cuts before the emotions came back. The silk had already pulled and bloated her neck and jaw. She slid her gloved hands under the skin and pulled. Her technique and speed were improving, but the sound of squelching, tearing Velcro still made her grit her teeth. By any means necessary, the deed must be done. No one can be fairer than the Queen.

Gamble Donna Phart
Chapter 7

2 **006**

Gasp. "Antonio! What on Earth?!" A ten-year-old Antonio ducked into his mother's mid-sized closet. He was doing his best to take her dress off and put her shoes back, although he had already been caught. He heard his mother rampaging toward him, her purse and keys still jangling in hand.

"No, Mommy, wait!" Young Antonio's muffled yell barely audible from deep inside the closet. His mother practically tore the closet door off its hinges as he attempted to throw her bracelets and earrings to the side. He was hoping to do anything to make this nightmare easier. "Wait, Mommy, I was just playing!"

She grabbed him by his arm, yanking him up hard enough that his shoulder felt like it popped out of its socket. "I told you to stop going through my things! My Jimmy Choos!" she exclaimed, as she dramatically fell to the ground cradling the shoe, one heel ripped and dangling.

"I didn't mean to, Mommy. You scared me and I tripped!" Antonio wailed. The shame and fear radiated from him, leaking from his eyes.

"You shouldn't have been wearing them in the first place! Can't I have anything?!" Now yelling, she threw the pair back in their box and grabbed a stray wire hanger. "It's bad enough I have to work double shifts just to keep food on the table since your good-for-nothing father left us. They finally let me go home early and this is what I come home to? My son, my *boy,* wearing my clothes?! Like some kind of . . . pervert?!" She crumpled on the floor, overcome with emotion.

Antonio didn't know whether to comfort his poor mother or to make a break for it while he still could. He felt just as hurt. He was only playing. What was so wrong with that? He wasn't hurting anyone. He wanted to be pretty, just like Mommy. He wanted to be strong, just like Mommy. He wanted to be royalty, just like Mommy.

He sniffled and whimpered, "I'm sorry, Mommy. I'll never do it again."

His whispers broke his mother from her trance of self-pity. Rage filled her face. Antonio's fight or flight kicked in and he dove for the closet entrance as his mother leapt in the wrong direction. He ran through her room, dodging the garish bedroom furniture as he heard the monster screaming from inside the closet still. As he made it over the threshold of his room, he heard her footsteps speed after him. He slammed his door shut and bunched his *Dora the Explorer* rug underneath his door, his trusty way of keeping his mother out of his room whenever she was being scary. The bottom of the rug showed its age due to how many times he had to use it. He sat with his back against the door, the only way to keep the rug in place and his mother out. He braced himself as she began pounding on the other side.

"Not my son! Not my little boy!" she screamed between her hits to the creaking wood. "You are not a faggot! Do you hear me?! Girls wear girls' clothes and boys wear boys' clothes!" He was trying not to listen. She told him that people say mean things when they're mad. She always told him this after she had already said the mean things. After she had already hurt him. After she had already made him not want to live in this world anymore.

He buried his head in his arms, resting them on top of his knees. Her anger still threatened to split his door in half. Tears rolled down his chin and soon all he could hear was his own breathing. His happy place was where he could look any way or be whoever he wanted to be. He could be a boy and dress like a girl if he wanted. He could be pretty if he wanted to be. He could look like the beautiful girls in the magazines. It was his favorite place.

Mommy said you should always look your best. He would sit on her bed and watch her put on makeup with amazement. Sometimes her lips would be red, sometimes pink. Sometimes her hair would be long, other times it would look like a seashell. Every time she stepped out of her closet, she could be a whole new person.

Why was it ok for Mommy to become someone else? It used to be her happy place too. She was in beauty shows with other gorgeous women. She won all the crowns. Then Daddy called her names and broke all of them. She said Daddy broke her heart into a million little pieces and that he doesn't love either of them anymore. Ever since he left, she only goes to her mean place.

Antonio slowly opened his swollen eyes, blinking away the last bits of sparkle from his happy place. He heard his mother shift and exhaustively pushed off of his door, then her door slammed a moment later. He stared out his window from the floor, it was dark out now. His face and most of his shirt were finally dry. He was safe. She never made it inside. He should have been relieved, but he knew this would happen again. At least he had his happy place, and the shimmering gold cuff that was still shining on his wrist.

October 22, 2022, Saturday

"No . . . wire . . . hangers. What's wire hangers doing in this closet when I told you, no wire hangers EVER?"

Antonio woke up on the couch in a cold sweat, gulping for air. He must have left the TV on while he took a disco nap before his gig that night. He didn't expect *Mommie Dearest* to be playing when he woke up. *A little too on the nose,* he thought as he hit the power button on the remote. The TV screen went black, leaving him in silence with his thoughts. The movie must have been the cause of the flashbacks. That, or the conversation from yesterday. Regardless, he had no time for a panic attack right now. He had to start getting ready.

Antonio hobbled to his room but felt his heart still throbbing in his ears. He sat on his bed and charged his phone, willing his nerves to calm themselves. He sucked in air and exhaled it gently between pursed lips.

Antonio looked around for five things he could see: the black trench coat hanging on his door, the blonde wig sitting on his desk, the Queen Bey *Renaissance* poster, the crown from Miss Gold Coast 2020, and the dark sunglasses that were the finishing touch for his *Dressed to Kill* homage look tonight. Four things he could touch: the stubble growing on his chin, his dad's straight razor that he still used to this day, the sheets on his bed, the carpet beneath his pedicured feet. Three things he could hear: the air conditioning finally kicking on, some asshole honking outside, some Norteño music from the mom-and-pop Mexican place down the street. Two things he could smell: his Febreze plug-in and the cherry lip gloss he had just put on. One thing he could taste: the last swig of Red Bull from the can next to his bed.

With the end of the grounding technique completed, he felt his heart rate drop back to normal, his breathing calmed. He let out one more exhale and prepared to begin his transformation into Miss Gamble Donna Phart: the killer who was going to take no prisoners tonight.

Freshly shaven and baking,[1] Gamble unplugged her phone from the charger. Her best friend, Evayda, must be back in town considering how many texts she had sent while Gamble took her disco nap.

Evayda Subpoena:

> I'm back bitch! Where is your fugly ass at?

> Remind me to tell you about the trade I linked up with in Denver, I still ain't walking right 3 days later.

> Bitch you better have paid your damn phone bill!

> What time tonight? Oh and bring my pink pumps I know your ass still has!

Gamble smirked and kicked the pink pumps back under her desk.

Gamble:

> Hey worstie! I go on at nine and ain't nobody have your busted ass shoes. I think you lent those to Reba last time.

---

1. applying concealer/loose powder and letting it sit or "bake" so it sets better

Bitch! Oh yeah, you right. She ain't responded to my ass either.

Girl, wait till you see my outfit! Mind if I get a ride gorgeous?

Don't pull that gorgeous shit on me heifer. Oh? Is the screeching culture vulture gone already?

lol yes Roger left this morning with his bf

The one that looks just like his ass? Conceited much? Well that's good, I didn't feel like seeing his lil narrow ass anyway. Especially after that raisins in the potato salad debacle, child.

lol girl! Let me finish beating this mug so I'm ready when you get here.

8pm SHARP bitch. I'll give you an extra hour so you can get that hairline right cuz last time that shit was on your eyebrows girl.

BITCH BYE.

Gamble heard Evayda downstairs honking at eight on the dot. She threw her phone in her bag and grabbed her keys before she hit the stairs sideways, trying her best not to break her neck in sunglasses and heels. She twirled out of her building, giving Evayda and everyone else on the street a show. The black leather trench coat was cinched around her *tiny* waist, the collar pulled up close to her Ray-Bans so all you saw were the sunglasses and a killer red lip.

"A trench coat, bitch?! Get your school shooter ass in this car already!" yelled Evayda out of her passenger window. Evayda's purple afro puffs matched her sequined top perfectly, her jet-black lip in a sneer.

Gamble strutted to her door and flicked the straight razor out of her pocket. "Don't get cut, bitch!" Gamble could barely keep a straight face as she got in the car.

"I know that is not a real razor, right?" Evayda asked, already knowing who she was talking to. Already knowing, of course it was real. "Leave it to your crazy ass to bring a weapon to a gig. That's what we doing now, huh?" She looked in her rearview before she pulled out of her parking spot. "I can't even blame Roger for this colonizer foolery 'cuz you were on this horror movie shit before I even met you."

Gamble laughed while she checked her lipstick in the visor mirror and repositioned the sunglasses on top of her head.

Evayda eyed a police car in the opposite lane as they cruised down the boulevard. "And if the cops pull us over and find that shit, you on your own, girl. Pam ain't seen JACK! I don't know nothing."

"We will be just fine, girl, you worry too much." Gamble blew herself a kiss and closed the visor. She turned to her friend who kept giving her the side-eye. Flicking the razor open one last time, she said, "Besides, you missed a spot around that Adam's apple, I think." Gamble giggled. "Want me to get it for you?"

Evayda glanced in her rearview mirror at her neck, "You lying bitch." Focusing on the road again. "Keep playing and watch how quick you'll be walking to the gig." Gamble cracked a smile and put the razor away for real this time. "And what the hell happened at Flamin' 'Mo's? When were you going to tell me? I had to find that shit out on the bobblehead twins' annoying-ass TikTok."

"I don't know, to be honest, we were all pretty shook up about it." Gamble's gaze swept the street and landed on the crowds lined up around the block of some random bar they passed. "I opened the show. It was amazing. Dyna even congratulated me, and, you know, it's like pulling teeth just to get a little compliment out of her."

Evayda heard the pain in her friend's voice as she spoke. "I just can't believe she's gone. She was the first person to show me how to pad right. She said my ass used to look like I had a full diaper." Evayda sniffled and fanned her eyes, eyeing Gamble doing the same. "No crying, girl. Mama would want us to keep it moving and get these coins. She would want us to honor her by not showing up onstage looking busted. Now if only someone could pass that note to Yanita."

Evayda chuckled and waited for her friend to join in. She quickly glanced at Gamble who seemed like she had retreated into her mind at that moment. Evayda had to snap her acrylic fingers in front of her. "Gamble! Earth to Gamble! I was talkin' shit about ol' Yanita Dentist!"

Gamble instantly snapped out of her funk. "Yanita Prenup!" They both laughed as Evayda pulled up behind the venue, Rude Illusions.

Evayda screamed, "Yanita Talent!" as she parked and they both stifled their laughter, fanning their eyes so they didn't mess up their makeup. "Before we go in, I want to tell you something very important. Okay? I'm for real-real, not for play-play. All right?"

Gamble's smile dropped from her face. "Girl, what?"

"Hand me my purse behind you, I want to give you something that has helped me my whole drag career and I want to pass it on to you now. Big sis to li'l sis."

Gamble's eyes started to tear up. "Girl! Don't you go messing up my makeup!" She snaked her arm behind her and felt for Evayda's bag. She handed it to her and started to fan her eyes. "You do too much for me, girl."

"I know, baby, but that's because I only expect the best from my sisters," she said, unclasping her clutch. "Ready?"

Gamble nodded her head with glee and held her open palms up to her friend, closing her eyes and thrumming with anticipation. Evayda placed a small package in her hands and feverishly waited for her reaction. "Open!"

Gamble's mouth was already locked in a smile. Her eyes shot to see an open pack of gum in her hands.

"Breath check, bitch!" Evayda screamed. "'Cuz it's hot! Burnin' hot! Like a tire fire and microwaved bootyholes!" Evayda howled and bounced in her seat, convulsing in laughter.

Gamble's face dropped for the second time now. She balled her fist around the pack of gum and attempted to choke her worstie who was too busy cackling to notice. They both laughed and calmed down eventually, checking their makeup one more time before they went in. Gamble closed her mirror and dropped the gum into her purse. "And I'm keeping the gum, you rude bitch."

"That's good, baby, 'cuz you need it more than me." Evayda shook her purse. "Besides, more where that came from. I got mints, gum, "skrips." You name it. No reason for your breath to be burning my nose hairs when I'm around."

Gamble pushed the door open. "With all the hair in that big-ass nose, I'm doin' you a favor, bitch."

Evayda laughed and slammed her door. "See? We got each other's back. It's us versus the world!"

They walked arm in arm toward a crowd of cackling hags circling the lone light source in the alley like moths with fake lashes. It was hard to make out who was who in the smokey haze, but they both could hear the unmistakable hoarse mouth of the one and only Yanita Shower. The pair groaned in unison as they pierced the tobacco-scented veil.

"Well look what the cat dragged in," Yanita remarked greasily before taking a long drag off her cigarette. Evayda and Yanita gave cheekbone and a smoky air hug.

Evayda eyed Yanita up and down and said, "Oooh, I love your heels, Mama."

Yanita gasped and did a little step-and-turn for the group of NPCs surrounding them. "Givenchy," gushed Yanita. "Big Daddy got them for me last week in Milan."

Gamble subtly eyed them, hiding her envy as she followed every rhinestoned detail. Evayda was staring at them, too, before she replied, "Maybe next time he leaves for another *business trip*, he can get you a pair that fit."

The gaggle of wild turkeys surrounding them yelped in disbelief. Yanita's soul retreated along with her dangling pinkie toe as she attempted to readjust her foot in the strappy little number. Determined to distract the random birds in her entourage, she quickly fired back at Evayda. "When did you get back in town, bitch?"

"Just last night, had to support my girl," Evayda said as she squeezed her friend's arm with hers. "Didn't want to miss her first time opening here."

Yanita let out a single laugh and faced Gamble for the first time during this exchange. "Aww, I guess you didn't see the Facebook post, huh?"

Gamble innocently asked, "What post?" She pulled her phone out but saw no notifications or texts.

Yanita's mouth contorted in an exaggerated crocodile smile, which seemed to cause her some discomfort. "They decided to have me open the show tonight . . . Gamble is on after me." Yanita scrunched her face as her pearly whites blinded the entire back alley.

Gamble wasn't sure what was more shocking, that she got bumped so last minute or the fact that Yanita's new veneers were about two sizes too big for her head. Gamble was known for her signature gap but was always a little self-conscious about it. Kids were cruel and quiet little Antonio was an easy target growing up. She wanted to get it fixed one day, but not with the prices she saw online.

To see Yanita before her with a whole new set of chompers, knowing that must have cost a fortune—like, you just won *Shantalle's Slaying Dragazons* (now streaming on all platforms) kind of fortune—was just salt in the wound. All is fair in love and drag, but this insult had Gamble ready to take off a heel and dot Yanita's eye.

Feeling her friend's body temperature rising with the puffs of her chest, Evayda shot back. "That's okay, girl, she can wake the crowd up after you waddle off-stage."

Yanita gasped. Evayda motioned for the pigeons to part so they could move past them. "Well we'll see y'all inside. Good luck, girl, hope you don't choke onstage." Knowing full well that wishing someone about to go onstage "Good luck" was the equivalent of praying for their death.

Yanita remained speechless as Evayda moved past them, pulling Gamble in with her. Yanita and Gamble came face-to-face as she moved through, prompting Gamble to venomously yell back to her rival, "Break a tooth!"

Yanita Shower

Chapter 8

OCTOBER 22, 2022, SATURDAY
"Girl, you're on! They've been calling you for the last two minutes!" Suzee Ho Maker yelled at a barely coherent Yanita. The young queen must have been nervous being the opening act for the first time. She grabbed her shoulders and gently guided her to the stage. That's when she smelled the strong stench of Southern Comfort wafting from the teetering girl. Yanita forced her absurdly bright smile as her new veneers and swollen gums threatened to blind the room. Lying her ass off, Suzee offered a final "You got this!" before giving her a shove toward the light. The fledgling drag queen almost rolled her ankle in the Givenchy stilettos but she finally made it onstage. Her music queued up and Shantalle's "Bitch Betta Have My Honey" (now available on iChoons!) began to play.

After about the sixth lip sync miss, Suzee decided to get lost in thought instead of witnessing this travesty. She wished she had never agreed to take Yanita Shower's offer to coach her in her first year of drag. Big Daddy's checks cleared, but as she kept trying to tell Yanita, an inebriated elder once said, "Money can't buy you class." Sometimes just listening to reason, or at least the person whose help you were paying for, could do the trick too. Perhaps not using the same played out songs would help, or songs that you knew the words to. Those expensive heels sparkled in the stage lights, but not if you got the wrong size and your pinkie toe was hanging out for the world to see. Wigs that could be a down payment on a car and makeup could take you far, but not if it looked like you put both on in the dark.

Suzee didn't like to be shady, though. That was just her nerves talking. A flash of skin caught Suzee's eye as Rico, the club's number one go-go boy, popped what his mama gave him to the beat of the music. Hopefully the sheen of a baby-oiled ass cheek could distract the crowd a little from Yanita's lackluster performance.

All that protein powder and broccoli was paying off. Suzee looked out at the crowd and saw three measly singles wadded up on the stage. Yanita seemed to be having enough issues as it was just staying upright as she gyrated her hips in a gown she could barely move in. The fact that the gown probably cost more than anything Suzee had owned in her whole twenty years of drag didn't bother her, though.

Suzee was too busy texting Reba again. The nervousness in her stomach threatened to ruin her tucking panties. They'd received nothing but radio silence from her since Thursday night and it was now Saturday. This was totally unlike her best gal pal, who called or texted her daily. She asked friends in the crowd when she arrived at Rude Illusions, but no one had seen or talked to her either. Everyone was a little on edge ever since the fire at Flamin' Mo's and the list of casualties. Still, something wasn't right here. She knew her chosen sister wouldn't have just ditched her that night. She definitely would've gotten back to her by now. Reba knew how dangerous these streets were out here for a drag queen. Suzee just hoped that *these streets* didn't happen to her best friend.

The last time she saw her was on Yanita's balcony that night, sucking on her coffin nail, as always. Before the tragic news hit and everyone piled out. She didn't remember seeing her leave. That strange, sparkly masked girl did reek of cigarette smoke, but like Mariah, Suzee didn't know her. She needed to find her, maybe she would know where Reba ended up?

Yanita emerged backstage, a scowl on her face. "My fucking head and my teeth hurt, girl," was all she could muster. Yanita dropped a *very* small handful of singles on her station and tried to pull her wig off, with no luck. "Ohmygawd, girl, can you help me get this shit off?" She rambled with stray wisps of hair in her face and mouth.

Suzee came around, pushing Yanita's hair back. "Wow, that is *really* stuck on there. I don't even see the pins. Don't tell me this is all glue."

Yanita's voice surfaced from below between a tight wince. "The bitch on YouTube said to use glue if you planned on rolling your head around!"

"Yes, baby, but how much glue did you use? The whole bottle? This shit is STUCK to your scalp HARD."

"I used the rest of the bottle; it was only like, halfway full. Look, over in the trash can. It was the only glue I could find."

Suzee groaned. It was about time for her to clock out of this shit show. She walked to the open trash can and stared at the empty yellow tube sitting at the top of it. "Bitch, I know you are fucking with me. You did not use this! Gorilla Glue?! Do you not watch the news?!"

Yanita had a guilty scowl, like she was lying to her teacher at school. "It was all they had back there! I thought the girl on the label kinda looked like Mulva Vagenstein so I figured, why not!?"

Suzee did her best to remain calm and assess the situation. She gave her wig one last good tug, jolting Yanita with it. "Babygirl, they are going to put your ass on the Internet for this one. You better hope all the alcohol in your system starts to pump out of your pores and loosen that shit 'cuz it is *not* moving for me."

Yanita was near tears. "This is the last shit I need, girl. My fucking mouth feels so swollen right now."

Suzee stepped back from li'l Miss Trainwreck and forced a smile. "They look good, babygirl. And beauty is pain, right?" She winced as the Chiclets in Yanita's mouth looked like they were trying to invade her whole face. "Besides, I know you were tired of everyone saying your teeth were still social distancing, or you could eat an apple through a fence, or when they were calling you Princess Snag-gletooth behind your back." She smoothed her hand over the young girl's back, offering her some comfort.

"They called me Princess Snaggletooth? Those bitches." Yanita painfully smiled again, displaying her kitchen-tiled mouth to the back room. "Well now they can just stare and eat it.[1]" She knocked back another shot and rubbed some on her aching gums.

"Babygirl, I think we need to cut you off. You're not driving home, right?"

"I don't drive, Mama. Big Daddy is sending me a car."

"Oh!" She laughed. "Well! Fuck us poor bitches with a bus pass, huh? You lucky bitch."

"You can ride with me, girl, but I told him not till later so I could get my drink on."

"I'm good, love. I want to stop off at the police station since they keep hanging up on me when I call. I'm just worried sick about Reba."

"You already know the cops ain't going to do shit when it comes to this part of

---

1. eat their hearts out, especially when feeling confident

town, girl. The fire department didn't even show up till half of Flamin' Mo's was coming down," Yanita slurred.

"I know, I know, but I have to do something." Suzee sighed.

"We all know they don't give a damn about us. How many of our sisters have gone missing and the cops looked the other way? We have to look out for ourselves in these streets." With that, Yanita poured the last of the Southern Comfort into her glass and chugged it.

Suzee sighed. "Don't I know it, babygirl, don't I know it."

It was last call and Yanita was still celebrating her "victory." The bartender cut her off an hour ago and was giving her daggers as he wiped down his counter one last time. Rico slinked out of his cage with an odd grimace on his face. Yanita and the bartender both rubbernecked as he hustled to the back. "Dumb as a box of rocks, but I *loooove* to see him go," Yanita lamented to no one in particular. The bartender dusted his flannel off before opening the bar counter that had held him captive for the last six hours, the urge to piss hitting him all at once. Yanita looked around at the empty chamber, enjoying the silent cessation of vitality as the bar drifted off to sleep. Her phone dinged, reality chiming in her ear. She forgot to text Big Daddy back. He would be pissy all night.

Big Daddy

> *$2000 FOR A DRESS?? Back in my day, that could have bought a hooker, a burger, and a house. We need to talk when you get here. $20k for new teeth and now this?*

> *That card is canceled for the time being . . . maybe you need an allowance cut til you learn your lesson . . . What's good for the goose is good for the gander.*

Marcus:

Yanita clicked send and rolled her eyes at her phone with contempt. How long could she keep this up? *Till the money dries up, of course.* How long will Big Daddy turn a blind eye to Marcus's indiscretions? Marcus already knew Big Daddy checked his whereabouts and his calls online. Money can buy you security, but not the kind that quieted the mind of an aging sugar daddy, apparently. Marcus was sure he knew where all the cameras were in the apartment, but squirrelly eighteen-year-olds only knew how to do one thing right, and that was *not* listening. Braylon or Graylon (he could never tell them apart) got Marcus caught, but Big Daddy would forgive him eventually. He frowned as no text came back and grabbed his bag off the barstool next to him. *Where did Rico's stupid, thick ass go, anyway?*

The lights dimmed as Yanita walked through the doors to the back, the only sound was her heels on the linoleum. The darkened hallway seemed to be rocking back and forth, the heft of the leftover alcohol weighed on her mind. She turned the corner toward the dressing area, rubbing her still sore gums. The bathroom door burst open as the bartender almost collided with the statuesque drag queen. Their collective scream shocked them both, the bartender's eyes wild with panic. He gasped for air before yelling, "Girl, Rico blew that fucking toilet up! My fuckin' gawd, I thought I was going to pass the fuck out." He had his hands on his knees, catching his breath. "I would wait, baby, it smells like a busted sewer main in there." He stood up and fished his keys out of his overly skinny jeans as he made his way to the alley exit. Yanita unruffled her feathers and scowled in the direction of the restroom. *Not another fucking toilet. Say it ain't so, sweet baby Jesus.* She sulked as she began to gather all of her stuff from the setup area. She regretted leaving her makeup in her "dressing room" that was now swimming with whatever Rico had left behind for his last act.

She scrolled on her phone for five to ten minutes, hoping that would let it air out some. Her texts to Big Daddy showed he had left her on read, the petty old dinosaur. She held her breath and stepped inside, expecting bad but getting so much worse.

The tiny bathroom was all the fine establishment that was Rude Illusions had to offer their talent in terms of dressing rooms. One toilet stall, one urinal, and two floating sinks with a warped piece of lumber used as their makeup station. Tears welled in Yanita's eyes, not due to her accommodations but from the acrid fumes attacking all of her senses. She rifled through her bag, producing her sweet pea body spray and dousing the air with twenty or thirty sprays.

She tried her damndest not to inhale through her nose, but even breathing through her mouth felt like her tongue was coated with the thick bathroom air. The already moist floor seemed more slick than usual under her brand-new heels. Her internal sobs cut short as she almost slipped traversing the off-colored body of water rippling from the direction of the malodorous stall.

Rico is officially off the menu after this ordeal. There's no way I would ever go near anything that produced the noxious sewage that was now saturating her gown. No matter how round it was. How did all that come out of that little man, anyway?

She pussyfooted her way to the pathetic attempt at a vanity, throwing her bits and baubles into her designer makeup bags while still trying to hold her breath. The sound of the back door slamming jostled her still tipsy mind. "What the hell?" *They never pick me up in back. You aren't catching my fine ass in no fuckin alley, I know that.*

Puzzled and annoyed, she grabbed at the last of her things while her double vision caused her to clumsily knock one of her bags onto the contaminated floor. She yelped in anguish as powder compacts crackled and sloshed in the runoff from the overflowing toilet. She dumbly bent down to salvage anything that didn't hit the damp wretchedness.

The door to the bathroom swung open, scraping disintegrating tufts of toilet paper and mahogany waves toward her. She gagged and screamed out, "What the fuck, bitch, don't you see all thi—" She stopped mid-sentence as the figure stood in the doorway. "Girl, wha—" she babbled in confusion as the pink ski mask shone bright in the hazy air. The glare from the jewels shined like a beam from a lighthouse cutting through fog.

The disdain on the Queen's face was momentarily interrupted with disgust as the fetid air soaked into the soft fabric of her mask. A look of condemnation blaming Yanita for the stench was overshadowed by a look of hatred in the Queen's eyes.

Her boots abruptly whomped through the shit pond toward her kneeling target. Yanita was stuck in frozen bewilderment as the Queen's knee plowed into her jaw. The impact rocketing her head against the edge of the sink. The "two-piece and a biscuit" did a "double homicide" on her balance and coordination as pain swallowed her skull.

The Queen swiped at her face but Yanita was already toppling to the slick floor. The Queen audibly snarled as the rage poured out of her. The fall splattered them both with liquid awful. One queen scrambled for equilibrium, the other for bloody annihilation. Yanita worked to get back on her hands and knees, to make sense of this living nightmare. Her temple was already ballooning, her head swirling with thoughts of her ruined gown, these terrible heels, and a bitch in a mask who *obviously* got a BeDazzler for Christmas.

The Queen faced her as Yanita threw herself into the Queen's lower half. The spray of fecal water surged, splashing the walls as their coupled form collided and rattled into the side of the stall. The flimsy walls threatened to throw them both into the cesspit of go-go guano. Yanita hit the swampy ground, her injuries throbbing. Her triumphant counter merited no fanfare.

The Queen pushed off the rickety wall segment, attempting to regain her composure. The revulsion of the wet feces smeared on her boots, coupled with the anger of this kill going awry, fortified her reserve. She gritted her teeth and forked her fingers through Yanita's wig, balling her fistful of hair before slamming it onto the side of the urinal. The unexpected pull ripped patches of hair and skin from Yanita's scalp. An exhausted wail eked out of Yanita, her new smile catching the flickering fluorescents one last time. The Queen pulled Yanita's ringing ear to her juicy pink lips before whispering, "SMILE."

The few remaining bits of Yanita's wig still clung to her inflamed, pulsing scalp. Even in the clutches of the Queen, it held fast as she slammed Yanita's pearly whites onto the porcelain ridge of the urinal. The first slam removed her top front teeth and one canine, loosening her bottom row. Trickles of blood flecked with teeth fragments began to dribble down her chin as the damage and pain caused her body to clench her jaw in defense. Her muffled screams were drowned out as the Queen slammed Yanita's mouth again on the blood and urine spattered latrine. This collision cleared her bloody maw of all but her molars. Her mouth was a babbling cascade of saliva and gore, spilling onto her chin and neck. Her gurgled screams waned as shock rippled through her once pristine body.

The Queen was not yet appeased. This girl deserved a death as extra as she had been in life. She released the loosened wig, trickles of blood seeping out from beneath it. She grabbed the cowl of Yanita's tacky gown like she was scruffing a cat and dragged the fading queen toward the stall, kicking the door in. Chunks of shit and toilet paper swam in the bowl like an overflowing lava lamp. The last bit of fight stirred Yanita, just in time for her to experience her jaw being clamped onto the outer rim of the trickling filth fountain. She choked as the dysenteric swamp water flooded her nostrils and mangled jaws, making her sputter and gag. Her arms flailed uselessly. Yanita's palms never caught traction on the glistening tiles as the Queen raised her knee to her chest. The force of the Queen's boot plummeted down onto the back of Yanita's head. The blow wedged the two pieces of her skull onto the porcelain. The rim smashed through what remained of her jaw. The impact instantly nutcracker-ed her gaping gullet. Her final bubbles surfaced among the other shit smears.

The Queen clung to the wall. She exhaled in relief, still trying not to breathe in the disrupted stench. She turned to stare at Yanita's lifeless head bobbing for turd apples in her watery grave. She could stay there for all she cared. Yanita was never really competition, just fodder for the judges, but the Queen took no chances. She would not dirty her blade on hackneyed mediocrity. She wanted to save its honed edge for those who truly deserved to be removed by royalty.

Gamble Donna Phart

Chapter 9

2 **008** Little Antonio skulked down the long, darkened hallway. Usually a bustling discord of laughing and yelling, the empty silence made the rows of lockers appear longer and more ominous. The sound of prattling and sneakers skidding sent him nervously down a musty staircase. He had no choice but to cower and hope he would go undetected while his tormentors passed him. Antonio had never been in this part of his school. The door that he was ducking next to appeared to be locked with no light showing through the frosted glass. His heartbeat quickened as he heard footsteps at the landing above him.

He didn't know why the four boys hated him so much or what he had done to deserve it. One of them used to be his friend. They had even spent the night at each other's houses for a whole summer. This was back when all he wanted to do was watch *Dexter's Laboratory*, even though his mom disapproved of Dexter's mom's waist-to-hip ratio, claiming it was unattainable. So Antonio found a way to always end up at his friend Cody's house when the show was on. That became their thing. This was the same Cody who started hanging out with the main bullies of the school. The ones who would actively search for Antonio, knowing he had something they could easily pick on. Today's offense: besides sitting at a girls' table at lunch, was letting them put purple nail polish on his nails.

It felt like the second the polish dried, just as his girl friends were putting their lunch trays away, he saw the boys circling. Diego grabbed the back of his neck. Then he whispered in Antonio's ear that they were going to find him after school and gay bash him into the ground. (Whatever that meant.) The school had a strict anti-bullying policy. They hammered into all the kids' heads: tell a teacher and ask for help. So when he went to a group of teachers that day to ask for help, he thought they would finally put a stop to all this. Especially since he still had Diego's nail marks on his neck as proof.

Except the first thing Miss Williams did was grab his hand and stare at his purple nails with her ashy, unmanicured hands. She wasn't listening to anything Antonio was saying. She just whispered something into Mrs. Daniels' ear, and they both smirked with their bad dye jobs and kitten heels. Mrs. Daniels leaned down and loudly whispered in Antonio's face to "Try to be a little less flamboyant" with hot, cigarette and coffee-scented breath. Antonio backed away while the two raised their over-plucked eyebrows and placed their hands on their turkey waddles in judgment.

Antonio should have known better. He should have known that adults say a lot of things but only mean them for certain people. People the same as them or who will be like them when they grow up. Something Antonio would never do. Pastels? He'd rather die.

The sound of feet on the stairs caused Antonio to try the cobwebbed door one last time. To his relief, it scraped open and he was able to slip in just as he heard movement behind him. He spun around and pressed it closed, aware his bullies were only inches away from him. He tried to calm his breathing but the pitch blackness inside and the kicked-up dust made him shake uncontrollably. Unbeknownst to him, baby's first panic attack just set in and began thrashing his insides like a wrecking ball. Through some miracle, his overstimulated brain told his fingers to flick the lock just as the assholes attempted to open it. After a few more tries, he heard their footsteps retreating back upstairs. He slumped down on the gritty floor while the stars in his eyes faded away and he was finally able to get a better look at his surroundings.

The dark room seemed to be a storage for tables, chairs, and random gym equipment. Drop cloths were draped on top of the tallest items, creating a world of ghosts and shadows that were not helping Antonio's preexisting mental state. His brain chose that moment to revisit how frightening the darkness seemed after he opted to stay up and read one more chapter in Stephen King's *Night Shift* last night.

When his mom worked double shifts, he started digging in the still-packed boxes of books for things to read. This was when he stumbled upon his dad's collection of Dean Koontz and Stephen King books. Antonio would read them all night until he heard keys jingling in the front door. That usually gave him just enough time to bookmark where he was and ditch the book under his mattress before his mother would ominously stand outside his door and pray. The silence was the loudest noise he'd ever experienced. When she eventually went into her room, the tiny sobs and whimpers were no reprieve from the inevitable fits he had witnessed on the other side of that wall. Even the most talented horror authors would find it difficult to portray the insidious degradation of someone you loved and trusted becoming the one you feared most.

His breathing was back to normal and his eyes were somewhat used to the dark now. He shakily stood up, bracing himself against the door as he kept his eyes glued to the dark outlines in front of him. The darkened silhouettes reminded him of *The Blair Witch Project*. At this point, he was rethinking which side of this door might have been worse.

He felt for a light switch on either side of the door. It clicked unresponsively, of course. He bit the side of his lip and mustered the strength to find a path through the dank pit of darkness to what seemed like dimly lit windows farther down. A few steps in, he kicked what felt like a large file cabinet that sent a chain of clamor throughout the murky dark of the room.

The pandemonium within his prepubescent brain's imagination, certain he had just told the Blair Witch where he was hiding, gave him the speed and agility of an alarmed cat. The shot of adrenaline allowed him to fly over and across everything in his path. Even the bony claws of the cackling hag couldn't touch him till he abruptly hit the other side of the room in a huff of fear, sweat, and dust.

This side of the room had covered windows that let in just enough natural light for Antonio to find a way out. A single *CLANG* behind him made his skeleton leap within his skin and nudged him closer to a set of double doors. The dust caked on the push bar made him gag, but the sliver of sunlight made it worth it. He pushed through the floating specks of dust until the jangling of chains stopped him in his tracks. Luckily, they were attached to the door and not a would-be attacker or witch behind him, but it still stood in the way of his freedom at this moment.

The chain was wrapped around the outdoor handles of the storage room for security. He reached back to try and free the other door, allowing him a little more space to squeeze his arms through. He struggled as the smooth metal skinned his shoulders and hips, but with one final push he fell to the concrete floor on the other side.

Lying on the cold concrete for a second, trying to catch his breath and cough up whatever had coated his lungs in the dusty dungeon. His knee burned, prompting him to sit up finally. On closer inspection, his knee was skinned from the fall on the ground. Bright red blood dribbled down onto his socks. It almost looked pretty if it didn't sting so much. He brushed the gravel from his gnarled tan skin as he heard voices echoing on the side of the school.

He quickly rose to his feet and listened, trying to determine which way they were coming from. Multiple boy voices came from his right, so he took off running to his left. Ducking behind the wall, next to some low bushes, he cupped his hands over his mouth as he squatted down trying not to be seen. His knees burned, but his whimpers would give him away if he removed his hands. Even the crunch of the leaves brought tears to his eyes. He watched his bullies try the chains on the door. They noticed the smears of blood below them. The boys took off running in opposite directions, giving Antonio the chance to finally make a run for it.

Sneaking out of the bushes, he prepared his lungs for more punishment when a flash of movement out of the corner of his eye caught him off guard. He stared into the face of Cody, equally stunned. Cody's eyes darted to the direction his friends were, his mouth half open in a confused stupor. Antonio's equally frozen face didn't hide the pleading his eyes were making to Cody. A sparkle of sadness, pain, maybe even regret trickled down Cody's cheek.

Antonio took a step back from Cody, his nerves unraveling. Their eyes locked, placing Cody under Antonio's spell as they stared into each other's eyes. The same green eyes Cody had seen up close when they both experienced their first kiss together.

Cody lost their staring contest to wipe his nose on his sleeve. That spark of uncertainty was all the distraction Antonio needed to take one more step back, turn, and run toward his home as fast as humanly possible. Cody's look of recollection quickly contorted into hate as he ran back to his friends.

Once he had made it off school property and was sure he wasn't being followed, little Antonio gave his exploding lungs a much-needed break. He stopped to rest at the city bus stop across from his favorite clothing resale shop. Even though most of the clothes inside were bland (except for the smell), the store always put its most glamorous finds on the mannequins in the front window. He stared at the flowing gowns, fluffy feather boas, and the tallest heels he'd ever seen. Seeing all this beauty made him forget he was running for his life just moments ago and that his white socks were dark red with blood from his skinned knees. Ah, the resilience of youth.

He used to take this bus, before his mom told him he was old enough to walk the twenty to thirty minutes home. He knew it was because of money being tight. Not wanting his mom to worry, he told her it would be good exercise for him. He wanted to tell her how much it scared him to walk alone because kids would follow him or make fun of him when he walked past. He only had his headphones for a few days before one of the kids yanked them right off his head. He had to tell his mom he lost them so she wouldn't worry, but all that did was make her yell at him more than usual.

Antonio missed seeing his mom truly smile. He missed when they would stay up and watch horror movies together and poke holes in elaborate death scenes. He missed having the person whom he admired most look at him like he was her most prized possession. Someone that she would do anything for. His mom was his security blanket. They only had a wall between them but she made him afraid to bridge that gap. She was so close, yet so far away, just when he needed someone in his corner most.

The city bus came to a screeching halt, jolting little Antonio from his dream world of lip gloss and plunging necklines. The three o'clock bus meant he had to make it home before his mom did. Antonio returned to his trek, following the boulevard of stores until he was near their neighborhood. He felt his heaving chest to make sure the house key was still on the chain around his neck. He gritted his teeth as the pain returned to his knees, now ugly paint strokes of drying scabs.

Mom's new job with the church had her working late hours, but Wednesdays were always her early days. She would put on her prettiest dresses and her make-up was on point for mass. She did her best to try and talk Antonio into coming with her, so he could meet the reverend and talk to him about Antonio's "problems."

She always said it was his choice, but she also made it a point to unplug the TV when she left if he decided to stay home. Which just gave him more time to read and create nightmare creatures to look for in the dark.

Antonio's feet and knees ached, he just wanted the day to be over. Turning past the corner to one of the backstreets of his neighborhood, he saw a familiar van creeping slowly. His body kept chugging along, even though the van sighting had his Spidey sense tingling. Momentum took over when his exhausted legs threatened to snap below him. As fate would have it, he caught himself on a light pole just as the van came to a halt beside him.

A greasy-looking man peered out of the van as Antonio winced in pain. *The LordsWay* name, address, and phone number were written in cursive below his hand.

"Angelica told us to pick you up from school," said the scuzzy-looking man as he stubbed his cigarette out on the oversized side mirror. "Where were you? We waited until one of your little . . . friends told us you were walking home."

Antonio's eyes darted from him to the back side of the van. "Where's my mom?" The logo for the church was a big gaudy cross with their slogan *Change is Possible* wrapped around it.

The man said, "We are taking you to her now, boy." He shifted in his seat and dropped the snuffed cigarette butt, still emitting a thin line of smoke. "Now get in." The van rocked and the sliding door opened. A man with adjoining eyebrows stepped out, squinting in the light. He looked Antonio up and down, appearing as if he had to hold back his disgust, and motioned for him to get in the van.

"She didn't tell me anything about this," Antonio said in a shaky voice. "I'm almost home anyway"—he took a step back and looked for anyone else on the street—"and I have homework I need to do."

Unibrow glanced up and down their side of the street, seeing the same empty sidewalks before he grabbed Antonio's wrist. "You can do your homework at church." He pulled Antonio forward, his body responding like a whip pointed toward the open door.

Antonio's breath snagged in his throat as he instinctively grabbed the side of the door to catch his balance. He bolstered himself and said, "I'm not going. You can't make me! Mom said it was up to me."

The tobacco-stained beast slapped his ring-bearing hand on the door and muttered, "Let's go."

Antonio's grip was slipping as the unplucked man released Antonio's wrist and instead wrapped his entire arm around his torso. With one quick move, Antonio was lifted up and into the van. His open mouth let out the beginning of a scream when the sweaty paw forcefully closed his jaw and carried him deeper into the windowless van. He held Antonio's head tightly against his musty body and slammed the door with the other.

"Don't hurt him, just keep him quiet. I promised Angelica," said Ashtray up front as he lit up and put the van in gear.

Antonio tried to pry the unwashed man's crusty hand away from his mouth, to no avail. His eyes were wild with rage, panic. His nose burning with the smell of a thousand locker rooms surrounding him.

"Just drive." The creature's voice strained against Antonio's ear and his hot garbage breath assaulted his face.

The van lurched forward, with Antonio's muffled screams fading from his sapped energy. He eventually succumbed to his exhaustion while the van passed The LordsWay church and kept going.

October 22, 2022, Saturday

The blaring car horn snapped Gamble back to the real world. The van following her down the street caught her off guard and almost made her dive for the bushes. She nearly lost her balance as she blinked repeatedly and attempted to revive some neurons.

"Shnap out of it!" yelled a familiar voice from the darkened passenger side window.

Gamble recognized that horrible Cher impression anywhere, bringing a huge sigh of relief.

"Hop in, bitch! I know them hoofs is painin'!" yelled Suzee Ho Maker from her Econoline van. Gamble barely hesitated before pulling the door open. "I was trying to get your attention, girl. I wish I knew you needed a ride before."

"Since when did you get a soccer mom van, Miss Maker?" Gamble asked while putting her seat belt on and staring at the pine tree air fresheners dangling from the rearview mirror.

"Shut up, bitch, I'm borrowing it from my brother while mine's in the shop." Suzee laughed before checking her blind spot and pulling off. "I'm hoping Amanda Scrümi doesn't screw me over too bad. She heard the noise Bessie was making at our last gig and told me she would take a look at it for me. Isn't she a sweetheart? With her big ol' man hands."

"Who? Amanda?" She paused. "I don't know her," Gamble said, biting her acrylic pinkie and looking away.

"Ooooh, girl, you so shady! I thought Amanda got along with everyone. What's the tea?[1]"

"Ain't no tea. She just kinda stays in her lane and I stay in mine. She don't check for me, I don't check for her. You know how it goes."

Suzee smiled in schadenfreude, sniffing new bones to be collected.[2] "Ohhh, so y'all tryna FUCK, huh?" Suzee gripped the steering wheel with anticipation.

"GIRL, SHUT UP!" yelled Gamble, visibly offended. "We might have matched on a dating app here or there, but nothing ever happened. Besides, that was before I knew we were competitors. Now I want her head on a stick."

"Youch! So it's like that, huh? You girls make me glad I got out of the game when I did. Y'all a little too cutthroat for me. I don't know how . . . Reba . . . still does it."

The laughs stopped and a cold silence filled the interior of the vehicle.

Suzee distractedly pulled her phone out and looked at her empty notifications. "I know y'all don't really talk, but have you seen her out since Marcus's party? Or anywhere?"

Gamble sucked her teeth and said, "No, ma'am, Pam. Why? Where is she? I thought she was supposed to be doing the gig at Stiffies on Monday with us?"

"I haven't heard from her at all since the party. It's just not like her to ghost me like this," Suzee said, holding back her sobs. "I just feel so helpless. First Flamin'

---

1. the truth/news/info

2. gossip/secrets to hold on to

Mo's, now this?"

Gamble heard the hurt in the voice of someone who was like a drag mother to her. She bit her lip and nervously asked, "Have you gone to the cops?"

"Oh, fuck these pigs," Suzee snapped as her sorrow flipped to anger. "I just got back from the police station. This asshole looks me up and down and slides a missing persons form to me. Wouldn't even listen to a word I had to say. Just made me fill it out, then slapped it on top of the pile. I was so mad I wanted to spit."

Gamble let out a deep sigh and grabbed her friend's hand. "I'm sure she'll turn up. Maybe some trade whisked her off her feet and they're fucking the weekend away as we speak."

Suzee caught the tear before it ruined her makeup and laughed. "For her sake, I hope that's true." She sniffled. "Even though that trade would have to be blind and have a thing for yetis, cuz you'd need a cage to catch that Bigfoot hairy bitch."

October 21, 2022, Monday

"Girl, what the hell is a Hyundai Sonata?" Elektra asked, into her phone jammed onto her shoulder while she continued to grab all her leftover swag bags. "A black car with an *H* on the front? Okay, next time just say that, Jenellica. Like I'm supposed to know what every damn car looks like. Mm-hmm, I am walking out now. "

The statuesque Nubian queen's signature bald head glowed under the bookstore lights. Her custom-made spiked metal collar glistened as the lights flickered off bay by bay. The black leather catsuit with built-in cape would look garish on anyone else, but it looked regal on the Amazon princessa.

With an armful and her bag slung over her shoulder, she stepped her black leather boots out of the storefront and into the chilly evening air. "Oh, it's here already, girl. Yes, black Hyundai." She attempted to wave at the driver before crossing in front of the headlights of the Black Honda Civic.

The doors unlocked just before she pulled the door open, threw her things in, and plopped into the back seat. "It was dead, girl. I only signed maybe ten books and most of them were for other queens." The driver uttered some greeting but she didn't catch it, her phone to her ear while she dug in her purse for her cigarettes.

She muttered, "Uh-huh" in response, casting a side-eye to the front seat. The driver was wearing a pink bedazzled beanie and trench coat.

Somebody got a BeDazzler for Christmas.

Elektra scrunched her face, "I need to get a car if I'm going to be doing appearances like this, girl. An Uber ain't cute for the doll."

Every few blocks, the streetlights would dance across the face of the driver for a millisecond. Elektra obliviously prattled on. "My preorders were shit but sales will be through the roof. You know these hos love some good spilled tea." A flash of emerald green eyes caught Elektra's as she glimpsed in the rearview mirror. The split-second stare caused her some unease, or perhaps it was a jolt of déjà vu. *Are we getting off the freeway?* "Did you upload the episode or not, Jenellica? It's almost ten." Elektra craned her neck to see what exit this was. "Uh-huh, well you tell that heifer to bring her own mic, not my fault she sounds like she's eating the side of her face." She dug around in one of the swag bags for something to munch on. The ding of a text notification rippled through the silently smooth car ride. "Did you text me? Hold on." The flash of headlights illuminated her frozen, confused face as she peered at her glowing screen.

Uber:

Your Uber has arrived!

Elektra didn't have time to process any of this new information before the hot pink beanie was pulled over the face of her driver. The squeal of brakes and the force of the stop rocketed Elektra's brow into the back of the headrest. A light show of pain flashed behind her eyelids from the small bones and cartilage in her nose folding in on itself. All the contents of the back seat, including her, were thrust forward. Blood flowed as her face began to slump down the rear of the seat and her senses attempted to regain some sort of agency over her trembling body. Blood trickled from the bored holes in her décolletage made by the sharp points of her snug metal collar. The loud, crackling sound of the stun gun jolted her back to a dazed consciousness just as the prongs stabbed into the soft flesh behind her ear. Darkness enveloped her.

Elektra willed her eyelids open. She longed for an escape from the black nothingness she was suspended in. The sound of duct tape, shifting equipment, and high heels striking the concrete floor invaded the void as blinding white light horizontally sliced through the black veil.

Pain blossomed from the center of her skull as a glob of black blood forced itself out of her collapsed nostril. Pained moans escaped her mouth as she attempted to shake free from her restraints. She glared at her bound wrists, then her surroundings as she regained the ability to focus. Her eyes finally rested on the familiar masked Queen standing before her.

"About fucking time," spat her attacker, her voice a little too sultry for the occasion. The masked Queen gave a cautionary glance at Elektra's bound ankles and wrists before heading into the back of the dilapidated garage. Elektra's eyes transitioned from panic to rage as she screamed and tried to bite through her duct tape gag. She continued to thrash, knowing it was futile. All she could do was try and figure out where she was and how she could get help. Dust that was caked on the floor floated around the garage, possibly a storage unit, behind the Queen's trail of boot marks. Elektra's vision seemed to waver as she tried to note anything familiar in the room besides the mistaken Uber parked next to the large roller door.

Heels clicking concrete and scraping metal snapped Elektra's attention to the source of the commotion. The jerk made her neck ache under her custom-made metal collar, measured and forged to her exact dimensions. The brash piece of jewelry was guaranteed to catch the eye of every onlooker in the room. She demanded three-inch spikes, custom-ordered and honed to fine points that were now coated with her dried blood.

The Queen trudged a rusty cart covered in a crusty drop cloth toward Elektra, the wheels barely able to spin. With a final groan, the Queen sat the cloaked apparatus only inches from Elektra's thrashing body. A dirty smirk crossed her pouty lips as she dusted the grime from her leather gloves, letting the dingy particles drift toward the incapacitated prima donna.

Elektra shook her duct tape throne with blind fury as bloody spittle spattered past her makeshift gag, commingling with the dust. The Queen removed her black trench coat with a flourish, revealing a catsuit and corset that Elektra would have eye-fucked *hard* had the situation been less sanguinary. Elektra's eyes fixated on the drop cloth as the Queen pulled, letting it slide and drop. A chalky cloud puffed around Elektra, coating her clammy, bloodied skin.

Unprepared to hold her breath, Elektra hacked and wheezed when the stale bits invaded her nostrils and throat. The grainy tears in her eyes obstructed her view, prompting her to squeeze and flush them. Terror roared through her body as the murky shroud cleared, finally revealing a pair of jumper cables and a car battery.

The tears caused the duct tape to loosen around her cheeks, enough for Elektra to gnaw at the gag, suck in a deep breath, and let out a muffled scream, "WHY?"

The Queen drew closer, ignored the inquiry, and placidly clutched a jumper cable in each hand.

Elektra writhed for freedom, shrieking again, "WAIT! WHY? TELL ME WHY?!"

Elektra's screams seemed to penetrate the Queen's leather-clad exterior. Her screaming set off a chain of firecrackers in her synapses, her swollen brain throbbing against the walls of her skull. The Queen paused, looked into the straining, tear-soaked eyes of Elektra, contemplating her response.

"Gamble deserves the crown," the Queen said breathily, as if she were speaking in a dream sequence.

"Gamble?" Elektra murmured. "GAMBLE?" she repeated, slurring her words, rocking back and forth, testing the pull on her restraints again.

The Queen let out a labored exhale, bringing her lips close enough to Elektra's bruised cheek to smell the fear evaporating off of her.

Their opposing eyes met as the Queen cooed in her ear, "There can only be one Queen." The combination of the decree with the snap of metal on metal stunned Elektra, while the confusion and lethargy that came from a brain hemorrhage set in.

The weight of the jumper cable clamps only pulled the collar down slightly—that custom piece was not going anywhere. The Queen traced the cables back to the cart, turning in time to see a stream of viscous blood bubble and leak out of Elektra's crushed nostril. She uncapped the terminal covers on the car battery, wanting to appear as if she knew which end went where. She waited a beat for more refusals from Elektra but knew it was now or never. The Queen hoisted the jumper clamps, their fangs gaping just before the gleaming terminals.

"Time to fry," she huffed as she finally made contact, snapping Elektra's head back like a Pez dispenser.

The Queen stood back, watching her elaborate electrocution scene unfolding before her. Elektra's painful screams came out more like strained gasps. The Queen had anticipated sparks, sizzles, flickers that turned to flames but instead, she stared at the contorted face of Elektra, her eyes twitching but not yet smoking.

Her bald head was not glowing as electric currents undulated beneath her skin, nor were her eyeballs about to explode out of her charred skull. The frustrated Queen stepped out from behind the battery cart, needing to get a better look in case one of the cable clamps came loose.

The room seemed to fill with a smoky aura that finally penetrated the Queen's mask as she drew near. The smell of burnt hair and . . . shit. A large amount of heat seemed to be emanating from Elektra's clamped collar and the car battery.

Her neck and chin had quickly turned an alarming hue of rust, darkening by the second. Smoke was certainly starting to emit from the quivering queen, as well as the smell of rank booboo. Elektra, wanting to go out with class, had indeed voided her bowels.

On closer inspection, her face was aghast in pale anguish. The faint electric currents in the car battery had only been successful in paralyzing the very muscles that the roasting queen needed to breathe . . . for the last four to five minutes. The Queen was disappointed to say the least, realizing too late that Elektra was already dead. The few jerking movements the Queen had witnessed must have been tremors from the car battery still attached.

Now was not the time to dwell on couldas, shouldas, wouldas, but you could read the disappointment on her face, mask or not. It was hard to tell if the battery was out of juice, so the Queen readjusted her leather gloves in order to unclamp the cables from the battery.

Just then, as a faint sputter spattered out of the corner of her eye, she gasped in disbelief. Had Elektra survived, after all? She squinted through the thick, pungent smoke that blocked her view as a flicker of light illuminated Elektra's roasted head.

Flashes of fire rose up around the dearly departed, broiled beauty as her hairless head ignited. The Queen felt the warm glow through her mask, prompting her to stop pouting a little. The flames on the side of Elektra's enshrouded face made the Queen smile—her favorite Madeline Khan moment.

The Queen strolled to retrieve her trench coat before the stench of shit and scorched flesh permeated the material. She was deep in thought as she walked to her car, ruminating on all of her careful planning going up in flames just behind her. She really botched this one, but all's well that ends well. No trophy this time, but she knew she would learn from her mistakes. The count was six girls eliminated, for good. Now only six more to go.

Gamble Donna Phart

Chapter 11

OCTOBER 24, 2022, MONDAY

"Well, if it isn't Miss GD Phart!" Edema Kanklez said, wrapping her arms around Gamble. "Look at you, girl." The pair parted so Edema could get a better look at Gamble, who wore a navy blue romper that looked markedly similar to something Michael Myers would wear, paired with platform boots to finish the look. Edema snapped her fingers. "I see you out here hurtin' 'em, Michaela Myers."

Gamble grinned ear to ear. "Okay, Miss Va-va-voom!" She marveled at Edema's floor-length crushed velvet gown. "I am gagging, I love all the green."

"It's the color of envy, you know. Gotta keep all these hos mad," said Edema, with a side smirk. "And that's . . . "

They both joined in, "ON PERIODT." The old friends double high-fived and interlocked their fingers in delight.

"You go on next, right?" asked Gamble, motioning for a drink at the bar.

"Yeah, after Xtra Mayonessa." The sound of skin slapping and sticking to laminated wood created an offbeat metronome from behind them. "I hope they mop up during intermission because the last thing I need to do is slip a disc walking on a greasy stage." Edema looked toward the stage with a furrowed brow and winced. "I don't think that girl's parents taught her how to bathe correctly. She makes me itch every time I see her." They both shuddered and looked away, patting their wigs in disgust.

"Wanna come back with me while I get ready? We need to have a kiki," said Edema, as she stood up and gathered her such and such.

"Yeah, I'm doing Stiffies in two hours but I need to pick your brain on what I should do to my hair for the pageant," Gamble said, grabbing her drink.

"Ma'am, how am I going to look giving my direct competition pointers?" Edema laughed as they both headed toward the back.

Before they made it to the dressing room, a dark figure in head-to-toe black vinyl emerged from the office. Both girls stopped and stared before letting out a collective scream.

"HOOOOOO!" Edema yelled, as the pageant-queen- turned-dominatrix, Heaux B. Hayve, shyly covered her mouth and gasped.

Edema hugged her and eyed her up and down. "It's giving me *Hellraiser* . . . but fashion . . . I like it."

Gamble absentmindedly took mental screenshots of Heaux's entire look, from her tight bob to her corset bustier.

Edema pulled away from her old friend and said, "Oh shit! Gamble, this is the *legendary* Heaux B. Hayve of the Haus of Fyre." Everyone went silent, all eyes began to go glossy. "Nope. Nope. Nope. We are keeping it moving, y'all. Dyna wouldn't allow *any* of us to smear our makeup, especially this close to curtain call." Edema snorted back her tears. "This is Miss Gamble Donna Phart. She's one to watch, she's coming for all our necks."

Gamble was overcome, starstruck. Heaux gave Gamble cheekbone and said, "I love that name. So very few clever names out there anymore. Then you hear ones about mayonnaise? Heaven help us." Edema stifled her laughter and Gamble bit her lip.

Gamble said, "I saw one of your last shows when I first started out. I've never seen hair teased so high in my life."

"Aww, aren't you sweet?" Heaux remarked as she grabbed Gamble's hand and motioned for her to spin around. "Brains and booty, my favorite combination. I look forward to joining you onstage."

The crowd in the bar all collectively gasped and a *boom* followed by a record skip rippled through the speakers.

"We got a drag queen down! This bitch has fallen and she can't get up!" yelled the MC.

"Say what, now?" asked a dumbfounded Edema, next to an equally slack-jawed Gamble eyeing Heaux.

"I just filled out all the paperwork," said Heaux with a smirk. "With Mama gone, I will have to represent the Haus of Fyre one last time. It's what she would have wanted." She wiped her little button nose with a tissue.

"Well, I have some preparations to make, now don't I? I'll catch up with you two at the pageant."

The shiny, slick siren strolled back out into the bar, leaving both queens gooped,[1] mouths agape.

"Fuck" was all a stunned Edema could utter. Then, after a long pause, "Girl, why don't you go get us another drink real quick? I need to text Dixie."

Gamble silently agreed, still lost in thought. Edema sashayed back to the dressing rooms while her acrylics furiously tapped her phone screen.

Until now, Gamble felt like she was guaranteed a win at the pageant, but to have an old pro make a surprise comeback could throw a wrench in everything.

Gamble returned with two Long Island iced teas, setting one down on the makeup station while her eyes met Edema's in the mirror. Heaving a sigh, Gamble said, "Bitch . . ."

"I know, I know," said Edema before she gulped down half her drink. She came up for air to finish. "We'll deal with her later. I can't take all this before I go on." Edema stared in the mirror as Gamble picked a stray sequin off her back. "That bitch. The audacity," Edema added while she looked in the mirror.

"What did Dixie say?" asked Gamble while she babysat her cocktail.

"Nothing yet," Edema replied while scrolling her dry phone. "She's going to choke when she hears, though. I'm going to see her tonight, and she's going to want the whole rundown."

Gamble almost choked herself before replying, "Bitch, is you serious? You too?"

Edema squeezed her *mitties* together in the mirror. "Nothing wrong with a girl getting a little help in the ass and titties department. I did the girls last time; this time I'm getting me a Kardashian ass."

Gamble shook her head while she drank. "Girl, you have more ass than three of me! You don't need it." She stood up and shook her ass in front of the mirror to both their amusement. "I would just worry about what Dixie is putting in you. You know her cheap-ass will cut corners everywhere. Remember when she walked out onstage in just pasties and a G-string and said she was a smiley face?"

Edema made a face like she'd just opened a jug of spoiled milk. "I still have nightmares of that night. I was in the front row and she almost took out my eye

---

1. amazed, stunned, shocked

when she hit those splits," Edema said, staring a mile away like she was lost in a war flashback.

Gamble cocked her head and winced. "Anyway, just be careful. Text me when you're done, if you're still alive." They both snickered. "Wait, isn't Elektra's book thing tomorrow? Are you not going?"

"Yeah, she's mad at me still." Edema chuckled as she applied her lipstick. "She ain't texted me all day. She'll get over it eventually."

"I was going to go but I'd have to Uber over there and I haven't been trusting these Uber drivers lately," Gamble said, as she tapped glitter on her eyelids.

"You can't trust anyone lately, beloved," Edema said, as she pulled her dress up and rearranged her cleavage. "Just keep your head on a swivel and watch your back."

A commotion could be heard over the subdued EDM playing throughout the bar. Both girls noticed and started grabbing all their shit.

"You good?" asked Gamble as Edema grabbed her purse. "What the hell is going on out there?"

They both hurriedly shuffled back out to the bar to angry shouting and the music cutting off. A crowd was forming around the bar, all the hens seemed to be clucking at once.

"Who found her?"

"How could this have happened?"

"Where the hell is my chiffon?"

"And she JUST got that fucked-up mouth fixed!"

Edema pushed through the theatric throng when she saw some grown-ass man and Suzee Ho Maker in the center of the commotion.

Suzee's eyes were a muddy mess of ruined makeup. She was sniffling now while the tall glass of "Whew, child" was attempting to comfort her. As soon as Suzee and Edema's eyes met, Suzee started howling and crying in elderly ho.

"She's dead, Edema!" Suzee wrapped her arms around her stunned friend.

Edema asked, "Who's dead!? Somebody get her a napkin, please!" Edema held her old friend tight so her makeup wouldn't stain her dress.

After a few tries to catch her breath between sobs, Suzee exclaimed, "Yanita! They found her dead at Rude Illusions this morning!" Suzee's face contorted into ugly Kim K crying face, and she collapsed on the bar in a fit. "My poor baby! She could have been a st—" Suzee paused the waterworks to reminisce. "She was so young!"

Edema gasped in mild shock at the news and recognized that the strapping young man was Cisco, a.k.a. Amanda Scrümi. She had never seen Amanda in boy drag before, let alone in his work clothes all greasy and blue collar and tempting like this. Cisco turned to her, anger and hurt in his eyes and his square, manly jaw quivering. Edema couldn't miss an opportunity to console the young man or cop a good feel, so she opened her arms to offer him her motherly bosom.

Cisco pulled away from the embrace. "I just wanted to come tell y'all. I have to get back to the shop. I didn't want to text the news."

That *skrong* deep voice almost made Edema flood her basement as she went in for one more uncomfortably long hug. "So thoughtful!" She squeezed his arms. "So strong!" She turned to her still blubbering friend, getting all cried out on the bar top. Gamble took the initiative to rub Suzee's back while she wiped her tears away, trying not to smear her makeup more. "We are so appreciative of this Cisco." Edema pulled a cocktail napkin out from under Suzee's pile before it got wet. "Let me give you my number in case you need someone to help you get through all this."

Cisco gave Edema a look of disbelief before barking, "Girl, if you don't go over there and help your friend! Somebody is DEAD."

On cue, Suzee wailed and latched on to Edema, allowing Cisco to escape while he could. He tried to part the Childboo Sea while yelling back, "I'll text you if I find out anything else!"

Edema yelled back, "Okay, baby," while she tried to fix Suzee's torn-up mug, prompting Cisco and Suzee to both look at her in bewilderment.

Suzee collected herself and uttered, "I can't believe it."

Edema, watching Cisco go out the door, said, "Girl, me too! Now I understand why I always thought she had such a strong-ass face. Mmm mmm mmm."

Suzee pulled away from Edema. "Can you be serious for ONE minute, Darius?"

The crowd oohed and dispersed.

"Not the government name."

"Darius?!"

"I found my chiffon, if anyone cares."

Gamble ordered the three of them drinks and asked Suzee, "What the hell happened?"

Suzee grabbed the drink as soon as it hit the bar. "They won't give us many details. All I know is they said the janitor found her in the bathroom at Rude Illusions this morning right before he retired." She took a second to sip her drink and collected her thoughts.

"Mama, you know I don't believe it until I see it with my own eyes," said Edema, finally showing some emotion. "This just doesn't sound right. We just watched her flop onstage a few days ago!"

Suzee was about to go on a tirade disagreeing with Edema, but she had a point. She'd never seen so many patrons walk out on the dance floor and take their tips back as she had before Yanita's final performance.

"This is just too much. First Dyna, now Yanita." Suzee blew her nose into a napkin and handed it to Gamble. "I know ALL these hos' phones are not broken! Something is going on and I don't like it."

Gamble reached over the bar to drop the pile of soiled napkins in the trash can. "Nobody is going to fuck with Reba, she's the broadest broad I know. Remember when she pulled the entire judging panel with her teeth for her talent?"

"Exactly!" added Edema. "They had to give her the win, but that's when they started doing drug tests again for contestants."

"Yeah,"—Suzee sniffled—"I miss my jolly queen giant. I pray she's okay. Oh shit, Edema! We are eating into your time! Get on up there, girl. I'm sure we could use something to lighten the mood."

Edema looked at all the smiling faces around her. "I do hate to disappoint my public." She checked her face in her compact and walked to the stage.

Gamble yelled out, "Wake up, Lance, Edema needs a song!"

The crowd rose to their feet. Gamble put her arm around Suzee. "C'mon, Mama. No more tears tonight, okay?"

Suzee grinned and fanned her eyes. "What would I do without my girls?" She stood up and joined the crowd waiting with anticipation for Edema Kanklez.

Lance, the MC, cued up Edema's music as she did a mic check. "We are strong. We are one. We are nothing without each other. Can I get a HOT DAMN?"

"HOT DAMN!" the crowd yelled back.

"This one is dedicated to the talented, the unforgettable Amanda," said Edema throatily.

"YANITA, YOU BITCH!" howled Suzee, with a disgusted look on her face.

"Oh shit! I mean Yanita. My bad," Edema apologized, before she started her number.

Dixie Wrecked

Chapter 12

October 24, 2022, Monday

"Now you listen here, Thiccy Ricardo, I ordered my food over an hour ago. Not my fault you don't know your way around the Hills," the voluptuous drag queen in the velour tracksuit said through the wrought iron gates of her palatial condo. "You want a tip, you better come feed me my Popeyes while I'm in the tub," cracked Miss Dixie Wrecked to her DoorDash driver.

"I don't think my girl would be cool with that," said the Dominican with the tight fade. Though he seemed to be thinking it over once he spit out his perfunctory answer.

Dixie leaned against the column as the gate began to rattle open. Her blue bundles blew in the slight breeze. "What's your girl gotta do with me?" She batted her eyes and giggled as her gate started to screech and clank noisily. "Just give it a second, it likes to act up," she cooed, seductively puckering her lips at the poor man. The gate made a loud crashing sound and stopped in its tracks.

"HO-ASS GATE!" She slipped off her *chancla* and hit the inanimate object with the baby blue slipper repeatedly. "DON'T YOU SEE I'M TRYIN TO—" As if commanded, the gate started to open again, emitting grinding noises as it moved.

After the gate squeezed open enough for "Ricky" to hand her the food, he said in a hushed tone, "Ain't you a dude, though?" His eyes unapologetically scanned the drag queen's exaggerated curves, hourglass figure, and blue glittery beard.

"What gave me away, boo?" Dixie cracked dryly, stepping closer to her prey of the day. "I could be your last delivery." She coyly turned and rubbed her ass against him. "These Hills have thighs. It would be a shame if you got lost in them again."

Ricky said frustratedly, "I got lost because there's no reception out here. I couldn't find the damn place."

At this point, Dixie was close enough to see his drawn-in patchy beard. A shame really, he needs more protein in his diet. Which she was trying to help him with.

"That's one of the downsides of living up here, Papi, the reception is horrible." She thrust her bountiful bosom toward his face, slipping her hand in her hairy cleavage to pull out a warm, sweaty one-hundred-dollar bill. "But these Hills ain't all bad, you know."

Ricky was dangerously close to wishing he was in Dixie, but the cash so close to the taco meat snapped him out of her spell.

"Nah, fam, I gotta go." He backed up until he almost cleared the fence.

Dixie knitted her brows and yelled, "Getcho ass on, then. Go cut some coupons witcha li'l girlfriend or whateva." She hit the gate button on her keys, beginning the slow, scraping sequence.

Ricky fired back as he crossed the gate threshold, "Okay, Uncle Phil."

Dixie scoffed and tucked her hair behind her as she marched in his direction. "You know what, not-so-pretty Ricky? You not that cute."

The gate pushed past Ricky's face, rattling and chugging as it went. "You look dusty."

Ricky turned and walked down the curved sidewalk.

"And your hair is uneven!"

Ricky crossed the street to his black Hyundai Sonata with the Uber sticker in the window as Dixie continued to berate him. "Eat you some spinach and maybe that beard will finish growing in, RICKY!" The gate finally jerked back into place.

Dixie stared at the rusty, dusty, crusty gate with displaced anger.

"This motherfuckin' gate is going to be the death of me," she said *sotto voce* as she grabbed her phone out of the back pocket of her track pants. The ass used to say JUICY, now it just read ICY from closing the fridge with her hip too much.

She texted maintenance *again,* instantly getting back a *Not Delivered* error message. Irritated by the whole situation, she turned to go back inside when she heard the click of heels abruptly coming her way. Her eyes shot up as the Queen brazenly walked up to her gate.

"Bitch, what the fuck?" Dixie spit, stumbling backward, almost losing her balance. With disdain and shock, she eyed the towering Queen. From her boots up to her black catsuit, trench coat, and hot pink rhinestone ski mask.

"What in the BeDazzler for Christmas?!" she exclaimed. "Bitch, I don't know who sent you but I don't do walk-ups," she barked as she caught her breath.

Dixie's tone came down a little. "You makin' it hot with that little getup anyhoo, girl. Text me and I'll see if I can get you in next week."

Something about the glare the Queen was giving to Dixie made her blood run cold. She stepped back, further inching up her driveway. As much as she hated that punk-ass gate, it seemed to be keeping this wild animal off of her at the moment.

The Queen smirked and broke eye contact as she walked backward and out of sight. Dixie slow blinked at this whole fucked-up afternoon and chalked it up to hunger. She headed inside, cold Popeyes in hand.

Dixie was not only THE bearded lady, but this genderfluid stunner had ass, ass, and more ass, with a brain too. She even had a sixteen-week CNA training certification to prove it. She took her hippopotamus oath seriously. That's why when she heard her good Judies were getting "enhancements" in dirty back alleys, she said, "Not on my watch." Not when her nice, clean garage was available and her skilled hands were made to augment.

It took her a few botched procedures, but she eventually got the hang of it. Eventually all the doll babies knew that if your wagon was saggin', or your ass needed more mass, or your chesticles weren't their besticles . . . Dixie would wreck you good. She might not have been the best . . . or most knowledgeable, but she was cheap and she would keep pumping whatever you needed until she got it right. Except she didn't do any of the above . . . in case the cops were listening. For all they knew, she was selling flat tummy tea.

Dixie Wrecked emerged from her bedroom, showered and fresh as a bearded daisy. She was on her second velour tracksuit of the day. As she walked down her stairs, she tied her hair up in a ponytail. Her phone dinged as she entered her kitchen. She read the text from Edema Kanklez as she dug around in the crumpled Popeyes bags on her counter.

Edema:

> *Leaving now. Elektra hasn't responded back yet, but can a bitch get a group discount or what lol*

Dixie:

> *I would have to charge Mr. Clean extra, she built like a lollipop with that big ass head. Lol I still ain't forgot how she nudged me out of second place at the Summer's Eve International way back when.*

Dixie resent her text to maintenance about that bitch-ass gate and it miraculously went through. *Praise the Wi-Fi gods.* She had an hour before Edema arrived. She had to get everything ready in the garage. She grabbed one more Popeyes biscuit to keep her strength up. Edema was getting the Onion Booty Special, so Dixie would be in "surgery" for over an hour if she didn't have any complications. She checked the time and bit into the infamously radioactive-yellow biscuit as her phone vibrated in her hand.

Edema

> *GWORL. You won't believe who was at the gig tonight talking about one more show for Dyna. Wait for it . . . you ready?*

> *Miss Heaux B. Hayve!!! I said BIIITCH!!*

Dixie inhaled in shock, a flaky hunk of neon yellow biscuit caught in her throat. Dixie instantly tensed her entire body and gripped her phone. Her eyes widened and watered as panic set in.

Each attempted breath burned and forced the chewed bolus deeper into her airway. She stood up from her kitchen island and used the edge of the counter to move herself nearer to the sink. As she got close, the thought of city tap water made her shudder. She was seeing stars as she remembered the open water bottle in her purse.

Pained wheezes escaped her open mouth. Her vision started to go fuzzy. Capillaries began to burst in her eyes. Her acrylics scratched the plastic lid of the water bottle. With her last remaining strength, she hunched over the counter and sucked the room temperature water down. With her last gulp, the dry biscuit—now hydrated—finally unclogged from her throat. She gasped for air as her chest filled with burning embers. Her eyes now just puddles of tears. She regained her composure and summoned the strength to unlock her phone and text Edema.

Properly recovered and rehydrated, her flip-flops flicking echoed in her driveway as Dixie waddled to her Escalade. She opened the colossal back door and pulled out several bags from Home Depot filled with assorted plastic caulk tubes. She grabbed them all and slammed the door closed with her hip. The jolt of the movement caused the pointy nozzle of one of the caulk tubes to stab and split the thin plastic bag open. Two tubes hit the driveway and started to roll down the steep descent. Dixie cussed and threw the remaining bags in her open garage while she huffed laboriously, chasing the tubes that had gone astray.

The copious amount of silicone that she had injected herself with was attached and hardened to her ribs. Her girls looked great in a gown but all that extra weight was killing her back. With a pained grunt, she picked up the lost tube that stopped just past her behemoth truck.

Dixie exhaled in exasperation and checked the time on her phone. Edema should be here in thirty minutes and she still had to get everything prepared.

Last year's get-rich-quick-scheme was massage, but she mainly got older women with arthritis showing up for a rubdown instead of the line of muscle-bound "menseses" she had envisioned circling her block. That didn't pan out, but at least it let her use her massage table as a makeshift operating table. She even got that crumple-crumple medical exam paper to complete the illusion that this was all legit.

She started to cut the tips off the caulk tubes at a sharp angle like YouTube had instructed her to. They were ready for her caulking gun to extract and mix their contents in a *sanitized* paint bucket. She found a blend of Fix-a-Flat, industrial silicone, and liquid concrete worked the best and kept her prices down. When her clients asked what it was, she told them the truth . . . silicone. *wink wink*

Besides, not everyone needs to know how the sausage is made. Just pay up and enjoy your donkey booty and don't say shit if the cops ask you anything. Dixie slapped on her nitrile gloves and started to stir the milky gray mixture. Globs of overflow dripped down her slew of syringes like candle wax as she poured the concoction into them. Edema was a big girl, but she wanted more dump in her truck, so ten vials should do the job. She capped the syringes with their plungers to stop the gelatinous goo from clumping and drying out.

With her cell phone in hand, she opened her garage door and texted Edema.

Dixie: *My gate is acting up so park on the street and text me when you get here XOXO*

Edema Kanklez pulled past Dixie's gate and parked across the street in front of Dixie's cute li'l McMansion or whatever. She texted Dixie and grabbed her purse as she marveled at the view all around the place. Her house looked like a palace, no neighbors to be seen. Edema stepped out and around her car to look at the hills and trees that sat below the steep ravine just past the sidewalk. She had on a T-shirt, flip-flops, and some purple sweatpants that she knew she would be filling out better once she left.

"It's pretty, huh, bitch?" Dixie yelled, startling her zaftig friend.

"Almost as pretty as me, bitch!" Edema replied, cautiously looking both ways before crossing the street.

"You good, girl, nobody drives back here unless they lost," Dixie said as she gave her friend some cheekbone. "And good luck getting reception up here, bless their hearts . . . even though today is a whole other story."

Edema basked in the opulence of Dixie's home as they walked up to her front door at the top of the hill. "You made it, girl, you are living in The Hills in a house made of ass money."

"Child, if you only knew the half of it." Dixie giggled as she ushered her friend in. "Anyway, I want all the tea on this Heaux B. Hayve sighting," she said, as the massive front door clicked closed.

"Here, take this now, 'cuz I ain't going to lie to you. This shit stings," Dixie said, handing Edema a pill and a full glass of water.

"What is it?" Edema asked as she gulped it down.

"Just a Valium. It'll take the edge off. Just like last time." Dixie took the glass back from Edema. "I need you somewhat coherent in case I need you to move around or anything. Your chest was just pump and go. Booties are a bit more work when it comes to shaping and movement." She grinned at her friend and exhaled. "You ready to do this, girl?"

Edema nervously jumped up. "Yes, bitch, let's go before I change my mind!"

Dixie motioned for her friend to follow her and yelled, "Time to blow that ass up, babygirl!"

Dixie was putting on her gloves while she explained everything to Edema one last time.

"Once I get both sides equal, I will move the silicone where it should be. All you have to do is lie there while it molds itself into place. After about an hour, you should be good to go," Dixie assured her friend as she put on her face mask with splash shield. "You'll probably be knocked out anyway. Valium puts my ass to sleep every time."

Edema held the towel around her lower half as she sat nervously on the creaking massage table. The worry started to melt off her face the more she listened and Dixie knew that meant it was time to get started.

"Towel on the table and then I'll have you lie down flat on your stomach," Dixie instructed.

Edema followed her directions and Dixie grabbed the bucket full of syringes and warm water.

"Let's begin."

An hour had already passed and Dixie was sweating up a storm. Almost all of her syringes were empty and *one* half of Edema's ass looked great. The other just didn't seem full enough. This is about the time that Dixie realized she didn't have enough to fill both sides. She had perfected her concoction of liquid concrete, industrial silicone, and Fix-a-Flat down to a science. Yet somehow, she was off. A tube of liquid concrete sat half used in her trusty caulking gun, but she had somehow miscounted and was one tube of silicone light. She nervously retrieved her phone from her soggy cleavage to check the time. She was glad Edema was groggy and face down, unable to see how worried she looked. She had enough time to run back to the store to get more but that meant Edema had to stay here while everything got settled.

"Okay, babygirl, listen to me, listen to me, okay? I have to run to get a little more so we can finish up your right side, okay? It looks great, though. You are going to be making all the boys cry with this onion booty, all right? I'll be RIGHT back, I promise."

Edema mumbled back in babbling approval.

Dixie grabbed her keys and purse, opening her garage door before she walked out into the crisp air. Her frazzled mind was trying to think of the quickest way to Home Depot as she got in her truck and started it. She drove a few feet closer so she was in range to open the gate. When, of course, that trifling-ass gate decided to groan and stick in place. Just as she was beginning to full-out rage on the bitch-ass barricade, she noticed a single shining tube of silicone sitting at the base of it.

"There you are!" Dixie jovially exclaimed.

Her eyes filled with adoration for the gate that she had misjudged so harshly. With no hesitation, she leapt out of the front seat and followed her headlights to her savior. Just enough silicone to finish Edema off and save both their asses. Her worries were finally assuaged.

The hum of her mega-truck muffled the sound of heels on her driveway amidst her own frantic flip-flopping. Just as she shambled to retrieve the lost tube, she felt her ailing back achingly give out. The sound of her herniated discs slipping sounded remarkably like a truck door slamming shut. Pain radiated through her body as she attempted to hobble closer to her gate in order to use it to stand up straight.

The sound of her truck's gears shifting and the gas being slammed down was just another part of this dream sequence turned nightmare scenario. She was barely upright when the sound of screeching tires snared her eardrums as she tossed a cautionary eye toward her speeding automobile. Allowing a split second to see eye to eye with the rhinestoned-pink-ski-masked-freak that was about to have the audacity to mow her down in her own truck. *Fuckin' BeDazzled Bitch*, her last thought as her body was crushed against the wrought iron wretchedness.

The impact of the strike forced her body up slightly as her hips caught and crunched against the thick bumper. Bits of bone and chunks of meat were mashed into the grill of her designer SUV. Small clumps of milky silicone mingled with blood began to drip onto the driveway in a fluorescent pink puddle beneath her. Sections of her ribs were protruding through her signature concoction of industrial fillers, pulping through the mangled gate. The only part of Dixie that did not seem to be wrecked was her skull, which had somehow maintained its shape while being pressed almost completely through the openings in the gate.

Dixie Wrecked's mangled form, the dented gate, and the idling vehicle took a sigh of relief as all the excitement seemed to dwindle. The Queen opened the car door and exited the vehicle. Content to admire her handiwork while the instinctual urge to be a spectator at a car accident beckoned to her.

Dixie was a leaking, oozing pustule that seemed like it popped between two dirty metal fingers. Shoulder joints were inverted and hip bones pointed in all the wrong directions. If this was a game of Twister, bitch would have won for sure.

The mutilated "Most likely to break some necks" had most likely fractured hers in more than a few places. Her chest, or what parts were still in place, allowed only very small sporadic movements. The Queen grimaced at the blends of red and purple collecting beneath the dying drag queen. She knew Dixie's suffering wouldn't be too much longer . . . but just enough that she deserved. The Queen blew Dixie a farewell kiss and gave her, the mammoth SUV, and her creaky gate some quality time. She had a patient to check on and deliver some tender loving carnage to.

The click of the Queen's heels faded away in the background leaving the remaining consciousness Dixie had to ooze out. The disfigured queen felt the hot headlights squeezing the last few particles of air out of her lungs. The truck was still running and seemed to still be in gear when a thunderous *CLANG* erupted from the gate.

The force and the persistent push from the behemoth-on-wheels appeared to have set the gate back on track. If the contents of Dixie's skull weren't swelling to immense proportions, she might have giggled at this turn of events. That would be if the gate hadn't continued to open back in working order. The pickets in the gate ground against Dixie's disfigured derriere allowing her body to just barely come free of it when it reached its fully open position. The parts that weren't still attached to the ridges in the truck's grill slowly melted into dangling strips of flesh attached to the undercarriage as the immense truck crept past the driveway and into the street.

The land yacht silently cruised over the curb and sidewalk while gravity continued to press more of Dixie's pulverized limbs into the tread of the slowly rolling tires. The headlights shone over the grassy bluff as the vehicle picked up speed. The increased *rolling drag force*[1] peeled Dixie's lolling head down and into the path of the craggy sports utility tire. The pressure on her already swollen brain caused her skull to expand, macerate, and crunch while the tire trampled the last spark of life out of her. With her insides now on the outside, her exposed silicone hit the cold night air. The hardening silicone glued the last bits of her to the bumper as she and her charioT plummeted into the dark forested ravine

---

1. Yes, that's what it's called. I shit you not.

below.

Gamble Donna Phart

Chapter 13

2 **008**   The bump in the road jostled little Antonio out of his nonthreatening dream state. One he wished he could go back to when his sense of smell and urgency returned. He attempted to hop up and out of the second row bench seat, but the arm of the disgusting man pinned and held him in place. Before he could react, the smelly man bent his arm and jammed his elbow in Antonio's face.

"Keep quiet, Tinker Bell, unless you want me to put you back to sleep," the lummox said greasily.

Antonio wasn't particularly shocked at the formulaic insult. His mother taught him that those that name call also usually pronounce the *L* in salmon . . . so just ignore them. She learned that in her pageant days. She said years of dealing with pageant girls gave her a surprisingly tough skin. She could be loving and caring when everything was going her way. Yet, his loving and caring mother was the reason why he was sitting in this filthy church van in the first place. *Were they really taking him to her? Was she really behind this?*

He was jolted out of his thoughts when the van took a sharp left and seemed like it was now driving on a gravel road.

"We're almost there," said the driver as he pulled up to some kind of security guard attendant in the woods. "Keep your mouth shut, Angelica is waiting for us inside."

The driver honked and rolled down his window. All Antonio could see was a large wire fence, and just beyond it, a winding road through trees. He could hear footsteps crunching the ground and a gruff man's voice mumbling something. The driver said, "Another wayward," and nodded before the gate began to crank open.

Little Antonio felt a cramp just behind his belly button causing his teeth to grind against each other. Stars began to form in his eyes as the van lurched forward. His lungs felt devoid of necessary air. His arms were buckling under the goon's foul hold. He tried to take his mind off *where* he was going or *why* by staring at the throngs of green trees they were passing through.

The sun seemed to be setting, but the height of the forest made it seem even darker in the vehicle. Antonio's pulse was thumping in his ears. He clamped his eyes shut, praying he wasn't having a heart attack. It felt like they had been driving for hours through a million trees before finally coming up to a clearing. As they pulled forward, the last of the setting sun lit up a large chapel connected to a Spanish mission. The entire settlement seemed to have somehow been buried deep in this fantastical forest.

Antonio's heart raced in his chest. The van lurched up the large drive of the ominous pale building. Antonio's mother was placidly standing outside in a baby blue dress with red roses on it. A man stood next to her that Antonio didn't recognize.

The van came to an abrupt stop. The warthog holding Antonio finally loosened his grip. The van door slid open, allowing Antonio to finally suck in fresh air that he had been silently begging for. His urge to fly out of the smelly van was quickly dashed by the appearance of the strange man he'd seen standing with his mother. His linen suit only brought more attention to his bad tan and slicked back greasy hair. His sunglasses didn't hide the uncomfortable stare that Antonio felt burning through the thin tinted lenses.

The man cracked his nonexistent, flaky lips to reveal dingy beige dentures in a sinister smile as he reached a hand out to Antonio. "Hallelujah! Could this be our latest Christian soldier reporting for duty?"

Antonio scrunched his face at the creep blocking his way, looking past him at his mother. She stood still, posing for her newly arrived audience. Overcome with emotions, Antonio dipped and ran past the comically unaware cartoon villain. His mother's face remained calmly unchanged as he wrapped his arms around her waist with a death grip. She brought her hands up to his face and pulled it back so he could look into her eyes. Their emerald gaze was broken by her words. "Baby, you're going to get dirt all over my new dress." She winced. "My god, you're filthy."

Antonio's jaw trembled as he lowered his arms. He took a step back from his mother, waiting for an explanation that he felt he deserved.

"I'm sorry, baby, but it's Prada!" She brushed an imaginary stain away from her hip before meeting Antonio's gaze again. "Don't you just love it?"

Antonio's brows drew together and his eyes went shiny as the sound of crunching gravel came up behind him.

"This is Dathan," she said, her voice shaking the closer the presence behind him grew. "He's Mommy's new boyfriend."

A strong hand gripped Antonio's shoulder. "You can call me Reverend DL Cakes, son." The man turned Antonio toward him, with his vise-like grip still clamped on his shoulder. "We might have to clip those wings of yours if you are so adamant to fly away like that, son." Antonio glared at the forty-pushing-fifty-year-old man with rotten breath.

"You know, Genesis tells us of a wayward young man just like yourself. His name was Jacob. He was a little trickster and he lived up to his name." The man picked up Antonio's chin to look him in the eye. "I see you got your mother's eyes"—he sighed—"but also the eyes of Jacob. Do you know what the name Jacob means, son?"

Antonio shook his head reluctantly with doubt and hesitation.

The man took off his sunglasses and pulled Antonio close enough to smell the acrid scent of wintergreen, garbage juice, and decaying gums before uttering, "It means 'deceiver.' You see, Jacob was a deceiver *and* a trickster." His eyes bore holes in Antonio's skull. "Tricksters disrupt nature. They poke fun at what is normal and traditional, the way the Lord intended it."

Angelica interrupted the sermon, "Let's go inside, Dathan. I'm getting cold."

The man's nostrils flared, but his face didn't change. He yelled back, "You go on ahead, don't you see me and the boy are still getting acquainted?"

She turned but paused before she went inside. When she attempted to speak out again, he commanded, "I SAID LEAVE US UNLESS YOU WANT TO BE OUT ON THE STREETS TONIGHT."

Angelica balled her fists and exhaled noisily through pursed lips before she turned toward the massive wooden doors of the chapel.

Antonio broke his stalwart stone reserve and yelled, "MOM! I want to go home!" before his head was pulled back in place by his ears. Back to the sinister face of the Devil himself, whose hot breath threatened to melt Antonio's skin right off his skull.

"You don't have a home, son. This is your home now. It's either this or the street, so you don't have much choice now, do you?" Calmness returned to the leathery face of the crazed man as he slid his hands back to Antonio's shoulders. "Your mother and I think that with some hard work, you can be the face of The LordsWay ministries. Our greatest transformation yet, once we get you back on the path of the Lord."

A glob of clear mucus dripped from the man's brambles of nose hair. "I'm sure your mother has told you . . . the only way into Heaven is to do everything the way the Lord intended you to, right?" His intense stare was making Antonio's skin crawl. He turned his head away from the man and toward the chapel and the forest.

The reverend placed his mouth only inches from Antonio's ear and said in a sickly whisper, "Your mother certainly has the Delilah spirit, doesn't she? Just loves interrupting grown men when they're talking." Antonio felt bile burn the back of his throat as spittle flecked his cheek before the reverend continued. "As I was saying, Dathan means 'belonging to the law.' That's why I'm here on earth, righting the wrong. Fixing the evil. Correcting the sinners. One by one." He sniffed his runny nose. "I belong to the law and you belong to me, you little faggot. I'm going to fix you, one way or another, and if I can't . . . I'll stomp your ass into a hole deep enough no one will find you."

Once inside, little Antonio tried his best to get close to his mother but the reverend kept his claws embedded in his shoulder. Antonio looked around the entryway at all the painted floor tiles and tapestries depicting anguished saints lining the walls.

"It's beautiful, isn't it?" the reverend asked, eyeing the space. "I can feel the Lord himself emanating from these very walls." He ran his hands over the stucco with pride. "This used to be the St. Anthony Monastery. Named after the patron saint of lost things. Your mother named you after him. Kinda ironic, huh?" He looked up at the ceiling and smiled. "Out in the middle of God's country. Isn't that beautiful?"

He snapped out of sermon mode again. "Angelica," he called to her, "why don't you see if we can get our little prototype something to eat."

Angelica walked up to them with a quizzical look in her eye. "And where is the . . . uhh kitchen?"

"Two roofs down, my love," he said with mild annoyance in his tone. "You'll learn the lay of the land, just you wait. In the meantime, I'm going to give this young man a tour." They headed toward the enclosed courtyard. The reverend guided mother and son through the door, one with care and the latter with thinly veiled animosity.

Dusk was turning to nightfall as lamplight flickered through the hazy courtyard. Antonio was no longer a fan of silence, and the deadened sounds of nature in the ominous seclusion brought him no solace. The menacing calmness broke when Angelica's heels clicked on the stone walkway toward the adjoining building with the smoking chimney.

"About time we men had time to ourselves," spat the reverend. He finally released Antonio's shoulder, guiding him into the dusty courtyard toward a shadowy figure. Antonio rubbed his shoulder, sure that it would be black and blue by morning. "I trust you won't do anything stupid like running from me again. You know we are miles from civilization out here." He inhaled, his nostril whistling. "Yes, just us and the wilderness. Isn't that right, Elijah?"

Unibrow from the back of the van stepped forward, brandishing a knife and a half-whittled crucifix in his hand. "Yes, Reverend," the ogreish man replied, glaring at Antonio and stepping back in place.

A door on the farthest wall ahead of them creaked open. The van driver emerged with an unlit cigarette dangling from his lip. The reverend beckoned the man to come closer before introducing him. "And I believe you've met Saul."

Saul stared down blankly at the boy. The reverend said, "The Lord has eyes and ears everywhere, son . . . and so do I. Don't you ever forget that."

The remark caused a smirk to wash across Saul's face. Proof that he wasn't, in fact, one of the living dead after all.

"You are awful quiet for someone who's had green daggers pointed in my direction since you laid eyes on me, son. Is there something you need to get off your chest?" asked the reverend in a bemused tone.

Antonio looked at both of the men and paused to think before saying, "You talk like the big rooster from *Looney Tunes*. Your dentures are too big for your face, and you're not my father, so you can stop calling me 'son.'"

The two men exploded with laughter. The reverend wiped back tears and tried to collect himself. "There's that fighting spirit I knew was in there." He smiled at Antonio, who was staring dead at his mismeasured teeth. The reverend's lip drifted down slowly over his overbite, in defeat. "Fighting spirit gives me a lot more to work with, and there's a much bigger difference to be seen by all when I rip that spirit out of you."

Little Antonio sat on the beat-up mattress and looked around the desolate room that he'd been told was his. Besides the bed, the only things the cubbyhole contained were white stucco walls, a murky window, and a small desk with no chair. Antonio stood up to peer out of the cloudy window while he held a damp towel wrapped around his body. His wet hair dripped on the glass, slicing a line of clarity through the window film. He drew a stick figure with a skirt in the film with the leftover moisture. Suddenly, the door loudly unlocked and the reverend charged into the room.

The reverend threw a handful of dismal-looking brown clothes on his bed before barking, "You have two minutes to get dressed unless you don't want to eat tonight."

Antonio picked through the pile to hold up a pair of woodland camouflage pants and a matching shirt. His face was pinched like he had just bit into a ripe lemon.

"One and a half minutes, and counting," the reverend yelled before slamming the door behind him.

A few seconds later, the reverend kept his hand on the small of Antonio's back, guiding him down the stairs. Antonio was trying to hold the oversized pants up as they walked.

"We'll see what other clothes we have from donations later," the reverend said as he pushed open the double doors in front of them. Antonio walked into a moderately sized cafeteria with tables and chairs. From his vantage point, he could see an older woman busy working in what looked like a small kitchen area in the back.

The reverend pulled a chair out from an empty table and motioned for Antonio to sit while he went to the back.

"Plate of supper for one, if you don't mind, Sister Abigail," the reverend said while he rested his arm on the serving hatch that bridged the kitchen area from the dining area. "That is, if Saul isn't back there eating it all." A pan clanged and Saul emerged from a corner of the kitchen invisible from the small window. Sister Abigail set a tray with steaming food on the ledge. The reverend grabbed the tray in one hand and said, "Sister Abigail doesn't smoke and it smells like an ashtray everywhere you go, Saul."

Antonio looked around the room, staring at the ring of chairs across from the table where he sat. The reverend placed the tray on the table and slid it in front of Antonio. "Those are for Group tomorrow." The reverend paused and sat, expecting Antonio to inquire deeper but was met with silence. The corner of his mouth raised into a slight smirk and he shook his head before belting out, "Nothing better to stick to your ribs than Sister Abigail's chili! Eat up, boy, you'll need your strength for tomorrow."

Antonio raised his eyebrows and picked up his spoon. He dug through the "chili" like there was a prize at the bottom. The jabs at the bowl were the only noise echoing through the wide space.

Antonio dropped his spoon and asked, "Where is my mom? Why are you doing this?"

A look of victorious satisfaction crossed the reverend's face as he steepled his hands before him. "Son, have you ever felt lost? Confused?"

Antonio looked down and thought to himself. "Sometimes . . . but isn't that normal? I'm becoming a grownup."

"Well, yes and no." The reverend paused. "Have you ever felt broken? Like something about you wasn't right?"

Antonio continued to look down and his mouth quivered. "Sometimes . . . is that why I'm here? Because I don't feel right?"

The reverend put on his best straight face, and said, "Son. If you don't feel right. If you feel wrong . . . That's because you are."

Antonio's face turned stone-cold as he fought back a tear. "No, I'm not. You don't know anything about me."

The reverend replied with a heightened sense of righteousness, "I know you are a boy who likes to dress like a girl." He paused to enjoy the look of betrayal on the young boy's face. "Do you see any other men wearing women's clothing?" He paused to see if the sullen boy was paying attention.

After a long silence, Antonio replied a quiet, "No." He sniffled and said, "I just like fashion. My art teacher says that I can be a clothing designer someday."

"Son, don't listen to a woman who gets paid to clean up crayons and finger paint all day."

"My art teacher is a guy."

"Good Lord in Heaven, they got them in the schools too." The reverend put his face in his palms. "Talk about the blind leading the blind." The reverend continued. "Son. Normal people don't feel lost, or broken, or that they weren't right. God wouldn't let them think that way because he loves them just the way they are."

Antonio laughed, but the tears welling up in his eyes betrayed his current mental state. "So you're saying God doesn't love me."

"I'm saying God is telling you that something about you is wrong. Something about you is not like everyone else and once that thing is fixed, those feelings will go away." The reverend glanced over to see if the young man was believing any of this. "He wants you to be normal. He wants you to be happy. He wants you to have a wife and kids. Like we were all made to do."

Antonio's eyes looked lost and downcast beyond belief. The reverend knew now was the time to strike. "You are here to have what's wrong with you fixed so God will love you again, because the way you're going . . . If you stray any further from what the Lord has created for you, he will strike you down. Hell is a scary place, son. We need more good, honest, Christian men in the world. I'm afraid the Devil himself has been whispering in your ear and it's my job to stop him in his tracks. You love your mother, don't you? Isn't it selfish to let people see that she birthed an abomination? Some freak in a dress? I know you felt dirty, you felt shame putting on girls' clothes, right?"

Antonio held his head in his hands with tears streaming down his wrists. "Yes,"—he coughed—"I didn't want her to see me."

"That was the good Lord trying to warn you that you were going down the wrong path. That was the Devil thinking he was winning. We will bring you back to God's love. He will welcome you back . . . once you shame the Devil for what he made you do. Are you prepared to do that? For your eternal soul? For your lovely mother? For our new ministry?

Antonio looked up with fear and hatred in his eyes and said, "Yes."

Edema Kanklez

Chapter 14

O CTOBER 24, 2022, MONDAY

"Dim the lights, Daddy, Mama wants to sing a little song just for you."

The houselights dipped down low. Waves of sultry saxophone began to fill the smoky room. The downbeat kicked in as the spotlight shone on Edema Kanklez, a vision in a low-cut, shimmering purple gown. Every eye in the room was a roadster following all her dangerous curves. Her pin curls look like caramel rosettes on her supple brown (okay, fine . . . chocolate) skin. She pulls her cream-colored gloved hands from her *tiny* waist up to the microphone and cradles it while she belts a buttery note that melts every heart in the room.

Her voice is as smooth as the iridescent pearls glowing around her *dainty* neck. With her voice thoroughly warmed up, the instruments stop. The music yearns for Edema's voice to give it a home. She takes her cue and belts out loud enough to shake the rafters:

"I have a cute faaaace

Chunky waaaaist

Thick gams in shaaaape

Humps shakin' both waysss

Made ya do a triple taaaake."

The room erupts with applause and wolf whistles. Edema bats her eyelashes and blows a kiss to the crowd. Her eyes twinkle in the light, the sounds of the room buzzing. A faint clicking begins to materialize. Edema's showstopping smile wilts. The clicking of heels shakes the room. Screams contort the alarmed faces in the crowd. The clicks stab her temples with white-hot intensity. Edema lets out a shriek that snaps her back into the reality that is Dixie's garage.

Edema jolted back into her body. The clicking heels of the Queen seemed like they were right on her swollen ass. The spike-heeled boots appeared in front of her stupefied eyes as she peered through the hole of the massage table. Before her stood the Queen, with a look of wonder mixed with hesitation.

The Queen leaned down to get a level look at what appeared to be two very different-sized ass cheeks.

Edema's bassy baritone voice boomed, "Peekaboo, bitch! I see your ass!" The horizontal, lopsided drag queen's cackle echoed throughout the open garage. She wiped the drool from her cheek and groggily lifted her head before the pain in her ass and thighs shot up her spine.

Their eyes met. Edema now seeing the rhinestoned ski mask sent her into a fit of laughter. "What are you going to do? Rob my ass? I ain't got no damn pants on, bitch!"

The Queen sneered in disgust. Her eyes began darting around the garage for anything that would prove helpfully homicidal to her. To her dismay, the garage was an excess of Costco impulse buys. The Queen sidestepped a bucket full of used dirty syringes to look at the shelves lined with cleaning supplies and paper towels. Who in their right mind needs a six-pack of liquid weed killer?

On second thought, she grabbed a jug and dropped it in front of Edema.

"Bitch, is you the gardener?" Edema continued to be ever so tickled.

The Queen looked toward the open garage door as a scraping and clanking maelstrom could be heard amidst Edema's nonsensical jibber-jabber and raucous chuckling. The Queen dug in another corner and found bleach and ammonia. She shrugged her graceful shoulders. Ingenuity is the mother of invention, right? She set those jugs next to the prostrate, yet disproportionate, prima donna as well.

"Ohhh, you're the MAID, now I get it." Edema wheezed a wet cough and laughed uproariously. "Miss Dixie, I am out of lemon Pledge!"

A sudden racket of crunching trees and a dull *crash* sent the Queen running out to the driveway to see what all the commotion was. She came back cursing under her breath as she grabbed the bucket full of syringes. Edema remained incredibly amused, oblivious to the dangerous predator just inches from her.

"Thank you for the BeDazzler for Christmas, Miss Dixie!" Edema erupted in an uproar of shrieking hysterics.

The Queen was outraged by the nerve of this prone plebeian princess to continue to joke in the face of death. The Queen screamed out, "KEEP LAUGHING, BITCH!" before she kicked the wobbly massage table with all her strength.

The strike caused both front legs to fold inward, rocketing Edema forward. Her top half skidded toward the garage floor. Her legs curled over her back like a scorpion's tail, sending hot fire through her swollen ass and hamstrings. That rude awakening seemed to have snapped Edema out of her hazy stupor and finally silenced the howling hyena. The Queen heaved the tilted massage table over with the strength of a Jersey housewife, rolling Edema to the ground with it.

Edema lay on her back, with the wind knocked out of her from the abrupt landing. Keenly aware, too late of the danger she was in. The Queen kicked Edema in the ribs and straddled the downed drag queen. She grabbed a tacky used syringe out of the bucket next to her. Edema fruitlessly pawed at the Queen's face while she jammed it into the plastic bottle of bleach.

The fumbling didn't detract the Queen from pulling the plunger back and engorging the syringe with the corrosive toxic chemical. In one quick motion the Queen reeled back, switched hand positions, and plunged it into Edema's chest. Edema screamed out in fear more than pain as the Queen shot the bleach into her flesh and chest cavity. To add insult to injury, the sadistic Queen cranked her wrist to the right, lodging the broken needle in the muscle. The smell of bleach began to permeate the area as the stream of acrid fluid continued to pour out of the punctured jug.

As Edema's body began to quiver, panic set in, anxious about what this foreign chemical was about to unleash on her already debilitated body. Her skin began to itch. A metallic taste formed in the back of her throat. Her already short, labored breaths seemed to become even more so as uncertainty flooded her mind. The burning in her throat caused her to hack, forcing the sensation to travel further up to her mouth.

The Queen already had another syringe in her grip, taking advantage of the flailing, faltering, fizzing Edema. She tried to reach the ammonia, but did not want to give up her position holding Edema in place. Her stretched, gloved hand was able to grasp the side of the weed killer and pulled it closer to her. While the Queen jammed and filled the second syringe, Edema continued to thrash and pull at anything she could get her hands on. Edema was finally able to grab the leg of the shifty card table Dixie used for mixing as the Queen readied Edema's next injection.

Gooey paint stirrers, wire cutters, and Dixie's caulking gun tumbled down onto both of them, almost knocking the blue-loaded syringe out of the Queen's hand. Her catlike quick reflexes allowed her to deflect the falling debris and bury the needle deep into the other side of Edema's chest. Edema's wails were drowned in phlegm and defeat. The Queen's tongue traced her teeth as her thumb shot more hazardous chemicals into Edema's already brimming body and snapped the needle in place once again.

Edema felt like magma filled her chest. Her arms and shoulders felt numb and were no longer following her commands. She felt her jaw start to shake, leading to her entire body eventually convulsing unbeknownst to her. Edema watched powerlessly as the Queen eyed the fallen contents of the table. The Queen grunted, reached above Edema's head and pulled the caulking gun loaded with the industrial silicone in it. The sharp, slanted tip glinted as a glob of thick, murky goo dribbled out of it. Edema sucked in an inhale to scream one last time, anticipating the Queen pointing the barrel of the gun at her and pulling the trigger.

If anything could be said about the Queen, it was that she lacked mercy about as much as she lacked predictability. The Queen speared the Bondo bayonet into Edema's open eye with enough force to prompt a spray of blood and ocular fluid to geyser up. The thunk of the nozzle cracking skull caused Edema to scream her pain into oblivion. The Queen reeled back a few inches and jammed again and again until she felt the bony back of Edema's crunchy eye socket. In her enfeebled state, Edema's body was decommissioning. Her ability to fight back was stunted by the tip of the silicone mashing bone fragments into her perforated brain sac and the hilt of the cross guard shattering her orbital bone. A bead of sweat ran out of the Queen's hot pink mask as she pulled the trigger into the jammed space she created in Edema's dome-piece.

Click . . .

Click . . .

Click . . .

Usually the sound of a close call from an armed assailant was instead the meek, steady sound of Edema's skull being packed with the sticky, odorous silicone. The irony that the same material that promised to fill out Edema's jeans was now filling her sinuses and cutting off her air supply. Edema's face looked like a sputtering, overflowing bowl of cherries jubilee. Perhaps she could use that drag name in her next life, because the silicone was already overflowing from her swelling brain and out of her nostrils and mouth. Edema's movements came to a shuddering stop. The Queen pulled the squelching caulking gun from the expired queen's wrecked hole of a head. Threads of syrupy red spider silk clung to the weapon as it clanged to the ground.

With a heavy sigh, the Queen's knees popped like water in boiling Crisco when she stood from the deep knee squat. She hadn't noticed until it was almost too late, the chemical-dense air she had been sucking in made her a little woozy. She quickly stepped around the dearly departed Edema, her heels slapping through the puddles of bleach and ammonia. She raced out the garage door and sucked in lungfuls of fresh air.

Her eyes and lungs felt like they were on fire. She rested her hands on her knees to summon her strength. After the brief pause, the Queen looked around cautiously at the silently ominous night. She followed the trail of gore out the open gate and ripped off her mask as she glanced around for any witnesses. Satisfied by the isolated solitude, her heels clicked through the street and past the sidewalk. Her face sparkled from the beads of sweat lit up by the glow of the ridiculously large taillights bathing her dewy visage in red. Regardless, she marveled at her view of the entire LA skyline from here. She soaked it all in and couldn't help but reflect on all that she had accomplished on such a beautiful night.

Gamble Donna Phart

Chapter 15

O**CTOBER 25, 2022, TUESDAY**

<u>7:03 p.m.</u>

Gamble:

Did you hear about Specific O'Shawn? :(

Evayda:

OMG girl, don't tell me! Dis TEW much, my heart can't take it.

Don't tell me they got her too??

Gamble:

No bitch. Well I mean yes bitch. She dead but she wasn't killed. She choked on a crab-cake @ Drag Brunch and they couldn't revive her. :(

Evayda:

BITCHHHH NOOOOO. Not dying in day drag! Nobody deserves that. :(

Gamble:

I hope her mortician is good with a putty knife cuz they said her foundation looked like chunky peanut butter toward the end.

Evayda:

I hope your VIP section in hell is far away from my VIP section in hell cuz I can't stand your disrespectful ass.

Gamble:

LOL what time??

Evayda:

9 p.m. Outside, or I'm leaving your ass there.

Gamble held a bronzed chest piece and long white skirt to her body, waiting for Evayda's ever-critical eye to tear it to shreds.

"And the headdress is the same bronze?" Evayda asked, raising an eyebrow as she studied her friend's pageant look.

"Yes, ma'am. I just did another coat, it's drying on the balcony." Gamble said, biting her lip in anticipation.

Evayda nodded and rubbed the white chiffon sleeve material between her fingers. "And hair up or down?"

Gamble swallowed and answered, "Black, straight, twenty-two inches, my queen."

Evayda smirked and looked her friend in the eye, pausing to let the sizzling pot that is Gamble's head boil over. "You are going to look *stunning,* dawling!" She snapped her fingers in succession. "You aren't going to let these girls have a single crumb onstage."

Gamble hung the pieces back on her closet door and leapt at her friend. They hugged as Gamble exclaimed, "Bitch I hate when you do that shit to me! I was like fuck, there's only a few days left so if it ain't right, I'm SOL."

"It's all amazing, booboo, Mama is very proud," Evayda added. "Just make sure you swing those arms, I want to see those sleeves flow like you have Beyoncé wind fans about to knock you over. You hear me?" Evayda turned to strut a line down

Gamble's modestly-sized bedroom in her black one-piece bodysuit hugging every curve she created.

Gamble pulled back and did her signature walk with her arms snaking around her. "I won't let you down, Mama . . . Are you still doing the *Kill Bill* lewk?"

"You already knowwww. Embezzla Froque is going to drop it off at the hotel. All yellow leather, smooth as butter."

"Ain't that cutting it a little close?"

"Girl, when ain't she cutting it a little close? She lucky she does such amazing work and her detail is always on point, 'cuz chiiild . . ." Evayda patted her newly twisted cornrows. "When has a drag queen ever been on time for anything?"

Gamble grabbed her boots from her closet and gave Evayda the *welp* face: pursing her lips and nodding with a side-eye.

"Bitch! I knew you had my pink *fuck me* pumps!" Evayda yelled as she stepped behind Gamble to peer closer.

She playfully pushed past her friend and grabbed her shoes from the closet floor. "It be your own damn people, I sweatergawd."

Gamble laughed as she sat on her bed and pulled on her knee-length Timberland heeled boots. "Oops?"

Evayda held her pumps in her crossed arms. "Is that what you're wearing?"

Gamble looked up exhaustively as she pulled her bootlaces taut. "Don't start bitch, you know how I love Freddy. Besides, not all of us can pull off a Lane Bryant catsuit."

Evayda began typing on her phone but still responded with a whispered, "Bi-iiiitch."

Gamble stood up and smoothed down the back of her short red and green knit sweater dress. It looked remarkably like something you'd find at a Goodwill on Elm Street. She pulled on a leather fingerless glove with a mesh full glove inside, topped with four long shiny nails on the fingers from her nightstand drawer. She stepped up to Evayda, doomscrolling in Gamble's doorway. "Silver nails too!" She fluttered her phalanges in Evayda's face like a bothersome gnat.

Evayda looked up and scrunched her face. "The only nightmare around here is your hot-ass breath, girl! What did I tell you?! Hand me my purse, I know I got some gum in there."

Gamble scoffed and picked up the surprisingly hefty black mini shoulder bag.

"Are we ready?"

"Gum first, baby. You are not about to be funkin' my car interior all up to be damned," Evayda said, not even looking up from her phone. "Why is Dixie's punk ass not texting me back?"

Gamble opened the flap of Evayda's purse, almost dropping it in place. "BITCH!" she screeched in shock, "You do not have a pistol in this Michael Kors bag."

"I sure the fuck do, and it's Fendi, you whore," Evayda said, snatching her purse out of Gamble's hands, Gamble still in shock. She pulled the smooth, matte black metal piece out of her purse. "Also, this is a Glock. I ain't robbing no stagecoaches. Look." Gamble pulled back suspiciously. "Let me be serious for one second, okay, for this one millisecond of our friendship." Evayda pointed the gun away from Gamble with her finger off the trigger. "You ain't ever allowed to touch this, but in the case of an emergency . . . a.k.a. some crazy muthafucka is chasing our asses . . . this is where the safety is." Evayda pointed to a mechanism that ran along the trigger itself. "I ain't going to show you full-out 'cuz this bitch is loaded. Just know, it's like a double trigger. You pull once to engage and then again to put down whoever is in your way. Got it?"

Gamble gulped nervously but watched Evayda's demonstration. "Weren't you the one who JUST gave me shit for taking a li'l ol' razor to a gig?"

"Yes, but that's because you're a child. I'm two whole-ass years older than you," Evayda said, clasping her purse shut. "Did you miss the part where our friends are either missing or being found dead as disco?

"What's disco?" Gamble asked innocently.

Evayda kissed her teeth with disgust and pushed her friend out of her room. "Bitch, go gargle . . . and stay out of grown folk business."

Gamble and Evayda's eyes scanned the almost empty club. Dismal air filled the gig more than bodies did tonight.

"Let's get a drink," whispered Evayda as they crossed the barren dance floor to the bar. Only a few patrons were sitting at tables sprinkled around the stage. Two people sat at the bar, along with the owner who kept checking her watch.

Evayda ordered two vodka Red Bulls, hoping the kick of caffeine would revive the mood. The unease in the air was thick. Notes of confusion and dread, like smoke, permeated everything it touched in the moody space.

"So nobody is going to perform?" Gamble asked, breaking the tense silence. "Like, at all?" Her eyes darted around, hoping for a response but not expecting one. She turned to Evayda, nursing her drink, and asked, "Do you feel like going up onstage?" The bartender and the few lost souls at the bar listened in for her answer.

"Not until I hear back from Dixie." Evayda checked her phone again. "Doesn't feel right to just take her time slot when she's only a little late."

Gamble looked at her screen again. "I have a feeling I won't be hearing back from Edema. She said she would be recovering after her appointment with Dixie last night."

"So there's been no word from either of them now," Evayda said, her voice shaking as her nails clicked her phone screen. "No updates or stories or anything on either of their socials."

Gamble looked away and bit her lip, stirring her drink. "Should we . . . go up there?"

Evayda sighed frustratedly. "I don't even remember if I have her address." Her voice grew angrier the more she spoke. "There is something fucked-up going on here and shit is getting real." She brought her hand to her mouth to hide her quivering lips. "People don't just disappear. DRAG QUEENS don't just disappear!" She sniffled, then continued. "It's bad enough that we have the world trying to say that what we are is wrong. Trying to make it illegal for a man to put on a damn dress if he wants to. I spent three years of my life in law school, thinking I could make a difference. We went to how many rallies saying that these anti-drag laws were unconstitutional?"

"Too many to count," offered the bartender solemnly.

The rest of the bar clung to every word the stunningly beautiful drag queen spoke in her black bodysuit and black leather boots. The mind of the lawyer, Corbin Fowler, Esquire, and the voice of the drag queen, Evayda Subpoena, converged into one, delivering her final *that's that on that* statement before a jury of her peers.

"Even after the courts ruled that anti-drag laws were illegal, the cops out here act like nothing has happened. They still turn a blind eye when one of us comes up missing. Well, what about six missing . . . and two confirmed deaths? Will that finally make them get off their asses and see that some fucking psycho is targeting our sisters? Because I'm not going out without a fight. I wish some MAGA hat-wearing cousin-fucker would try my gay ass."

"Whose cousin is fucking your ass now?" Suzee asked, clomping up to the bar, purse first.

Evayda's reserve broke. She started to tear up as Suzee Ho Maker instinctively knew to open her arms and welcome her good Judy in for a hug. Gamble walked up to the huddled pair, pulling a Kleenex out of her cleavage. She offered it to Evayda, who snorted her tears and said, "No, thank you, boo, that's got tiddy dust all over it." The three girls chuckled and fanned their eye makeup.

"We have to do something, girls," Evayda said. "Nobody's going to help us but us."

"I've still got the van," Suzee chimed in. "We can go hunt us some bigots." She jangled the keys like a toddler in front of the girls.

"We need to go to the cops. They have to know something by now," Evayda added.

"I've already gone to the cops, love. Those fuckers won't tell me anything," Suzee spit with indignation. "They barely lifted their heads when I walked into the precinct. All they told me was it's standard procedure to check back after forty-eight hours."

"That's bullshit and they know it," Evayda said, before she downed the last of her drink. Incensed, she slammed her palm down on the bar, directing all eyes to her once more. "If you see something, you fucking say something." She cleared her voice so they could hear her in the back. "We are taking this old school. Everyone, don't go anywhere unless you have someone with you. OKAY? SEE SOMETHING, SAY SOMETHING! All right?!"

The patrons at the bar yelled back, "SEE SOMETHING, SAY SOMETHING!" in solidarity. Evayda smiled and grabbed Gamble's limp arm.

"C'mon, let's go. They're going to listen to us right now or these cops better be prepared to get their asses thoroughly chewed out."

"Oh my! That's one way to get our point across. I call the hairy one," Suzee said, jabbing her elbow into Gamble's side. "Gamble? Darlin', I made a funny about eating ass and you didn't so much as make a peep. You okay?"

Gamble blinked quickly in succession and sighed, lost in her thoughts. "There's just so much going on right now. I . . . I can't breathe."

Evayda stepped in front of her friend and grabbed her shoulders. "We got this, girl. Just close your eyes and gather your thoughts." She raised her eyebrows in Suzee's direction to get her attention and loudly whispered, "When she gets like this, you just have to calm her little hamster ass down. If not, she'll be flopping around on the floor like a fish."

Suzee gasped and put her arm around her shallow-breathing friend. "Deep breaths, sweetie, come back to us."

Evayda rubbed Gamble's shoulders. "Think of something you want. Anything. Focus on that."

Giggling like a schoolgirl, Suzee interrupted the two, "Some dick?"

Evayda pursed her lips and snapped in front of Gamble's face. "Ignore that ol' dry coochie heifer. We're gunna find her a date ASAP." Evayda sensed Gamble's breath starting to normalize. "Think of the crown, sweetie. Think of the scepter and the crown for the Miss Trick'd and Treated winner."

Gamble's gaze finally returned to meet Evayda's, finding her way back to the real world. Evayda's mouth slowly grinned and she let a heavy sigh out of her nose. "Now picture getting runner up 'cuz your ass still don't know how to put eyeliner on right."

Gamble's eyes met Evayda's in a look of joyous adoration. "You fucking bitch."

Heaux B. Hayve

Chapter 16

O CTOBER 25, 2022, TUESDAY

"How much for you to just tap dance on my balls for a little bit?" asked the patron as he annoyingly fiddled with the popper of Heaux's whip.

"It's twice as much now that you're tap dancing on my last nerve," hissed Heaux B. Hayve as she snatched the handle of the whip out of his grasp. "And if you have to ask, you can't afford it, darling." With that, the shapely dominatrix dismissed the married traveling salesman or whatever and moved on to the VIP section of her world-renowned Blaq & Blu BDSM club. She paused and waited patiently for her sentinel to lift the velvet rope. Security might be twice her size but gentle as lambs. That is, until she snaps her finger and instructs them to crack some skulls.

She beckoned the brute closer with her gloved digits. "Get rid of Men's Wearhouse by the bar. Smells like traveler's checks to me."

"Tiny" nodded and did as he was told. Mistress B. Hayve liked the strong, silent, stupid type. That's why she kept him around. She vamped her way through the lounge with the ceiling speaker's ambient beats, the shrouds of smoke pierced momentarily by laser lights, to the low couches occupied by some of her top clientele. The guests couldn't help but notice the lithe leopardess, spotted in head-to-toe-faux perambulating toward them.

The moderately attractive man in the polo/khakis/wedding ring combo leaned forward to gesture for her hand. Heaux cooed and placed her hand in his as her PVC outfit squeaked out a giggle. His lips smacked the back of her leather opera gloves. "Good evening, Mistress, to what do we owe the pleasure?"

"Just making sure everything is to your liking, Sergeant." She grinned and batted her eyelashes at him and his barely legal, scantily clad twink seated next to him. "And to your specifications."

"Oh, everything is *exactly* as I like it," he said as he grabbed the boy's bony chin and stared into his glazed-over eyes. "Does he have a brother?"

"Not for another year, Sarge. I'll keep you abreast of his birthday closer to the date." It took years of practice but her face would not reveal disgust anymore. Who says the love of money is the root of all evil?

Sensing that someone was watching her, she turned toward the entrance. Her personal assistant was trying to flag her down. A laser beam struck her rhinestone biker hat, showering her customers with a galaxy of stars emanating from her heavenly body. She grabbed its brim in an effort to tip it toward the sergeant when he pulled her close once more.

"Sorry to hear about your friends, Mistress. If I had known they were friends of yours I would have intervened sooner." His hot, flammable breath could charm the paint off a wall.

"That's on the other side of town," Mistress B. Hayve said, "and none of my business." It was her business. Dyna Fyre was not just her drag mother, she was basically her chosen mother figure ever since she got into town six years ago. Dyna blessed her with her drag name and never shamed the side hustle.

The last time she spoke to her fairy drag mother, Dyna mentioned the upcoming pageant. Heaux was saddened to hear it would most likely be Dyna's final presence onstage, but said she could be in the audience to shout the house down boots.[1] Now the only person who could pull her out of her shy (when she wasn't crushing testicles with her heel) little bubble was a charcoal briquette in the morgue. She'd never felt so alone.

Cutting the pleasantries short, before her assistant had an aneurysm. Her smile melted into a scowl as she turned away from the VIP table. One girl missing was a sad commonality. Two meant security escorting you to your car was a must. Three meant the gayborhood would rally the Guardian Angels. Four meant the cops would *finally* start sniffing around. It's why she had to establish her own place, with her own rules and clientele. Being reserved meant she could hear and observe what no one else took the time to notice . . . and it's every ho for herself out here.

Mistress B. Hayve crossed the velvet rope once more to where her apprehensive assistant was waiting for her. "You rang?"

---

1. enthusiastic approval and excitement

Her assistant, Daniel, gulped. "There's a mess up there again. Mr. Zbornak ordered *The Roman Golden Shower Combo*. Now he's complaining The Roman Shower is not chunky enough and the Golden Shower is not golden enough. He's upsetting the other guests and security does not want to touch him." The Mistress had heard enough. "Don't forget you have a Haven appointment at eleven." Her assistant picked a stray hair off her shoulder. "Everything is already prepared for you. Make sure you read the packet."

"Ready and raring to go," Heaux mumbled. She walked past the bar and grabbed the cat-o'-nine-tails on her way to the elevator.

"A Heaux's job is never done."

When the elevator doors closed, it allowed her time to reflect on how she got to this exact moment in time. The family of Ho, a.k.a. Heaux, emigrated from Korea in the 1980s. His strict upbringing taught him the need for discipline in life. His mostly Korean community was practically run by strong women elders who embodied strength and beauty. Men cowered in their shadows. They were the perfect harmony of feminine and masculine energy. One that he loved to emulate as he grew into the Korean cross-dressing Ho. Work and school kept his nose to the grindstone during the day, but the nightlife and carnal desire called to him incessantly. One night, he answered that call and Heaux B. Hayve was born. Destined to make you gag, make you shake, but most importantly . . . make you hurt. The rest, as they say, is herstory.

The elevator doors slid open. Commotion could be heard to her right, joined by her heeled leopard boots clicking with silent rage. She followed the slime trail down the black-marbled hallway. It's times like this she wished they hadn't gone with the *classy* wallpaper as the recessed lighting above showed splashes already beginning to dry. Her boots aquaplaning in God-knows-what, she came to a stop at room seven. Door ajar. She gritted her teeth, held her breath, and stomped inside.

She witnessed an image sure to stay with her for some time: Mo, her senior security guard, cornering a yelling, cowering naked man in his sixties, glistening with every malodorous fluid the human body could excrete. Dillon, her top dom and piss play specialist, was attempting to wipe himself down with a towel in the other corner. Her presence sent the room into a tizzy of everyone yelling and almost slipping in waz and upchuck at once.

"SILENCE!" belted Mistress B. Hayve. "Dom Dillon, what's the story here?"

"He asked for the gag and tinkle, hold the stinkle," blurted the bewildered Dillon, wearing assless chaps.

The Mistress couldn't help but notice a shit on her floor, close enough to make her nose crinkle. "HOLD the stinkle?"

Dillon caught her gaze, his face full of shame, and attempted to explain, "He . . . frightened me . . . um, Mistress. He slipped me a hundo last time and told me to eat asparagus before he came in. I tried to, but it tasted like hot microwaved ass. I tried, though, I really tried! He said there wasn't enough barf, so I even took a double shot of ipecac just so he would shut up."

The Mistress stopped him with a midair hand slash. "The ipecac is supplied for *emergencies* only, Dillon. Taking a double dose is dangerous and irresponsible, you know that. That's how Karen Carpenter died, Beyoncé rest her soul. It's hard enough keeping a doctor on the books willing to keep us supplied and to deal with any emergencies, as it is."

Dillon pleaded with his eyes. "It won't happen again, Mistress, I swear to you. The minute I felt the bubble guts I knew I fucked up, but he wouldn't let me go. Then he started to yell about, 'What's good for the goose is good for the gander,' or somethin'. He started saying he was going to call the cops. I had to call Mo. That's when he freaked out and ran into the hallway and started banging on all the other doors."

The Mistress grimaced. "Hit the showers, then kick rocks for the night."

Dom Dillon grabbed his robe, thanked the Mistress, and hightailed it out of the room, slipping and sliding as he went.

The Mistress glared at the two grown men in the corner and stepped around the various gastrointestinal speed bumps. From the hallway, a thud, a crash, and "Owwww" could be heard.

"Don't you dare move, Stanley. Don't even look in my direction." She walked up and placed her hand on Mo's useless, oversized arm. "Get out of my way," she said as she sidestepped him. "But keep your ass handy." Mo moved to the door, awaiting further direction from his employer and master.

Mistress B. Hayve took a step closer to the quivering old man. His cheap toupee was slick and appeared to have little pieces of potato in it. "I could vomit just looking at you." He looked up excitedly. "Don't get your hopes up. You couldn't afford me." She cracked the cat-o'-nine-tails in her hands. "Your card will be charged for the cleaning and sanitizing of this entire floor, *twice* because you've disgusted me more than usual. You have one minute to explain yourself well enough to ever be let past my doors again . . . GO."

Mr. Zbornak babbled, "I paid for the pavement pizza, mellow yellow, no brownie. I even slipped Dillon an extra two hundred to eat asparagus the day before my appointment! I paid for stink, I wanted stink, damn it." He stared at her with a quivering lip. "You're not going to charge me for the brownie, are you? I can't afford the *Rooter-to-the-Tooter Special*. I just didn't want to get charged for it, that's why I panicked when the Hershey squirts hit the fan. I'm on a fixed income. I'm still paying alimony to my ex-wife!"

The Mistress let out a deep exhale and turned toward Mo, who met her gaze, "Get the cleaners up here, tell them I want a full hose down." She turned back to the dunce in the corner, still naked for some reason. "Get your pathetic ass out of my establishment. You are banned unconditionally for one year. Are we clear?"

Stanley shook in agitation, "But, Mistress, wait!" He fell to his knees, splattering the shit across the floor just as she started to walk out of the catastrophe. "Who's going to shit on my chest?" His eyes welled up with tears.

Mistress paused, not even dignifying his existence with eye contact. "Why don't you go ask your ex-wife? I'm sure she would be more than willing."

With that disturbing mess handled, Heaux got back in the elevator. That fiasco had taken up more time than she'd hoped. She had an appointment by special request approaching. The elevator hit the top floor, the penthouse, a.k.a. the Heaux B. Haven (if ya nasty.) She needed to get out of this outfit quickly. Who knows what odors were seeping into the fabrics. She exited the elevator and made her way to her *Playground* area. With the flick of her wrist, she slid her glove off and hit the light switch panel. The room came to life before her eyes.

The walls were all retrofitted in rubber paneling designed to be soundproof but also safe for anyone who would be strapped into the shackles that ran along the rows of rings and hooks. Along the opposite wall was a vast collection of toys that would make any depraved sadomasochist's heart flutter. Whips and chains and butt plugs, oh my! All shapes and sizes, there was something for everyone. The wall closest to her was adorned with an assortment of masks, ball gags, collars, and various lengths of nylon rope.

Each corner displayed furniture that IKEA wishes, but could never. A St. Andrew's cross in one, a spanking bench and punishment stocks in the other. Her personal favorite was the gynecological examination table and across from that were multiple swings and inversion tables with ceiling pulleys dangling down. The center of the large room held a platform with a bed and a chaise crafted with tufted leather and straps at all four posts. Heaux B. Hayve always said the only bridge between business and pleasure was pain with a capital *P*. Something she was a pro at.

Just inside the door, the stainless steel medical grade utility cart gleamed under the spotlights above. On it, an assortment of lubricants, XL sex toys, floggers, paddles, and a gimp mask. The shelf below had a funnel and plastic tubing for enema and piss play. She snatched up the invoice clipped to the side. Her eyes scanned the list of services and activities requested; it seemed this client wanted *The Works*. When her eyes hit the price total at the bottom of the invoice, she couldn't help but grin in anticipation. They'll get everything they paid for, that's for sure. The last few pages were just copies of all the limit lists and legal and medical releases. Before returning the packet to the cart, she noticed the word *SWITCH* next to today's date. Well well, it looks like the Mistress was going to get a taste of her own medicine tonight. She might have to cancel tennis tomorrow morning.

Her phone chirped a thirty-minute reminder before her appointment time. She clicked off the lights and exited the *Playground,* satisfied everything was ready for one hell of a night. Her shower playlist throbbed through the speakers of her "work boudoir," a.k.a her home away from home. Never one to miss an opportunity, she strutted through the overhead lights down the hallway. This was all part of her *that bitch* process, a way to work herself up. She peeled off her outfit, turned on the shower, and prepared for the beatdown of her life.

Heaux coughed through a cloud of baby powder, trying to get her strappy one-piece leather bodysuit on. The client specified a lot of skin, and the customer is always right. Heaux closed off the entire floor of the Heaux B. Haven when she had high-end clients. Even Daniel knew she needed to be in the right headspace, so privacy and quiet were all she needed. Which she regretted now since she needed zipped up. Hopefully Mr./Mrs. Moneybags wouldn't notice. At eleven on the dot, Daniel texted her.

Daniel

Client is on the way up, good luck.

He forwarded the standard contract agreement that would have to be signed before the fun began. Heaux checked her mirror and straightened the lines in her fishnets. Finally, she grabbed her lucky rhinestone biker hat before she winked in the mirror and hit the door.

Her nerves were cranked up in anticipation. She still got butterflies before every client. Her thigh-high boots demanded attention as they clomped toward the elevator. She stopped just as the *ding* and slide of the elevator door opened before her.

Her customer service smile only showed the smallest hint of surprise as the Amazon stepped through the doors. A full head taller than her, also in black leather. This seemed a little too good to be true. Who was paying who? Heaux admired her killer outfit. The pink rhinestone ski mask was a little *precious*, but who was she to judge?

"Welcome to the Heaux B. Haven, I am your ProDomme, Mistress Heaux B. Hayve," she said with a little more authority than intended.

The masked woman grinned and stared intensely at the petite dominatrix before her but stayed silent. Those piercing green eyes seemed so familiar to her. Heaux cleared her throat and pulled her phone out of her minimal cleavage. She swiped and presented her phone screen to the client.

Determined to reestablish the power dynamic, Heaux declared, "If you agree to all the conditions of the contract agreement, I just need a final signature here before we begin." The Queen paused, keeping her intimidating gaze on her Mistress before glancing down at the phone screen. Heaux resisted the urge to flinch when the Queen slid off one of her gloves and exhaled a small "hmm" through her nose. The Queen drew her finger with a flourish across Heaux's phone screen.

Heaux waded through the silence by stepping to the side and gesturing with her hands toward the *Playground*. "Follow me." She peered down expeditiously at the screen. "The Queen."

Adrenaline rushed through Heaux as the excitement mixed with fear took turns playing out scenarios in her mind. Every methodical step and hip sway was intended to distract her prey before they entered her domain. So why did she feel like the fly being cornered by this *zaddy* long legs? She detached her keys from the small ring just above her hip and unlocked the door. The lights flooded the room as they both stepped inside. Heaux stepped to the side and inserted her phone into one of two trays on the shelf inside.

"For your safety and privacy, we lock the door. Is that okay with you?" she asked.

The Queen simply nodded as her eyes darted to the vast assortment that occupied the room.

Heaux recited, "If you have a phone or anything sharp, please deposit it in the trays for safekeeping."

The Queen simply lifted up her hands and turned them in a circle to show she had nothing of the sort, in case she needed to be patted down.

Now it was Heaux's time to smirk. "I trust you. It's all about trust . . . right?" She got no response, just silence and the shifting eyes of the Queen as she eyeballed every blunt sex toy she could see in the room.

The dominatrix ushered the Queen to the utility cart. "A multitude of things to play with. Of course, you are welcome to use anything else in the *Playground* if you desire."

Heaux, perturbed by the deafening silence, was ready to do this. "Any other questions before we begin?" The Queen shook her head no and stepped up to her Mistress. Visibly startled, Heaux looked up at those verdant eyes staring sharply behind the sparkling mask. Both of their rhinestone accoutrements sending twinkling fireflies around the room.

"I guess I wasn't the only one who got a BeDazzler for Christmas," Heaux said with a confident chuckle that was instantly cut short by the Queen's face being only inches from hers. The startle caught her off guard, causing her to stagger down onto the tufted leather chaise. She gasped as she sat, but the Queen held her position above her, placed her hand on Heaux's shoulder and applied pressure, indicating Heaux was to stay put.

The Queen walked over to the wall and grabbed a ringed dog collar and a leather leash, then across the room to a wall of floggers and paddles. Heaux watched with anticipation at her selections. The Queen ignored the smaller paddles at eye level and went right to the larger, heavier, spikier paddles at the bottom. The Queen lifted one in her hands, testing the weight. She gave a few test swings, satisfied with the heft.

Heaux sat patiently on the chaise, looking away as the Queen returned, her heels clicking and growing louder in her ears, sending waves of anticipation through her body. The Queen roughly pulled Heaux's opposite shoulder closer to her and brought the dog collar before her eyes. Heaux bit her lip as the collar was lowered and secured around her throat. Once it was latched, the Queen attached the leash. Heaux was then pulled up and toward the corner with the punishment stocks and the spanking bench. Heaux followed behind her Queen diligently, but her eyes filled with trepidation when she saw the length of the spikes in the paddle chosen. A bead of sweat rolled down her back as she eyed the rows of sharp steel teeth that gave it its namesake . . . The Vampire Paddle.

Heaux did not hesitate as the Queen pulled her over and onto the spanking bench. The apparatus was black patent leather. It allowed the "spankee" to have their wrists and ankles strapped to the padded surfaces as if they were on all fours, while being fully supported. The Queen purposely placed the intimidating spiny paddle only inches from Heaux's face as her ankles were being secured. She couldn't help but wince at the almost inch-long steel tines shining in the lights above them. She began to mouth words but couldn't speak as panic strained her vocal cords behind the snug dog collar.

To her knowledge, The Vampire Paddle had never been used before. Only bought for the novelty and fear factor because all it would take was a few smacks for the blood to get out of hand. The Queen moved closer to her face, strapping her wrists to the bench.

At this point, Heaux was hesitant to jump to conclusions or try to talk the Queen out of using the bloodthirsty Vampire Paddle. This would either dissuade her or encourage her to use it, depending on her level of fuckedupness. Just as she was ready to voice her concern, the Queen got down at eye level with Heaux. She was instantly lost in the green fields of the Queen's eyes, fields of fervor and malice. The intensity only broke when the Queen threaded the leash through the loop just below Heaux's neck and pulled it taut, slamming Heaux's head down like a ton of bricks.

The sudden jerk sent pain shooting down Heaux's neck and shoulders. Her lucky hat toppled down, freeing her natural ebony hair. Her forehead made contact with some of the spikes on the paddle. Her hairline now had raised welts that were slowly expelling dark red, angry berries of blood. The Queen took the end of the leash, passed it through one of the loops on her collar, and cinched it tight, locking her head in place on the bench.

Heaux's eyes became glassy as she let out a small mewl of pain. The Queen hadn't heard it. She was already rolling the cart over to the whimpering, constricted offering. Seeing the black and red ball gag in the Queen's grips sent Heaux's mind atwitter.

"Wai-wait wait WAIT!" Heaux yelled, her voice full of alarm. The Queen continued to open the strap to the ball gag and grabbed Heaux by the back of her hair.

Heaux choked out, "My safe word!" She caught her breath as the Queen pushed the shiny red clown nose toward her mouth. "It's HOHOHO—"

The ball gag squeaked against her teeth, lubricated by fear-infused saliva. It strained Heaux's jaw as it nestled deeper against her molars, coming to a painful halt. Heaux inhaled a sob, tears running down her cheek and her nose dribbling. Her jaw felt hyperextended, like it was about to fracture at any moment.

The Queen fastened the strap behind Heaux's head and picked up The Vampire Paddle. She lingered next to Heaux as the trussed tenderoni unwound mentally before her. Heaux's low moan was cut short as the Queen planted a single kiss on her cheek. *Was this a gesture of good faith? Was this all to break me down?* Heaux's mind was swimming with rumination and lust as the trickle of hope promised to quench her thirst for answers.

The Queen let the paddle rest on Heaux's shoulder. An anxious shudder emanated through her body as the sharp spikes raked against her. The tines scored spider silk slices into the leather of Heaux's bodysuit. The few bits of exposed skin showed pink tracks that began to weep rivulets of merlot. The hot welt trails thickened as the Queen brought the abusive implement to Heaux's rump-roast. The Queen's eyes traced the crimson contours she had carved into Heaux's flesh. She lifted the paddle and positioned herself, watching Heaux brace herself for the first strike. Heaux felt the Queen reel back, causing her to inhale sharply.

The first hit caught Heaux off guard, and adrenaline flushed through her system. To her shock and awe, the Queen had answered Heaux's silent prayers and spared her, using the flat (safe) side of the paddle. The Queen swung again with more gusto, rocking Heaux's body against her restraints. The third and fourth were more like strikes and less like spanks. These strikes caused Heaux's ass and the backs of her legs to blush as the blood rushed to the surface.

Heaux could feel the Queen gaining confidence in her hits. The effect was aphrodisiacal to the ProDomme-cum-Switch. She had forgotten how arousing pain could be when doled out correctly. Heaux began to perspire more as her body temperature rose. Heaux's worries of her tuck coming loose were overshadowed by the anticipation of the next hit.

The redness of Heaux's skin flashed like a red cape before the Queen's bull horns. With the flick of her wrist, the Queen rotated the paddle. She slapped the sharp spines of The Vampire Paddle against the rosy skin with extreme prejudice. The shrieks of pain were muffled by the ball gag, but the Queen knew she could make them louder. Blood began to swell and spurt out of the oversized burrowed pores. The Queen grunted and prepared for another swing, this time aiming at the strawberry milky thighs. This slap hit at an odd angle, the tines of the spikes tearing flesh as it sank into the cavities they were meant to produce. Blood began to smear and trickle onto the leather bench under her. Heaux began thrashing and screaming through tears, but the Queen was just getting started. Gnashing her teeth, she paddled once, twice, thrice. Only pausing because she felt the hard resistance as the paddle began to puncture bone.

The imploring wails of the dominatrix were garbled as she repeatedly screamed, "HOHOHOOO" through her obstructed maw.

One of the Queen's (few) toxic traits was laughing at things at the most inopportune times. Blood spattered and mid-homicide, all she could think was how Heaux sounded like a *Pokémon* annoyingly screaming out its own name as its only way to communicate. Her shoulders shook with silent laughter as she adjusted her grip on the paddle handle. Composed and ready to return to the shredded drag queen doing her best impression of Santa Claus.

That thought caused her to guffaw. The insulting noise enraged the wounded dominatrix. Spittle dripped off Heaux's chin and the skin around where the restraints held her was deep, red, and angry. The Queen finally stifled her laughs and refocused on the task at hand. Her windup and swing dislodged a chunk of flesh that slid down the spanking bench and onto the floor. The Queen channeled her rage and let loose a barrage of hits that sounded like a meat mallet pounding steak into mince.

Crimson spattered the walls and the floor surrounding them. Droplets of blood were beginning to dissolve as urine began to trickle down the leather. Heaux was sagging in exhausted pain. Her nerve endings firing, being pulverized, sapping her of the energy to even scream as shock set in. The Queen winced at the visible flecks of bone among the maroon, beaten flesh of Heaux's glutes and hamstrings. She let the meat-caked weapon of ass destruction drop into the puddle of awful. Satisfied with this end, she moved on to her next priority: to silence Heaux for good.

The Queen tutted as her heeled boots clomped past the barely coherent drag queen, still nestled in the straps. The Queen's eyes studied the wall of dildos and butt plugs. All displayed from top to bottom, from smallest to gargantuan. *I always liked that word.* The Queen picked up a forearm-casted dildo with the hand in a fist. However, when testing its dexterity, she wasn't pleased with its flaccidity.

Her eyes lit up at a decent-sized dildo, about eight inches long but with an inflation bulb attached to the balls. She picked it up with fascination and gave the bulb a test squeeze or two. To her villainous joy, she watched the phallus grow in size and girth. The toy seemed to be capable of expanding to double its size while still being tough and rigid. The Queen tucked the sex toy under her arm with a satisfied smirk. She moved down the wall to her left where she had previously fetched the ball gag.

The pegboard hooks displayed a multitude of contraptions for the mouth. Some to silence, some to pry open. Some had metal jaw clamps and nose hooks.

The Queen's eyes stopped on the hot pink lip jaw spreader that would go perfectly with Heaux's tear-stained makeup. She squeezed the rubber mouth, pleased with how hard and inflexible it was. She attempted to insert the inflatable dildo into the mouth hole and achieved the perfect fit. The ending of *Cinderella* that Disney didn't want you to know about. "Cinderfella," if you will.

The Queen brought her armful of toys back to the sweating, pale mess that was once the belle of the drag ball. The queen set her toys on Heaux's sweat-soaked back. She was still moaning in anguish and anger. Heaux's head was resting on her ear, breaths huffing out laboriously around the ball gag. The Queen sidestepped the growing puddle and began to unfasten the ball gag from the back of her head. With the tension released, it erupted with a *pop* and deep sobs. Heaux's jaw quivered and slowly closed as the muscle was finally relieved of the pressure. Heaux swallowed hard and tried to plead for her life with the last of her strength, but the Queen had the mouth spreader in her hands.

The Queen snatched Heaux's splintered ponytail and pulled back, allowing a billowing howl to emit from the ailing drag queen. Seizing the opportunity, she angled the lips into Heaux's mouth. The Queen pressed and pushed the spreader into place. As she pulled harder on her ponytail, Heaux's whimpers echoed off the soundproof walls. The ridge of the rubber finally caught and pried open Heaux's still-aching jaws. With the lips in place, the Queen secured the straps behind Heaux's head. Heaux weakly tried to bite down or somehow evict the unyielding obstruction from her maw but was unsuccessful. More tears and drool lubricated her face, which would prove to be a blessing and a curse.

Angling herself above Heaux's head, the Queen brought her leg up and clamped the side of Heaux's head to the bench with the tread of her boot. Heaux let out an anguished howl, sobs unleashed with pained fear. The Queen balanced herself, keeping pressure on Heaux's head to grab the inflatable dildo. The shiny black dingus was positioned in her hand like a knife.

With one quick motion she stabbed Heaux's gaping mouth. The first five inches or so slid in easily, and the Queen proceeded. She knew a pro when she saw one, and she wanted Heaux to swallow every inch of her length. Heaux gagged and cried out against the intrusion. The Queen kept pushing and Heaux indeed took it all. *Someone's done this before.* The slightly larger balls were a bulbous speed bump before reaching the inflation tube.

Heaux attempted to buck the Queen off, but she maintained her balance as the Queen gave one final shove. The Queen's tumid balls lodged in Heaux's traumatized mouth hole. Lost in pain, Heaux prayed she would just succumb to her injuries. At this point, Heaux was sucking and blowing at any breath that she could catch. The obstruction fit snugly in her mouth and throat with only a hair of air to spare.

The Queen walked around in front of Heaux,

wanting to see the light in her eyes one last time. With much anticipation, the Queen snatched up the inflation bulb and squeezed two quick pumps. The hissing breaths ceased from the Queen's weeping blow-up doll, now replaced with muffled groans of twisted anguish. Two more squeezes caused Heaux's jaw to widen and her throat to expand. The Queen bit her lip and watched with bated breath as Heaux's eyes began to roll to the back of her head.

Pale pink streams of vomit began to bubble out from the sides of her mouth and nostrils. Heaux's pallor became a shade of *blurple* (blue and purple) down her distended throat. The Queen knew this sweaty fuck sesh was about to come to its messy climax. Wanting to give Heaux the most memorable nut she ever had, the Queen gave her three strong pumps to finish her off.

The black rubber was protruding from Heaux's hot pink mouth. Her jaw jutted forward just before it gave a dull snap, crackle, and pop. The pressure of the inflated dick blimp caused the jaw to further unhinge and made her chin and neck appear to be the same thickness. A final tear dribbled out of Heaux's vacant eyes and ran down her blurple bloated cheek.

The Queen stood back and admired her handiwork with hands on her hips. She casually reached into the cuff of her leather gloves. The opening flick of her straight razor gleamed in the light as the Queen began her depraved ritual.

Warm blood trickled down Heaux's face, pooling into her eyes and around the pink mouth spreader. Maneuvering around the spreader caused her slices to go deeper and cut through one of the straps. The Queen proceeded to trace her cheekbone and temple until the blade met its bloody point of origin. With the slicing done, she wiped the bloody razor on the leg of her pants before closing it and placing it back in her cuff.

The pull of the slick, bloody skin was hard to get a hold of, but the flesh was already freeing itself from the skull. As the skin tore from around Heaux's lips and cheeks, the entire contents of her throat poured out of her crooked jaw. The tumescent sex toy tumbled to the ground, now twice its size, along with a geyser of blood and vomit. The Queen grabbed the mass of skin that crested Heaux's nose like the top of a cinched garbage bag and gave one final pull. The sheet of flesh dangled in front of the Queen's eyes as she attempted not to breathe in the new scents that entered the room.

She looked at Heaux's beauty sitting in her hands. It belonged to the Queen now. A proper send-off for the little Ho. The Queen let a single tear absorb into her ski mask as she turned away from the fallen sex angel. Her beauty was not for this undeserving world, but at least she went out with a bang.

The Queen turned off the lights and closed the door behind her. *You live by the meat sword, you die by the meat sword*, the Queen thought as she called the elevator. She hoped it was as good for Heaux as it was for her.

Gamble Donna Phart

Chapter 17

2 ⁰⁰⁸

Little Antonio's stomach felt like it was eating itself. After three days with no food, his mind was too foggy to take him to his happy place. His body ached, blinking his eyes felt like he was shredding his corneas. So he did his best to keep his eyes closed throughout the night and the day. Even when he felt the fluttering of little vermin legs run across his fetal-positioned body. If that sensation wasn't keeping him awake, his hunger pangs felt like they were stabbing through his guts the entire time.

Every time he resisted DL Cakes's teachings or chose not to participate in Group, the reverend sent him to the *Box of Revelations*: a row of heavy wooden confessionals in the drafty old church. A pew pushed on its side and wedged in place to seal whoever was being punished inside. Antonio's tailbone ached switching from sitting on the cold floor to the tattered kneeler.

The large wooden doors of the chapel scraped the marble-tiled floor. The sound of unpolished patent leather shoes approached. A gnarled knuckle rapped on the confessional wall.

"Rise and shine, son," followed by the sound of the wooden pew scraping against the tile in front of the confessional.

"And on the third night, what did the good Lord speak unto you?" The adjoining door to the confessional creaked open. The reverend grunted before sitting down on the bench provided inside. "Ah, it's good to have a seat. Rest the old bones." The gleam on his sweaty skin shone through the perforated screen between them. "Oh, that's right. You don't have a place to sit on your side." He reached for his pocket square, using it to blot the sweat from his forehead. "Oversight on my part, apologies. We'll have to get to that after we get to the ventilation in here." The reverend side-eyed Antonio, whose back was facing him, sitting with his head in his hands. "Yup yup yup, I'm sure it gets mighty hot in here during the day . . . and cold as the Devil's heart at night. We'll have to rectify that before the next set of ne'er-do-wells."

Antonio groaned like his stomach took a bite out of his spine, causing him to shudder and hug himself tighter.

"Sounds to me like you might be ready to finally unbosom yourself." The reverend chuckled to himself.

"See what I did there? I said unbosomed, like unburdening yourself but also . . . the faster we unlatch you from your mother's teat . . . the faster we can get you suckling on some other li'l filly." He belted out another round of laughter until his top denture clacked against the bottom, causing him to abruptly close his mouth.

Antonio snorted, causing the reverend to stand with indignation. He slurped and said wetly, "SO YOU WANT ANOTHER NIGHT IN HERE, IS WHAT YOU'RE TELLING ME?"

The reverend pounded the back of his hand against the screen.

"Confess or you won't see another face or hear another voice for three more days. I can take your mama on a trip. She won't even know you're alive."

He sneered. "That's if the Lord decides he wants you alive."

Antonio sniffled, his tear ducts ached, his eyeballs felt like they were pockets of coarse sand. He opened his mouth to speak but felt shooting pain like barbed wire wrapping around his throat.

"Nice tall glass of ice water in the mess hall waiting for you." remarked the reverend as a smile crept across his face.

"Death is the ONLY penalty for homosexuality, what say you?"

Antonio shivered and croaked out, "Amen."

"I'm sorry, son, my hearing isn't what it used to be," the reverend said with thinly veiled glee. "Death is the ONLY punishment for homosexuality, what say you?"

Antonio mustered his strength and yelled, "AMEN."

"Sodomy is the only sin which caused God to rain fire from heaven on an entire five-city population, what say you?"

Antonio choked, "AMEN."

The reverend smiled, a single tear running down his cheek. "Homosexuality is a sin, just as pride is a sin. Gay pride is broadcasting abominable sin. Which is why God turns his back on them, delivering to them diseases and massacres. WHAT SAY YOU?"

Bits of gravel pressed against Antonio's forehead as his energy dipped lower. He could barely swallow but responded, "AMEN."

"YES, LORD. ANY HOMOSEXUAL SHOULD BE ASHAMED. ANYONE WHO EN-ABLES, SUPPORTS, CONDONES, LEGISLATES OR ATTEMPTS TO LEGISLATE THIS MOST HEINOUS SIN SHOULD BE ASHAMED. IT WAS YOUR ILK WHO BROUGHT HELLFIRE TO SODOM AND IT WILL BE YOUR ILK WHO FUELS GOD'S WRATH TO MAKE THIS GREAT LAND BURN NEXT. WHAT SAY YOU?"

Antonio's breath caught in his throat, but still he responded, "AMEN."

"REPENTANCE IS A GIFT OF GOD, BUT GOD TELLS US THAT REPENTANCE MUST BE ACCOMPANIED BY GOOD WORKS. WORDS ARE NOT ENOUGH. FAITH WITHOUT WORKS IS DEAD. DO YOU, ANTONIO, PLEDGE TO ESCHEW YOUR UNCLEANNESS, YOUR VILE AFFECTIONS, AND YOUR REPROBATE MIND NOW AND FOR THE REST OF YOUR LIFE?"

Antonio turned to face the reverend's voice, his vision going in and out. His cracked lips parted and with his last bit of energy, he shouted, "AMEN."

"Keep walking forward, I'll point you in the right direction. Onward, Christian soldier," said the Reverend DL Cakes with a grimace. He was basically holding little Antonio up by his arm, his shoulder joint threatening to pop with every near topple. Antonio's vision was blurring around the edges; every faceless person he stumbled past had an ethereal glow to them. Was he truly having a religious experience?

They entered the hallway adjoining the chapel and the reverend led Antonio to a bench under the window, where he breathlessly screamed, "Elijah, fetch me that wheelchair from the rectory!"

The cockroach of a man sauntered toward them pushing the antique wheelchair, not in any hurry.

The reverend yelled, "And get a move on before I blow out my hip!"

Elijah wheeled it in front of the bench.

The reverend was leaning against the hallway wall, attempting to catch his breath. "Well don't just stand there like a dummy, put the boy in the . . . blessed chair!"

Elijah unceremoniously grabbed Antonio by the same arm and pulled him into the chair. Antonio listlessly rolled his head like it was barely attached to his shoulders. His eyes hardly open from the shock of daylight shining through the windows.

"Wheel him to the mess hall. Quick," said the reverend, wiping his shiny forehead with his pocket square. "The last thing we need is another medical fiasco like last time. His mother'd have my head."

Once inside the mess hall, the reverend shuffled to the kitchen area while Elijah heedlessly slid the wheelchair up to an empty table and quickly departed.

The other boys from Group started filing in from across the room to the circle of chairs. They looked equally gaunt and downtrodden. The reverend yelled in their direction, "Give me a few moments, men, I'll be with you in two shakes!"

He attempted to keep the water in the glass he was hastily bringing to Antonio. "There, boy." He set it on the table as Antonio's bloodshot eyes widened in awe. "Sip it slow," he whispered, "you don't want to shock your system." He looked around for any eyes on him, moving his chair so the Group couldn't see Antonio's weakened state. "Sister Abigail will bring you a plate, all right? I want you to eat it slow and just take small sips of water, okay? If'n you don't, you're going to get the green apple splatters like you wouldn't believe. You hearing me, boy?"

Antonio was slowly blinking and looking around him. The glass of water was already almost empty when his stomach started growling like a wild beast unleashed.

"Look, I'll go get you more water but I got to get to Group." He looked over in the direction of the youths. "I don't like leaving them alone for too long. You'll be all right, just take it slow and when you feel up to it, come join us. I know the boys will be overjoyed to hear you have decided to join their journey to salvation!"

The reverend motioned toward the kitchen and headed over to Group. Antonio sat staring at the glass. He paused, then took the last swallow.

Sister Abigail set the tray in front of Antonio, taken aback by his ghastly appearance. She stood to the side of him and rested her hand on his shoulder, covertly feeling for his elevated heart rate.

"I hope you like shepherd's pie," she said, cautiously peering over her shoulder. "Everyone seems to like it." She sighed in relief as the reverend seemed occupied with Group.

Antonio had already shoveled two full spoons of food in his mouth before she could pull up a chair next to him. "Eat slow, my child," she said. "You don't want to make yourself sick." She watched the color return to his face slowly, his jaw working overtime to chew. "Wait wait wait," she said, putting her hand over his, pulling his spoon down. "There's a whole pan left, it's not going anywhere! Just slow down, let it digest."

Antonio forcefully swallowed and nodded, thanking the matronly woman sitting next to him. She pushed a lock of silver hair loosened from under her headscarf behind her ear. "How long were you out there?" she whispered to him. She kept her eye on the reverend, still with his back to them.

Antonio's breathing was returning to normal, his throat no longer full of razor blades like before. "Three nights. I think," he said slowly and quietly, glancing in her direction to see her reaction . . . to see if she could be trusted. Her brown almond-shaped eyes seemed warm and trustworthy to him.

She rubbed her hands together tightly. She glanced away, blinking quickly in succession, tears forming in the delicate folds around her eyes. Sister Abigail mouthed words like she didn't know what to say or how to say it. "You're Angelica's boy, right? How old are you?"

"Twelve," he said, eyeing his plate again, nudging her hand in a beseeching manner.

"Yes, yes, have some more. A few more bites." Sister Abigail bit the side of her mouth watching him eat. "I . . . I . . . I know it's not right. What's going on here. The reverend told me he was building a home for wayward boys."

She folded her hands in front of her, not taking her eyes off the circle of chairs in Group. "The things I've seen. The shape some of these boys come back in . . . it's not right." She removed a towel from her waist and folded it nervously. "Three days? In that chapel?"

She wiped her nose with the towel that looked dusted with flour. "I've been in there, and in this heat, it's a sweatbox." She looked at Antonio. Her watery frown turned into a grin. "You're a very strong young man, you know that?" She watched as he cleared his plate and looked at her.

"I have to be strong," Antonio said with a grin, the sparkle returning to his green eyes. He paused to take a gulp of water. "But I thought I was going to die out there."

Sister Abigail let out a low wail upon hearing the words coming from the virtuous little boy growing into a young man before her. She stifled the cry building in her chest with the folded towel and fought the urge to wrap her arms around him and tell him everything would be all right.

Just as she was about to throw caution to the wind and embrace Antonio when he appeared to need it most, a commotion came from the entrance to the mess hall. Saul looked toward them, then to Group as he quickly ran up to the reverend.

"Trouble at the gate, Dathan," Saul said, his eyes staring through the reverend's skull.

"That's 'Reverend' in front of the soldiers, Saul. You know that," DL said, to appear casually nonplussed. "What kinda trouble are we talking about here?" He stood and motioned for Saul to step to the side near Antonio and Sister Abigail.

"Big trouble, plain clothes are looking for you. *By name*," Saul said slickly out of the side of his mouth.

The reverend flared his nostrils and said, "All right, let's go." The pair headed toward the door before the reverend yelled to a startled Sister Abigail, "Keep an eye on the boys for me. I'll return shortly."

Sister Abigail eyed the boys before turning back to Antonio, "How about you join Group and I can get you more food if you are still hungry."

Antonio weighed his options and stood to join her when he felt his insides twist in an uproar. His face grimaced and he held his stomach as if he was fighting to hold his intestines in. "Bathroom" was all he could muster.

Sister Abigail looked conflicted but said, "Third door on your left." Antonio attempted to push his chair in when she coaxed him toward the door. "Go go go. The reverend will be occupied for a while, plenty of time for you to come back."

Antonio nodded, his face contorted. He walked swiftly but jerkily, as if bending his knees would be a gamble he didn't want to take. He ambled his body like a statue slowly coming back to life until he entered the third door on his left. His bowels felt like they wanted to explode whether he was prepared or not. The irony that he felt so much relief and now so much anguish from food after three days of hell was not lost on him.

Little Antonio washed his hands and silently peered out of the restroom doors. His prepubescent anxiety had made him an expert at mapping out his surroundings and memorizing the lay of the land. If the mess hall was down to his right, he knew the vestibule wouldn't be far. Which meant the front door wouldn't be far either.

Antonio made sure the coast was clear before he slinked down the hallway with his body pressed against the walls. The oil lamps had not been lit yet in the darkening halls. Once he reached the end of the corridor, he kept his eyes glued on the front door. Then shifted them back to the stairs opposite them. He nervously bit his lip, listening for any movement, certain it was now or never. He took a deep breath and ran for the front door, twisting the knob like his life depended on it, to no avail.

"Antonio!" said his disembodied mother's voice from the top of the stairs. "Did you finally go to Group? Did they let out already?"

He did his best to keep himself from crying as he turned and ran for the stairs. He wanted to yell out, bellow to his mother, ask her why she was allowing all of this.

She simply stood at the top of the stairs, like she had been waiting for him there the whole time. "Come see Mommy's new office," she cooed. "It's so me!" He finally reached her, his body still feeling some residual weariness as he hit the last stair. His body tensed, unsure whether he was expected to hug her or not.

Answering his question for him, Angelica turned and vamped down the hallway like she was the main attraction. He stumbled to keep up, his body and mind reeling, wondering what to do next. The hallway at the top of the stairs led one way, to an office with an adjoining library. Angelica passed through the threshold with Antonio tagging along soon after. He stepped into the room as his mother sat down at the massive desk.

She beamed with pride, pantomiming typing a letter and checking her makeup in a compact. She sat back in the large red leather chair, waiting for Antonio to pick up on the cue that it was time to compliment her. "See all the green, baby?" She glanced around the spacious office with a smile. "Dathan bought it all just for me."

Antonio looked around at the red and green decor in the otherwise wooden room. It looked like a gaudy Christmas display. He edged closer to the desk. "Even the stapler matches!" She held it in front of her eyes for effect.

"Why are we here, Mom?" was all Antonio could muster, emotions flooding his body.

"What, baby?" his mother asked blankly, her attention on the paperwork in front of her.

Antonio steeled his nerves and repeated, louder with his teeth clenched, "Why are we here, Mom?"

Angelica snapped at the tone and volume her little boy was using to speak to her, shuffling papers with simmering fury.

"You know why we're here, Antonio. We've talked about this." She studied her child for a response. "We have nowhere else to go, baby."

She took a deep breath, pushing out of her chair. "This is my chance at a fresh start." She corrected herself, "Our chance." She watched her son blinking at her in disbelief. "Dathan has a vision for this place, and he needs a strong woman by his side. He promised he would take care of me."

She walked to the front of the office to stand in front of him. "Your mother will be First Lady of the church." She posed in front of him in her Hervé Léger icon dress.

She gave her best pageant smile. "We love a title!"

Antonio continued to glower at her, ruining the mood while she was delivering good news.

"Antonio Angelico Agostino," she said, her face tensed. "A reverend and a First Lady are under a lot of scrutiny. All eyes will be on us to lead the flock to"—she paused, trying to remember the rest of the line—"rightness. Okay? I need you to be my little man, my little man who is going to grow up to maybe take over one day."

She sighed dreamily, thinking about her future, "Dathan isn't getting any younger. We stand to get this whole empire one day. It can all be mine. What's good for Mama is good for both of us, remember? If Dathan's treatments work on you, you'll be like our little mascot for the ministry! Just do what he says and he can help you. Dathan says you're lost. He just wants to save you."

"Did he tell you I was outside for three days?" Antonio's heart rate was rising.

"Yes, that retreat is to make you remember what it's like to be a man and to get back in touch with nature," she responded frankly. "Did you have fun?"

"I WAS LOCKED IN A BOX!" Antonio yelled, his face growing hot and wet with his tears. "I THOUGHT I WAS NEVER GOING TO SEE YOU AGAIN!"

"Oh, you're so dramatic, baby." She grinned. "I missed you too!"

Antonio swallowed hard and spat back, "YOU'RE NOT LISTENING TO ME. THIS ISN'T RIGHT, HE CAN'T DO THIS." He felt dizzy as he screamed.

"Lower your voice, Antonio. I thought you came to see me at work. Dathan said you were coming around finally."

"What if I called the police? I don't want to be here anymore!" Antonio said, his fists balled at his side.

"Go get my Blackberry, it's on the charger in the other room. Go ahead," she said, folding her arms and sitting back behind her desk.

Antonio's eyes widened, then narrowed on her as he crept through the interior doorway. What looked like it used to be a library was now a garish bedroom. A wall of gaudy dresses and fancy tops and bottoms hanging on racks were against the opposite walls. He scanned the bulky wooden bedroom furniture for anything with a cord plugged in. He eyed her dim phone on the bedside table and ran up to it. As he pulled it free of the charger, the clicking of heels approaching chilled his bones.

"Go ahead, try it." The throaty voice behind him rippled through the room's tall ceilings.

Antonio hit the side button and saw no service displayed. He still ignorantly tried to mash the keypad.

"I don't even get my text messages until we're almost at the gate," his mother said, snatching the phone from him and placing it back on the charger. "It's bullshit, but it gives me a reason to go see what else is around here until he gets phone and Internet put in."

Antonio looked around the large room. It looked comically wrong with the low furniture spread throughout it. Candelabras littered the tops of the dressers and bedside tables. Antonio aimlessly stuffed his hands in his pockets, allowing his mother to prattle on. Angelica spritzed some perfume on her wrists and rubbed them together. "Yeah, he has some kinda weird candle fascination," she responded nonchalantly, leaving the scent of *Princess* by Vera Wang floating behind as she walked back into the office.

Antonio lingered a moment, focusing on the movements of his mother before he chased after her. "Mom, I want to go home," he said, choking back tears.

"It's for your own good, baby. One day you'll understand. Dathan says I mothered you too much. Made you look up to me too much when you needed a man around as an example."

Antonio looked at his mother like she was someone else wearing her skin. "You told me we would be just fine, just you and me when Dad left." He glared at her. "Are we just here because he buys you dresses? In pastels?"

Angelica raged. "I am your mother and you will do as I say until you're grown enough to leave. Then you can go do whatever you want and be whoever you want to be, where people I know won't see you. Tomorrow is happening whether you like it or not. AND FIRST LADIES WEAR PASTELS."

Antonio fumed, filled with so much hurt and anger it felt like his head would explode. His heart shattered. He always thought his mother's love was unconditional, though through the years she had given him every inclination that was just a fairy tale.

Angelica walked up to her little boy, growing into a young man. She cupped his face in her hands and looked into *her* eyes. "When I found out I was pregnant, we were en route to the Miss California 1995 International. I was a shoo-in to win. We dropped everything the minute we heard your little heartbeat. My beautiful little baby boy." She paused. "I wanted a girl so bad. I just wanted a little doll to dress up. She would look just like me. I prayed for it every night while you were inside me."

She controlled her emotions, this was not waterproof mascara. "We wanted to wait to find out, but I still filled your nursery with anything pink I could find. Then we had you. Your father was so proud. I'd never seen him so happy. He couldn't wait to teach you everything he knew about being a man."

She dropped her hands and took a step back from Antonio, her eyes glistening.

"You wouldn't leave my side. You wanted to do everything I was doing." She sniffled and fanned her eyes with a slight snicker. "Your father said it was my fault. All the pink. I made you this way." She angrily reached behind her for a tissue. "I think he knew. I think that's why he left. He thought I got what I deserved . . . what I asked for."

She dotted her tear ducts with the tissue point, her mascara smearing. "Now here I am, almost penniless. Divorced. More wrinkles. More grays." She inhaled deeply, her rage pushing through her moment of hesitation. "With a freak in a dress for a son." She pulled her shaking hands away from her face. "The biggest regret of both of our lives."

The reverend cleared his throat, leaning against the door frame for the last minute or so. Angelica turned to face him and brushed off the imaginary lint on the front of her dress. Antonio's face was frozen in a tear-soaked frenzy, his jaw hanging open.

"It wasn't your fault, Angelica," the reverend said matter-of-factly. "Wasn't your ex-husband's or—" He looked at Antonio, snapping the boy out of his newest childhood trauma to add to the list. "Wasn't the good Lord's fault either." The reverend walked up to Angelica, placing his hand a little lower than her back. To his delight, she affectionately nuzzled closer to him. "This is the work of Beelzebub." His voice was hoarse and angry. "All of this . . . this GAY agenda. Trannies. Drag things. Vegans. Even these damn sparkly vampire movies. It's all dark sided!"

The reverend rocked his head back, chanting in place. Antonio winced, stepping back and out into the hallway, plotting his exit strategy. Angelica rolled her eyes and walked back to her desk.

"Here we fucking go," she mumbled under her breath.

The reverend stared off, looking at something miles away. He spoke sternly as he began his tirade, "No one whose testicles are crushed or whose male organ is cut off shall enter the assembly of the Lord!"

He seemed to be choked, more to say but his mind was elsewhere. He regained sentience from his delusional trance, patted his pockets, and looked around frantically for Angelica. Antonio remained in the hallway, his eyes shifting around while he wasn't being watched.

"I fucking knew it!" his mother yelled, the venom in her voice strong enough to scald Antonio a whole room away. She angrily backed away from the desk, papers in one hand from the once-locked file drawer and the reverend's keys in the other. "You fucking lied to me! This whole time! All of this, this all was a lie!"

Memories came flooding back to Antonio as his mother's screams ripped through his floundering mind. The resentment, the hostility, and the contempt crashed into him like a traumatic tidal wave. His body had become preprogrammed to detect the all-too-familar tone. Antonio's mind went into lockdown mode. He had to prepare for whatever his ruthless guardian—disregarding her duty to protect—was about to reactively dole out to anyone who displeased her.

Antonio felt like he was glued to the spot. The only parts of him that functioned were his eyes, seeing his mother screaming and the reverend trying to calm her down. Their screams and scuffling became muted, as if Antonio was underwater. His ears rang, hissed, and whooshed, but all he saw was his mother's hateful eyes practically glowing as her mouth twisted and gnashed between silent screaming. He heard his heart in his ears between short breaths. He tried to focus on extending his breathing, sucking the air deep into his belly. The more breaths he took, the more the movie playing out in front of him became unpaused.

His mother's shrill screams were elucidating, as liquid fear seemed to drain out of his ear canals. "FUCK. YOUR. JESUS," she screamed as she shoved the reverend away from her. "YOUR. BROKE. ASS. CAN. GO. TO. HELL."

The snow globe that his mind actualized was cracking as a flash of red and white flooded his vision. When his overwhelmed retinas refocused, he saw an oil lamp shatter on the ground in front of the reverend. Flames traveled like dancing electrical currents across the dusty area rug that lapped up the splashed oil with abandon. The Bibles and texts were already going up, flames rising like a scalding picket fence blocking the path for the reverend to escape.

Flickers of light caught Antonio's eye behind the huge desk as the heavy drapes behind it caught fire. The new source of light illuminated his mother, staring with an unhinged smile across her face.

She once told him, "Hell hath no fury like a woman scorned." In this moment, the green-eyed demon possessing his mother was a testament to that. The unbridled screams of the reverend were drowned out by the sounds of the creaking wood above them and glass shattering.

Seeing the flames spread thawed his *freeze* response as little Antonio felt his toes tensing. *Flight* finally took over as his legs moved him toward the adjoining door. The heat instantly hit his face like a hot oven, evaporating the tears from his stained cheeks. Angelica snapped out of her hateful trance long enough to notice Antonio in the doorway. Her face in shock and pain, twisted with regret.

Antonio eyed the only path clear of flaming debris that would take him to his mother. Hesitation filled his eyes as the flames seemed to be climbing higher and his lungs burned more by the second.

He braced himself, preparing to jump over the engulfed threshold to help his cruel mother. His feet had left the groaning floor when the wind was knocked out of him. His mother had trudged through the smoldering remnants and knocked him back into the smoky hallway. Hearing Angelica's tormented shrieks pulled his dazed stare to meet hers as fragments of flaring ceiling landed on top of her.

A whoosh of superheated air enveloped him, making him wince just enough to see his mother's agonized face engulfed by the flashover.

Antonio's body took over, forcing him to crawl backward on his hands and scrambling feet. He willed his body to go back and save his mom, but the heat from the bursts threatened to burn the skin right off him. Overwhelmed, he sensed danger creeping up as the inferno rose behind him.

He turned to see the wall adjoining the office beginning to crumble and flames peeking out of the blackening fissures. He army crawled to the stairs, looking back once more with a pained glance. His lungs felt like they were filled with black pepper; he couldn't stop coughing as he descended the creaking stairs. His body yearned for clear, breathable air. Smoke filled the stairwell, obscuring the view of the front door. Surely still locked, it appeared dark and sinister as his body pushed him to try again.

Down the hall, a commotion rang out that sounded like the reverend's two lackeys yelling. Instinctually, Antonio crept into the alcove near the door and slunk down onto the floor. Covering his face with his arms, he stifled his hacking lungs just long enough to stay undetected while Elijah shouted up the stairs. Saul could be heard screaming back from the direction of the kitchen.

Antonio's mind flashed to the faces of Sister Abigail and the other nameless kids who had suffered more than he had. He knew he had to put his self-preservation first in this situation. The smoke inside was getting heavier and darker. He began to feel soot collecting on him that sprinkled his face with a mix of tears and sweat.

The henchmen backtracked toward the kitchen, prompting Antonio to finally say a little prayer and try the front door again. It didn't so much as budge as he tried to crank it back and forth. He let his breath out, almost forgetting to breathe that entire time. His mouth took in a gasp of burning, peppered air. He knew his only other option was the hall opposite the kitchen. It had to be the hall that pointed to the chapel and the forest just beyond it.

The darkened hallway was more so as the smoke crept across the ceiling like shadowed creatures stalking Antonio in his weakened state. He wanted to get up and hurtle down the hall, but every time his head got a little above ground, he felt the heated gnat-like particles enter his mouth. The structure was now moaning and hissing, like it was trying to stay alive just as much as Antonio was. The loudest crash came from behind him. The stairwell glowed brightly as it crumbled in black and neon orange explosions. The flickers of the embers showed him the final aperture. His only hope. If the wooden monstrosity didn't open, this would be the end for him.

He felt his limbs go tingly as he reached up, grasped the handles, and pushed it through triumphantly. The cool, musty air of the chapel whooshed past his body to the flaming maelstrom behind him. He pulled his body through the vestibule into the darkened chapel, slamming the door, silencing the rumbling destruction behind him.

Antonio wanted to curl into a ball and breathe the fetid, non-choking air. The bright firelight rippling through the dark sky shone through the chapel's stained-glass windows. Antonio got to his aching knees and chugged along the last few feet to the large wooden doors. The light he could see creeping around the edges of the ancient doorway gave him a smidgen of needed relief.

With one final hacking cough, he inhaled a deep breath and trudged through the chapel doors. Before him lay a thicket of trees as far as the eye could see. With no hesitation, he dove into the only deep, dark forest he'd ever willingly enter. Survival was the only thing on his mind. Not the silhouettes of Sister Abigail and the small survivors she rescued. Not his aching lungs. Not the clunky Blackberry in his pocket slamming against his leg with every step.

Amanda Scrümi

Chapter 18

OCTOBER 26, 2022, **W**EDNESDAY

"I'm glad you have time to be a ho, beloved, I unfortunately have catalytic converters to install in the morning," teased Miss Amanda Scrümi.

Miss Xtra Mayonessa blinked slowly and sucked down more of her daiquiri. "Whatever. Ain't those the things people be stealing?"

Amanda snorted, chewing ice cubes behind her pouty red lip while swirling her near-empty glass. "Bless your heart, child. I think I understand now why there was nothing but sludge in your oil sump. You really went a whole year without an oil change?"

"Girl, the light said *CHECK ENGINE*. I thanked it for the suggestion. In the end, I had to choose between car . . . oil . . . or some bundles." Xtra shook out her braids. "And you know what I will always choose." She slurped and burped the last of her drink through a pink-lipstick-ringed straw. "Whew, I need me the little girls' room. Watch my purse, please?"

Some would say Miss Mayonessa was a little . . . slow. Maybe a little obnoxious, a little . . . rotund, but Xtra always forgot "rotund" ended with a *D*. So the short, plus-size queen just said she was "Built like a li'l jar o' mayo, and everything was better with mayonnaise."

Amanda moved her caramel bangs so she could see the time on her watch. "Hurry up, girl, I still need to stop off at the shop for inventory." Giggling, Xtra slid off the barstool and waddled through the crowd of people.

Amanda instinctively grabbed her homegirl's purse, noting its slightly greasy sheen. The bartender motioned to her for another but Amanda pouted and shook her head no. "A bitch gotta be up early. Maybe tomorrow night, Cliff." He winked with a "Hope so" smile and moved down the bar.

Amanda enjoyed the little flirtation game but knew entrepreneurship was the biggest cockblock for a working girl like her. The beautiful black swan, also the beautiful black sheep of this little drag community. Drag was her passion, it occupied her nights, but Cisco, the mechanic, paid the bills by day. Given the amount of Tangerine Clean he used on a daily basis to get the grease off his aching mitts, he was surprised he still had fingerprints. It was all worth it, though. Cisco worked his eight hours, rinsed the stink of the day off, then styled her wig while Amanda Scrümi's foundation was baking. He was the gayborhood's star mechanic. He scrounged and saved every sweaty single from their gigs and side jobs.

Last year, he finally made enough money to buy his own auto shop, right in the middle of his chosen community. Everyone knew the Body-ody-ody Shoppe was run by family and wouldn't gouge their customers, especially not one of their own. He couldn't tell what made him happiest: living his dream as a young queer business owner or being the spitting image of his Grandma Geraldine back in her heyday when he popped the lashes on.

"Miss Scrümi? With a purse? Would your . . . hammer . . . thing even fit in it?" teased the familiar voice behind her. Amanda turned toward the notorious Gamble Donna Phart. *Incredible talent, unfortunate name.*

"Not my style nor my grease stains, booboo. I think you know better than that," quipped Amanda. She eyed her up and down and met Gamble halfway for some mutual cheekbone. "'Hammer thing,' huh? That's the best you could do?" Amanda chuckled to herself. "I think you're a lot smarter than you let on, Miss Phart." She stifled her sophomoric sense of humor.

Gamble's toothy grin didn't falter as she chuckled and looked in the direction of the bartender. She seductively mouthed the words "vodka Red Bull" and winked before returning her attention back to Amanda. Gamble turned to the established drag queen, who was now staring intensely into Gamble's eyes. Caught off guard, Gamble recoiled and uttered, "Whew, she could back up a li'l bit," her nerve wavering.

Amanda smirked, arching an immaculate brow. "My bad, boo, I just wanted to get a closer look at your li'l blood drop earrings."

Sensing the need to defuse the tension, the bartender interrupted their exchange, "You killed that performance, Gamble. I never would have paired that *Carrie* look with the theme from *Mahogany*. Everyone was gagged!" He smiled and placed her vodka Red Bull on the bar between them.

"Awww,"—Gamble touched the bartender's hand— "thank you, handsome. I always thought the melody sounded so close to the opening of *Carrie* that I had to do my own bloody rendition. Plus, who doesn't love a Diana Ross ballad?" She soaked up the attention and took a sip of her drink.

Annoyed by this nauseating display, Amanda chimed in, "You know mixing uppers and downers will kill you, right, love?" Amanda's throwaway attempt to feign concern was written all over her visage.

Gamble was not afraid of a war of words; luckily, she came well equipped. "My young heart can take it, baby. It'd take a lot more than a drink to take me out."

"That's good, girl." Amanda softened. "That's really good. It's been a little too quiet around here after the Yanita news. I'm getting worried they're going to cancel the pageant."

Gamble almost choked on her drink. "They couldn't. They wouldn't, would they?"

Amanda raised her eyebrows and looked down at her nails. "Not this close. I already heard they went over budget with the venue as it is. They're probably scrambling as we speak."

A switch went off somewhere within Gamble. "If this was a horror movie, we would be running or looking for clues right now."

"If this was a horror movie, both of our brown asses would be dead already." Amanda crunched a particularly large piece of ice between her molars with an unsettling *crack*. "Beloved, it sounds to me like you know something I don't . . . What, or who, are we running from?"

Not missing a beat, Gamble countered, "Girl, I'm about as lost as you are. I've been too busy preparing for the pageant. The last thing I have time for is thinking about what my competition is up to."

Amanda looked at her incredulously. "The competition's still our sisters, sweetheart. How sweet is victory when you have no one to celebrate it with?"

Gamble stared off into the mirror behind the bar display, exhaling a subdued huff. "At the end of the day, I'm worried about me. I'm all I've got. There's only one crown going home with one of us."

Amanda sighed. She knew a mental brick wall when she saw one. "What happened when y'all went to the cops?"

Gamble kissed her teeth. "The same shit that always happens. They said they're looking into it but we shouldn't get in their way. Now that foul play is suspected, they are not fucking around."

Amanda shook her head. "So until then, just try not to end up dead or missing. Great." Amanda looked past Gamble toward the bathrooms. *Where the hell did Xtra go? Why am I still holding this greasy bag?* "I guess we'll just have to see how fate deals the cards."

Gamble downed the last of her drink and slammed the glass on the bar. She licked her upper lip and gave one last hateful glare at her reflection. "Yeah, well . . . sometimes you have to force fate's hand if you want it bad enough." Gamble fished a crumpled ten-dollar bill out of her red sequined clutch, slid it to the bartender, and blew him a kiss. "And speaking of, I have another gig to get to." She gave a deadpan smile to Amanda and patted her hand. "A queen's work is never done, right, sis?"

Amanda held her reserve. "Such is life."

"And life is a gamble, baby." Gamble laughed and gave a surprised Xtra a goodbye hug when she finally appeared.

Amanda let out a deep exhale as her stubby, unreliable friend made it back to the bar. "Mmm, something in the buttermilk ain't clean with that one."

"Whatever, girl, he fine as fuck." Snickering, Xtra grabbed her purse. "He can . . . clean my . . . buttermilk any day."

Amanda stared daggers at her portly friend the entire time. "Bitch, I gotta go. Make sure you get your drunk ass an Uber, or at least fuck somebody who can give you a ride home."

Xtra tittered as her towering girlfriend gave her a hug and hiccuped. "From your mouth to God's ears, henny!"

Amanda checked the time on her watch again, said her goodbyes, and begrudgingly made her final exit.

Amanda Scrümi was tired but worried about her first love/child more than anything. From the minute she walked the property to the day of their grand opening, her Body-ody-ody Shoppe was all she thought about. Other than where the hell had Wendy Williams run off to?[1]

After being in business for only twelve months, they were already expanding into collision and auto repair. The year saw big milestones, including the addition of her first full-time manager. Amanda was such a control freak, the only person she trusted to take care of her baby was her. That's why her nerves had been shot all day, knowing she had entrusted the shop keys to her new manager, Rachel.

As she sat at the red light, everything that could have gone wrong with the shoppe ran through her mind. She checked her phone but saw nothing but a dry inbox. The last message from Rachel was a *Thanks, boss!* reply to Cisco's text wishing her good luck on her first day.

The weird feeling she felt pulsating through her body . . . what could that be? Relief? Serenity? Was the universe allowing her the first carefree night she'd had since . . . over a year ago? And didn't she loan her pink pumps to that queen, Serenity Napkins?

She sighed and grinned, imagining the sweet freedom that could be in store for her. She turned the corner and saw the sign for her one true love, the Body-ody-ody Shoppe. As she drove to the back, she still marveled at the all-white building with a bubble gum pink roof and bay doors. Her contractor at the time asked Cisco if he thought it might be a little too much, and Cisco retorted, "We can only hope so." It still brought a little tear to his eye when he parked his cruddy old Kia (bought and paid for) in the *For Queens Only* parking spot. She might have chosen substance over style that time, but she knew big things were on the horizon for her.

The cold night air and the pungent smell of motor oil greeted her as she stepped out of the car. She only had to do an inventory check for next week and grab her doggie bag from the office fridge. Keys in hand, trying to remember when was the last time she ate. The thought bolted from her mind as the employee entrance door nudged open without the need for the key.

Puta la madre.

The lights in the shop stirred, illuminating the bays one by one as her heels

---

1. This was 2022. Don't come for me.

clicked the concrete.

I knew it, I fuckin' knew it. A bitch can't have shit.

Her anger caused her to pay no heed to the back light already on. The entire system was set to turn off lights that hadn't sensed movement in the last five minutes.

Amanda paused to listen, wary of intruders or scrap metal thieves. Only the hum of the unflattering fluorescent bulbs answered her. Relieved, she pulled out her phone. Ten p.m., too late to text Rachel, but she would be all up in that ass tomorrow. *Best believe*! She gave a perfunctory glance around the shop before going upstairs to her office where her phone charger and, hopefully, food awaited her.

> ### Beyoncé: Flaws and all.mp3

The sweet voice of Beyoncé floated out of the sound system below her, filling the interior of the shop. Enough so that Queen Bey's mezzo-soprano notes reverberated through her toes as she ditched the heels and switched to her "do work" sneakers. Her black baby doll dress was going to the dry cleaners, so it would be fine and the wig could stay.

Inventory shouldn't take too long. Three big jobs were lined up for next week, so she had to make sure everything was stocked and ready. Amanda grabbed her clipboard and set out to complete her task. She should be out of there before midnight if she played her cards right. She headed down to the parts department stockroom when she noticed the state her techs had left their workstations.

Her face twisted in annoyance. The velvety sound of R&B drowned out the sound of the stockroom door clicking closed and both sets of footsteps in the repair bay.

> ### Beyoncé: Love on Top.mp3

The state her fellow "grease monkeys" left their areas, knowing they had the best equipment in the industry, dumbfounded Amanda. She bopped her head to the beat as she was forced to clean up after grown-ass men in the name of ownership.

She picked up her clipboard again and finished the repair bay area check. As she headed to the paint prep/cycle area, her foot almost slipped out from underneath her.

If Amanda told Chris once, she told his dumb ass a thousand times: Any solvent or cleaner you spill on the floor needs to be wiped, then Oil-Dri applied. Why? Because if you don't, the shop floor stays slick and someone could slip. Like her ass almost just did.

Of course, Chris's station was out of Oil-Dri.

A queen's work is never done, huh, sis?

She smirked. She was going to have to step her pussy up next week. These girls were out for blood.

Beyoncé: Drunk in Love.mp3

She paused momentarily as she stood in front of the stockroom door, now slightly ajar. Her baby hairs prickled against her skin as the ghostly melody wafted through the charged air. She took a breath and peered down the big open space, suddenly feeling less alone than when she first arrived.

The farthest bay clicked off in response, the second soon after. The threat of the third going dark caused her to push through the stockroom door finally. She didn't feel like being left in the fourth and only light on in the shop, besides her office.

The light in the musty back room clicked on as her adrenaline began to pump. Amanda was *ret to go.* The stockroom was as long as the three car bays but not as wide. Wheeled trolleys stood akimbo throughout the dusty space. She nudged a few open boxes out of her path with her foot. Rachel would be spending most of her day here tomorrow and that's on periodT.

Amanda coughed into her sleeve as she made her way past the boxed car parts organized like books in a library. The dust seemed to have already been kicked up before she got there. She quickly checked the Original Equipment Manufacturer numbers of the shelved parts.

Aftermarket parts are for suckers.

Fillers, primers, and paint were in order. She knew some girls who could use some of this industrial strength shit. Bless their hearts. She smugly closed the flammable liquid storage cabinet. The magnetic *click* echoed through the silence in the dusty storeroom between her playlist tracks. A shimmer of light caught her eye as her attention moved to the masked figure standing in the doorway.

> **Beyoncé: *Videophone: the extended remix*.mp3**

The initial shock startled Amanda. She clocked the Queen's boots, catsuit, and ski mask. Then her eyes finally came to rest on the threatening ratchet in her gloved hand, registering that this li'l fight sequence was about to begin.

The brooding Queen pitched forward. Amanda threw her clipboard at her and aligned herself with the only entrance and exit the stockroom had. The Queen deflected the aluminum clipboard with her forearm. The sting flowing through her funny bone was anything but.

Amanda's sneakers slid and kicked up more dust as the Queen lurched back against the door, slamming it shut. Amanda felt behind her back, begging her hands to find something blunt to turn that pink ski mask red.

"That door is always closed." The dust particles tickled Amanda's nose as she tried to keep her eyes trained on the movements of the Queen. "Just take what you want, you not the first muthafucka who tried to rob us!"

Her now dust-caked fingers finally came to rest on the ball joint of the curved steel control arm that Hank absentmindedly left out of the box. *Bless him.*

The Queen raised the ratchet as she attempted to close the distance between them. Amanda's eyes lit up as she swung the control arm out and into the rib cage of the Queen. Amanda bum-rushed the extremely rude aggressor. The conjoined queens hit the back wall.

The ratchet knocked against the hollow door before it clanked to the ground. Amanda grabbed the Queen by the side of her rhinestoned neck and thrust her in the direction of the dusty trash can. The Queen tried to catch her footing as she slid against the wall. Amanda pulled the door open. "Fuck you and fuck the BeDazzler you got for Christmas, too, bitch!"

Amanda dove into the blackened shop-turned-concert-hall, as the true queen (Bey) imbued her with the fervor to live. The delayed luminosity gave her a millisecond to think as the bay lights finally blinked on.

My phone. The office. My keys.

The commotion in the stockroom made her bolt into the darkness to the stairs. The stalled lights would deter that freak in the mask and last season's Steve Madden boots, but Amanda knew her shop like the back of her—

The tread of Amanda's sneaker met the sans-Oil-Dri-spill like two lovers caressing in the night. The momentum of her sprint and the lack of friction caused her right leg to slide under her. The weight of her *petite* body plummeted down onto her *dainty* ankle causing it to twist to an unnaturally acute angle. Before more tendons in her foot and ankle ripped clean off the bone, her head careened toward the cast iron table vise on the edge of the workbench. The damsel in distress's body skidded across the shop floor when the harsh lighting flickered on, illuminating the blood seeping out from under her wig.

> ### *Beyoncé: Irreplaceable.mp3*

The Queen watched the entire embarrassing spill. Amanda seemed to have slipped in some of her own hubris. The Queen attempted to lithely stride with her hand gripping her screaming rib through her bodice. Her heels clicked to the beat of her favorite song. The bass line thumping over the speakers, drowning out the faint beeping coming from Amanda's direction.

The overhead fluorescent lighting was as unbecoming as a wig sopped with blood on a dirty concrete floor. The Queen scanned the area for something that could clean a bitch's clock once and for all. The blazing red toolboxes between each bay were as tall as she was; they *had* to have something sharp and murder-friendly.

Keeping an eye on the incapacitated, unmoving queen with one eye, she pulled a drawer open. Nothing but useless nuts and pointless bolts. The entire tool chest rolled away from her with an unintentional nudge. The Queen pulled a second drawer open and felt the entire cabinet begin to tip forward. She slammed the drawer shut in time to stop it from toppling onto her. Her peripheral vision caught movement coming from Amanda. Agitation flooded the Queen's mind. Her gloved hands grabbed the edge of the wheeled tool chest and aligned it with the writhing bombshell. Incapacitated was off the menu, but immobilized would do for now.

The music silenced itself, bitch didn't spring for Spotify Premium . . . obviously.

With a guttural roar, the Queen thrust the clunky apparatus toward Amanda. Full speed ahead propelled the weighted stack forward. The Queen struggled to keep it straight while chasing the trolley, finally sending it careening into the prostrate princess.

The wobbly wheel came to a cacophonous halt as it hit the rubber soles of Amanda's sneakers. The Queen quickly seized the opportunity and slammed her uninjured side into the hulking structure. It toppled with a resounding *boom,* combined with the wailing shrieks of shock and agony escaping Amanda's over-straining pipes.

The Queen walked around the wreckage of hurled tools and mangled body to marvel at her handiwork. Her joy was immediately rebuffed when a pry bar flew at her head. The heel struck her lower orbital bone, causing a natural crimson rouge from the apple of her cheek to the bridge of her nose. Ruptured capillaries bloomed beneath her mask. The stunned Queen cowered her head and bellowed into her shaking hands, "NOT THE FACE, YOU BITCH!" The Queen's words echoed off the walls and mixed with Amanda's equally loud screams.

Blood was trickling down Amanda's neck and chest, soaking into her dress. Her head wound was still leaking. She struggled trying to push the hardware off her lower half. The hard-edged top of the box was compressing her hip and tailbone. The more Amanda tried to pull herself out or push it off, the more pain exploded through her body.

The Queen finally recovered and launched at the struggling starlet, ready to elude any more projectiles. She purposely landed on the steel behemoth, crunching bone and metal beneath her. She pushed off, knocking another pry tool out of the astounded Amanda's quivering claw. The Queen shot one hand to Amanda's throat, the other reaching around her for any weapon in reach. She got her scrambling mitts on an extra-long screwdriver, switched her grip, and stabbed it into Amanda's solar plexus with all her strength.

A true Queen runs the chessboard and eliminates any threat that gets in her way.

The wet crackling sounds and the distant sound of sirens were drowned out by Amanda's exhausted screech. Amanda used the last bit of fight she had to keep the Queen's hands off her neck. The Queen straddled her waist, stuck in an uncompromising embrace with the obituary-waiting-to-happen when the Queen finally caught the sound of the approaching sirens. The Queen's swollen eye widened beneath the mask.

Amanda eked out a pained, vengeful laugh. "Apple Watch . . . BITCH." The Queen flipped Amanda's wrist to face her. Amanda's Apple Watch face showed

Fall Detection: Emergency Services Contacted.

The Queen's mask couldn't hide the panic written all over her face. She let

Amanda's wrist drop and eyed the pry bar she had dropped earlier. Tears filled the Queen's eyes as she screamed in frustration. Spittle foamed at the side of her mouth as she grabbed the tool and pulled it back like she needed a home run to save her life.

Full of vexation, she swung the bar at Amanda's head. The heel of the tool collided, rocketing uprooted teeth and a spray of blood. Amanda's lower jawbone dislodged and protruded, crunching and sloshing beneath pulverized skin. That final strike meant *lights out* for Amanda Scrümi, her body disengaging once and for all.

The Queen rose. Amanda's blood and her own soaking the pink mask. The rhinestones dappled with dried blood, still twinkling in the overhead lighting.

The Queen hobbled her way through the bays. Keys in hand, she unlocked the side door. She let the keys drop to the concrete before disappearing into the night to lick her wounds. Fucking technology. Fucking Car Bitch. Two more fucking bitches to go.

Gamble Donna Phart

Chapter 19

OCTOBER 27, 2022, **T**HURSDAY

"MOOOOM!" Gamble's scream exploded through the pitch blackness of her room. Her eyes wide and bulging in shock, the only thing visible through the weak light filtered in through her shut blinds. A mild rumbling came from the living room that sounded like shuffling feet and a decent amount of cussing. Evayda busted through Antonio's door, her face and silk headwrap illuminated by her phone screen. She felt for the light switch on the wall, annoyed and mumbling loudly. She flicked it on when her acrylics finally hit it, blanketing the room in dizzying light.

"Bitch!" Evayda yelled. "I thought you were getting killed!" She squinted angrily at her friend still somewhat in shock in her bed. "Gamble, come in, Gamble. Girl, not this shit right now. Can't you just be normal, at least while you sleep?" Evayda walked over and sat on Gamble's bed, putting her hand on her hyperventilating friend's chest. "Now I see why we were never sleepover friends. I'd never get any damn sleep, and I need my beauty rest." She looked into her friend's eyes. "Just breathe, baby, calm down."

Gamble gulped and blinked her tear-filled eyes. Her mind still reeling, she eked out, "I let her die."

"Let who die?" Evayda asked, turning away from her phone, momentarily intrigued. "Your mom?"

Gamble sat up in bed, her jaw open. "What? How did you . . . how did you know who I was talking about?"

"Bitch, you yelled out, 'MOM,' why else do you think you woke my ass up?" She patted the back of her headwrap. "Shit, I was sleeping good too. Even on that lumpy-ass couch."

"You're the one who said we had to be on the buddy system till after the pageant. I told you that you could sleep in Roger's room, I'm sure he wouldn't mind." Gamble reached across to her bedside table for her water bottle.

"I would mind. I don't know what his little scraggly ass does in there and frankly, I don't want to. It smells like wet chicken in that room. I'll take my chances on the couch," she said, standing up. "Well since I'm up, let me go pee. Then you can tell me what happened to your eye and how you killed your mama."

Gamble choked on her water. "Bitch! I . . ." She stifled a few coughs and stared off, deep in thought.

Evayda strolled back into the room, her face scrunched up while she rubbed lotion into her hands. "I don't know how you be sharing a bathroom with somebody that don't wash their legs. Couldn't be me. I'd be worried I'd catch scabies or some shit." She looked at Gamble, still staring. "Bitch, not again." She started to snap her fingers in Gamble's face. "What happened to your fucking eye?!"

Gamble sighed, wincing as she touched the tender bruising. "I told you. The fucking bar!"

Evayda scrunched her whole face like something stank. "Mmm-hmmm. Anyway. Finish the damn story, ANTONIO!"

"There's nothing else to tell. We just lost touch after—"

"After you killed her."

Gamble snapped, "I did not kill her! I was just . . . It was just . . . too much going on all at once and . . . " Gamble felt her heart sink. She brought her knees to her chest, holding back tears.

"Girl, I watch Lifetime movies. I know when someone wakes up screaming, 'MOM,' some fucked-up shit went down." Evayda rubbed her friend's shoulder, attempting to reassure her. "Let me guess, she hired the *wrong* wedding planner."

Gamble would have laughed if her head wasn't swimming. She was trying to piece her scattered memories back together. "I just never went into full details about everything with my mom because I didn't need you thinking I was crazy."

Evayda grinned and looked affectionately at her longtime friend. "Girl, I knew you were crazy the minute I saw your foundation blended like a black-and-white cookie. So let's hear it . . . and make it good."

Gamble exhaled, letting her air puff her cheeks, slowly releasing her breath. "I don't know where to start. I told you about the bullshit with the conversion camp.

I just never told you what happened after." Evayda nodded her head in agreement, nestling at the foot of Gamble's bed to get comfortable. "Did you ever hear about The LordsWay church? Up in NorCal?"

Evayda cocked her head with one eye closed, scanning her brain for recollection. "Yeah, wasn't it some kind of religious cult or something?" Gamble nodded her head in agreement. "Wait! The one that burned with people still in it?" Gamble solemnly nodded her head, looking away in shame. "That shit was all over the news when I was in high school, I think. They said it could have been one of the biggest brush fires if they didn't already have intel on the whole place. But it took forever for them to get fire trucks and shit out there. No way, that was the same place? I always figured your parents just, you know, were assholes. I didn't think it was all that."

Gamble continued to stare, eyes downcast, through the waterworks. "My mom was going to be the First Lady of the church until she found out the leader was broke and stringing her along the whole time. He just said whatever to have a First Lady half his age on his arm. Then she freaked out and set the whole place on fire."

"While y'all were still inside it?!" exclaimed a slack-jawed Evayda.

"Yup. When mom had an idea in her head, there wasn't much you could do to stop her. She was a Scorpio, so . . . "

Evayda instantly understood and nodded. "So wait, how did y'all get out of there?"

Tears squeezed out of Gamble's tightened eyelids. "I got out. She didn't." She sniffled, reached for a Kleenex, then continued. "There was no cell phone reception out there, no electricity, nothing. Everything was off-the-grid. Oil lamps and candles. Before Mom confronted the reverend, I grabbed her phone when she wasn't paying attention. He tried to calm her down but I saw her throw everything off the desk. The oil lamp started the fire. I tried to get to her but the room was already going up in flames. By the time I was able to get out, most of the building was destroyed. So all I could do was run to the gate in the dark and pray I got phone service.

That's when I made it out past the trees and all her text messages started dinging. All of them were from my aunt and uncle. I didn't know what to do, so I just clicked the text and it called them. I don't remember much else after all the police and fire trucks showed up." Gamble stared off again, reliving the moment in real time, just like in her recurring nightmares.

A loud crunching noise brought her back to reality. Evayda looked back at her, wide-eyed, licking her fingertips with a bag of Flamin' Hot Cheetos in her other hand. "Girl, then what happened?"

Gamble squinted at her friend in *bitch, wtf*. "Where did you get those from?"

"Roger's room," Evayda said nonchalantly between crunches.

They both looked at each other, heads cocked, lips pursed. Their furrowed brows conveyed their shared thought of *What was Roger doing with Flamin' Hot anything? . . . Are they evolving?*

Evayda sucked her teeth and said, "I don't know, girl. Finish your damn story."

"They questioned me and I told them everything. About what the reverend did to me, what he probably did to others." Gamble paused to think. "I blocked a lot of it out, thankfully. After that, the courts let me go stay with my aunt and uncle. Lots of therapy, lots of questions that I still don't have answers to." She blinked, "I think that's it."

"Damn, babygirl," Evayda said, "that's a lot of shit for one person to go through, especially so young. As much as I'd love to make a joke about it, this is the one time I know that shit's not funny." Evayda scooted closer to her friend and said, "I'm sorry you had to go through all that, but I'm glad to call you my sister." She wrapped her arms around her sniffling friend. "It's us versus the world, baby." A moment passed, cuing Evayda to let go and stand. "Now can we go back to sleep, please? Bitches got a funeral to go to in the morning."

"Girl, I can't believe you don't own anything in black that doesn't look like it's out of the streetwalker collection at Rainbow," Evayda said, looking through Gamble's closet. "I still say you should just go in boy drag. You're new enough, no one will say anything."

Gamble was holding sheer black dresses up to her body, frustratedly looking in the mirror. "That would just be easier. The rehearsal is tomorrow and we gotta get ready for that," she said, digging through the other side of her closet now.

"You'll be glad you did. Hope they don't recognize you because this is about to be a whole-ass spectacle," said Evayda as (he) laced up (his) dress shoes. Gamble was already ironing (his) shirt. "Watch out, world. Sisters from another mister are about to be brothers from another mother today."

"I hate boy clothes," Gamble said, itching her neck and nervously staring out the car window.

"Maybe that's because you look like Salt Bae out of drag." Evayda chuckled, seeing Gamble's nerves tightening up in front of her.

"Puta . . . Salt Bae is Turkish . . . or something."

"I thought you were some kind of Spanish? Did you ever tell us? Childhood trauma . . . ethnicity? Anything else you care to save for the very end, sis?"

Gamble side-eyed her annoying friend. "Peruvian father and my mother was Italian."

Evayda looked at Antonio's face. "Oh, okay, li'l caffe latte. I can see it." She chuckled. "I'm just Black." She pulled her visor mirror down and pouted her lips. "A vision in ebony."

"Bitch, watch the road!" yelled Gamble, gripping the car door handle.

"Whoops! My bad, girl." Evayda swerved back into her lane and closed the visor. "Calm down, we on our way to a funeral anyway. If we die on the way there, we saving them a trip."

"Whyyyyy, LAWD, whyyyyy?" rang out as the two entered the funeral parlor.

Dyna's final gig was packed to the gills.

"SHE WAS SO YOUNG!"

Disembodied voices shouting random farewells seemed to appear on cue every silent moment.

"She was forty-nine!"

Gamble and Evayda stood in front of a huge collage of all Dyna Fyre's successful club flyers.

"Oooh, she gunna haunt your ass for tellin' her business like that!"
tongue pop

Seeing Dyna's exuberant face brought a tear to both queens' eyes.

"And she just got her braces off too!"

The line toward the front moved at a snail's pace.

"Heaven gained another angel!"

By the time Evayda and Gamble got up front, the shiny red closed casket greeted them. A large glamour shot of Dyna Fyre stood sentry behind the casket.

"That angel still had my Mariska Hargitay wig too.

Fuck my life!"

After paying their respects, Evayda and Gamble looked for familiar faces amongst the sea of veils and day drag. Evayda's phone dinged just before the sound of hooves stampeding the worn hardwood floors shook the room.

All attendees startled as a blur of black and pink charged into the room aimed for the coffin. The crowd gasped as Suzee Ho Maker dove onto the casket with all her years and weight.

"Dyyynaaaa! My handsome Dyna!" The casket somehow stayed in place, even with Suzee suctioned to it like an octogenarian refrigerator magnet. "No, Lord, WHY? Take me! Take me instead!" Suzee continued to wail until it seemed people stopped paying attention.

A lanky heathen in a black large-brimmed fascinator strolled up and knocked on the casket, her good Judy arm in arm with her. "Now that's a sturdy coffin. Even under all that tonnage. Still holding up, see, Maybel?" She raised her voice in her hard of hearing friend's ear, "Maybel! I says, Maybel! When I go, make sure they bury me in one of these!"

The ancient pair of ravens hopped off into the horizon together, leaving Gamble and Evayda to ponder their own predestined *Death Becomes Her* fates.

As the viewing room was calming down, a "GOTDAMN!" filled the silence, followed by the sound of shuffling meat and crumpling plastic.

The room turned to stare at none other than Xtra Mayonessa in all her knock-kneed glory. The pallid princess's Converse laced-up heels were bulging in all the wrong places, the heel promising to snap off and take out an eye at the slightest provocation. She trudged down the aisle toward the casket like a slow-moving garbage barge with the stink lines and everything. As she made it up front, the crowd was atwitter with whispers once they realized the walking *Katamari* ball of trash was, in fact, wearing a large black garbage bag with all-too-generous-portholes cut out on the sides.

"Missy Elliot, she is not!" was yelled from somewhere in the back.

The front row thworped their folding fans all at once, causing the gay version of a sonic boom. The Sonique Boom, if you will, ricocheted off the funeral parlor walls. The pungent fetid air of a decaying carcass and sweet pea body spray offended their delicate powdered noses. A scent that noticeably wasn't there before the Hefty heifer invaded the room with her malodorous walk-by air.

"Dyna would have set that trash on fire!"

"The Ball! The Nerve! The Gumption!"

"I don't trust that fabric! One fart and she'll kill us all!"

After Xtra Mayonessa paid her respects. The Magic 8 Ball with a stubbed thumb for a head turned toward the crowd quizzically. Self-awareness was never the crinkling cretinous cow's strong suit. She seemed to have assumed they were talking about some *other* trollop in a trash bag.

"Wasn't yesterday garbage day?"

"Damn, we can't stand this bitch, huh?"

"Season two better be nicer! We ain't all this mean."

Xtra waddled past the first row and noticed Gamble and Evayda hiding behind their funeral programs.

"OMG! Not boy drag!" The under-bridge-troll cackled as she thumped closer to them. "You know I would recognize your fine ass anywhere, Antonio." She batted her askew eyelashes at him, thankfully blocking the view from the rest of the room.

Evayda crinkled her nose and blocked her nostrils with her finger. Her eyes squinted against her raised cheeks the more she examined Xtra's "outfit."

"Let's try and keep it low-key, Xtra," Gamble whispered from behind the program. "For Dyna's sake."

She nodded in agreement, "Oh yeah, gurl, I can't stand disrespectful-ass people at a function."

Evayda's eyes couldn't pry themselves off the chalky-looking sweat that dripped from the poorly cut holes in Xtra's "dress." With furrowed brows and her upper lip bunched up, Evayda asked bluntly, "You live in a fantasy world, don't you?"

"Oooooh no! Evayda?!" Mooed the livestock. "Girl, I ain't never seen you out of drag! Damn, you fine as hell too." She pulled back, taking in the two of them wearing their funeral attire and sucked her teeth. "Mm-hmm, you boys call me if you ever wanna make like an Oreo and get some double stuffin' in. If you catch my drip." She attempted to seductively wink at them after a few tries. "Maybe after the pageant. Y'all getting a hotel room?"

Evayda flared her nostrils and pointed her pinkie at the obnoxious ox. "Girl, if you don't get your oil slick ass out my damn face, you not going to make it to the damn pageant. I promise you that."

Xtra caught a millisecond of comprehension, making a face of confusion and possibly . . . gas?

Just before fisticuffs and/or flatulence hit the already telenovela-esque mood in the room, Suzee walked up to the girls. Still recovering from treating Dyna's coffin like a mechanical bull, but she was taken aback by the boy versions of Evayda and Gamble. "My my my, boys, I barely recognized you!" she exclaimed. "Not till I heard this exercise ball in sneakers yell it across the damn room!"

Evayda and Gamble sat back like children watching their parents fight in front of them. Several ooohs were released from the seating area behind them.

Xtra sucked in a deep inhale, giving the aging queen the look up and down. "Aww, gramma, as if you know what an exercise ball looks like."

The crowd behind them gasped.

"She is old," said a phantom voice.

Suzee did her best church grin, with her teeth clenching. "Oh, Mantequilla, our own little creature from the *snatched* lagoon." She paused and glanced down at Xtra's waist. "Well . . . *encased*, I guess, would be the better word."

Xtra looked like someone stirred her jar the wrong way, firing back, "Ma'am, this ain't the 1800s no more. You can't be body-shaming these days. Besides, ain't you next in line for a funeral anyway? Is that how you want to be remembered?"

A small pitter-patter of snaps could be heard in the back.

"Can we go home yet?" asked a perturbed voice.

Evayda chimed in, "Oh, wait. When is Yanita's funeral?"

The entire congregation yelled back, "WHO??" in unison.

Suzee blinked quickly and turned back toward Gamble and Evayda. "Anyhoo . . . listen, girls, did you get the email from the coordinators?"

Evayda was already scrolling on her phone. Gamble's face dropped. "They're not canceling the pageant, are they?" she asked, a choke caught in her throat.

"They can't cancel it, honey, even if they wanted to. The checks are cashed, the venue is already booked, and you can't return an engraved crown. I already called and checked," Suzee said, scowling.

"Yeah, I got the email," Evayda answered.

"Me, too," said Xtra and Gamble simultaneously.

"Okay, good. This is not ideal, to say the least, but the show must go on. Half of the girls haven't responded back to me yet," Suzee said with concern. "We just have to assume they are all showing up and they'll reply in *drag queen time.*"

Gamble was reading the email. "So what's changed? They bumped the rehearsal time slot up? Are we still doing interviews and all that? It says *full glam.*"

"Yes, I want you girls dressed to the nines. Full glam, hair, everything," Suzee said, "We need to get as many promo pics and as much good PR as we can. I'm talking to the videographer after I leave here, so look your best. At this point, it's full positive optics ahead."

Xtra blinked. "What's optics?"

"It means make everything look nice and pretty," fired back Evayda.

"We can pull this off, girls, I know we can," Suzee added enthusiastically. "Just think, one of you might be wearing the crown Saturday night!"

"Oh shit," Xtra said, checking her phone again. "I have to get ready for my last shift. I've got to go, ladies." She blew them a kiss before eyeballing Suzee. "Gentlemen." And made her exit.

Suzee glared at the back of the iconic ignoramus as she left.

The room took a final exhale.

Someone yelled, "See, that was her smelling like that!"

Xtra Mayonessa

Chapter 20

> *Duncan,*
>
> *We've had multiple complaints from customers overhearing you say, "Ew" when they ask for tuna salad on their sandwiches. Please remember that we are trying to sell sandwiches and cater to all tastes. You don't need to comment on their choices every time. Please refrain from doing this, effective immediately. Lastly, please stop using the deli slicer to open your hot chips. And a friendly reminder that all areas of the deli are under video surveillance for security purposes.*
>
> *Love you, sweetheart,*
>
> *Mom*

Xtra Mayonessa, a.k.a. Duncan, scratched her scalp with her yellow acrylic nail. She slowly blinked at the note taped to where her apron hung at the family deli. "I'm not reading that essay," she croaked as the door chimed, indicating a customer entering, pulling her out of her cognitive wasteland.

A middle-aged woman walked up to the counter, looked at the illuminated menu, and asked, "How is the tuna salad?"

Xtra, incredibly dumb as the day was long, gagged. "Ew."

The customer furrowed her brow and looked at her watch. "I'll just have tuna salad on wheat." Her eyes fixed on Xtra's nails, her hair, and her bovine stare. "Extra mayo, please."

It didn't take much to amuse the diminutive drag queen, but every time she heard her namesake, her irksome chortle became *extra* greasy. The customer, obviously feeling left out of the joke, faked a smile and stepped closer to the glass as her sandwich was being prepared. She peered through the glass at Xtra's acrylics, showing brightly through holes cut in her nitrile gloves. "Wow, I like your nails. They're so long!"

Xtra smiled and absentmindedly dropped the woman's sandwich in order to flash her nails so the woman could get a closer look. "Thank you! My girlfriend does them over at Heavenly Hooves on Lankershim and Cahuenga." She wriggled them in front of the now less-amused patron. "You should get you some, girl."

The woman laughed. "Oh no, not me. I don't think I could quite pull them off like . . . you . . . can." She glanced at her watch, hoping to end this exchange already so she could just pay and go before her lunch hour was up. To her relief, the zesty "sandwich artist" went back to working on her order, but at a snail's pace. The uncomfortable silence made the customer uneasy. She accidentally blurted out, "I don't know how you wipe your ass with those things," eyes widening and instantly regretting her words.

Luckily, the blonde dump truck of a dame laughed and said, "I just use the gloves they give us here." With her trademark vacant smile, Xtra flashed her gloved hand in front of the appalled woman, then put her sandwich in a bag. "Anything else, henny?"

Thinking made Xtra's head hurt. She tried not to do it unless she *absolutely* had to. That's why she loved working at her family's deli. She knew deep down inside that they would never fire her.

She might be dumb as shit, but she was no fool. She knew she was set for life. The Dungadoobar Deli would be hers one day. Then she could change the name to Xtra Mayo's Haus of Sandwich, even though her parental units weren't a huge fan of the name change. Mom made life so much easier for Xtra. She left her notes everywhere because she knew Xtra's brain was always . . . busy . . . with . . . things.

The notes like *LOCK THIS DOOR* on the back door, or *WE DON'T TAKE IOUS, WE NEVER DID* on the cash register, or *NO CALLING CUSTOMERS BITCHES EVEN IF IT'S*

NICE behind the counter helped a lot. Bless Donald and Debbie Dungadoobar for being so supportive and understanding about the emergence of Xtra. Even though, realistically, they were just glad to know that spending his adolescence so close to power lines hadn't affected their little drooling teenager, now all grown up.

Xtra's very existence made Charles Darwin roll over in his grave, but she was just "being Xtra." Duncan made people gag on whatever that smell was, but Xtra made people gag on her eleganza. She was still new on the scene but she learned fast. All the other queens pushed her into doing pageants with them because "pity votes were a thing" and "she was a shoo-in for Miss Congeniality."

The more practice she got, the better. So on nights she closed the deli, she had time to run home, Febreze the crotch of her tucking panties, and be on her way to the gig. She might not know all the words to the songs, and her wig might never be straight, but she was getting paid to twerk onstage in clothes that *almost* fit her. Plus, who didn't love picking money up off the floor?

Which reminded her to finish restocking the food prep area before closing time. She put her phone in her hairy, clammy cleavage and grabbed the XXL bucket of mayonnaise from the stockroom.

The food prep area was set up so she could refill everything and still see the front of the delicatessen. She had to slice the lunch meat for tomorrow's orders and refill the mayonnaise bottles, which all seemed to go empty on her shift. She doesn't know why everyone was shocked to see her squirt mayo right into her open mouth as a snack. Where do they think she got her drag name from?

Xtra peeled the white plastic lid back on the bucket of shiny, tangy, pus-colored goop. She did her best to stay strong, shoveling the oleaginous sludge into squirt bottles, never taking her uneven eyes off the congealed spatula. A glistening drip of drool passed her glossy lip and dribbled down her slick, pockmarked, razor burn chins.

Xtra glowered in the direction of the security cameras. The sign underneath that read *YES, WE SEE YOU* boring a hole in her vacuous soul. She felt herself go flush as a translucent globule of room temperature mayo flecked onto her eczema-dappled forearm, the unctuous fats lubricating the scaly skin beneath it. She slurped the now cold spittle from her lips as her eyes crossed and the dream sequence waves rippled in front of her vision.

Xtra's heavily shadowed eyes opened as the 8mm movie camera whirred and zoomed out, revealing a sepia-toned poolside paradise scene that reeked of old Hollywood glamour. Xtra's pouty lips blew a kiss to the lens as she ascended the diving board in her ornate one-piece that left nothing to the imagination.

The white suit was painted on her zaftig body, contouring every crevice, dimple, and inflamed ingrown hair she had. Her vintage swimming cap pulled snuggly over her Cro-Magnon skull and the pack of hot dogs on the back of her neck. Xtra maintained her perfect crooked smile, but she struggled to make it up the five steps of the not-so-high dive. The climb made her suit wedge itself into her musky undercarriage. So much so that the crotch looked like it had been chewed by wild dogs, but she maintained that smile. She finally made it to the apex, slowing to catch her breath and hack up a lung. However, the jaunty tune playing in the background never faltered as she regained her composure and posed before the diving board.

The movie reel changed into an aerial view. All of Xtra's drag friends looked at her and smiled as they awaited their MayoQueen in the pool below. The queens maintained their increasingly intense, toothy grins as they held their place in the twinkling waves of gelatinous mayonnaise densely packed into the in-ground pool. The scene returns to Xtra as she pounds onto the diving board.

In unison, the queens sing, "We are *gagging*, henny!" as Xtra gracefully dives into the vat of coagulating sludge warming in the sun. Less of a dive and more of a belly flop, the lukewarm waves spatter the queens, still gurning as their makeup is flecked with the tangy zip of nearly transparent salad whip. Xtra breaks the surface for air. Her head is a gleaming beacon of smeared makeup and curdy bits. She swallows her mouthful and beams.

She was about to begin her synchronized swimming number—*Esther Williams WHO?*—that would have the dolls screaming, when she was heaved out of her delulu by the sound of the hefty plastic bucket crashing to the floor.

Xtra's bountiful bosom had inched the slippery slop bucket closer and closer to the edge of the counter, resulting in the floor now being frosted with loads of liposuction leftovers.

A logical person, someone who wipes thoroughly, would have gasped in shock and did their best to clean up this disaster. Xtra's response was to blink slowly, grab a handful of napkins, and sprinkle them liberally on top of the mess. She wasn't the sharpest eyebrow pencil in the makeup bag, but in her mind, that would do for now.

Ever the stickler for safety and priorities, she had to get the lunch meat sliced before it was out for too long. Gathering all her containers and assorted meat products, she clicked the deli slicer on. The machine whirred to life, the metallic purr mesmerizing to her. Besides the mayo spatula in her mouth (when no customers were around), this was her favorite part of food prep. She cranked the blade thickness to thin, placed the ham loaf in the sliding food sled, and proceeded to convert it all into thin slices.

Xtra sidestepped the mayo mishap and put everything back in the under-counter refrigerators. The napkins were now absorbed into the oil slick that rivaled Xtra's forehead. She pulled her phone from her soggy cleavage to check the time. Milky meat juices commingled with her own meat sweats to create ham-prints on her screen.

If she wanted to make it to the gig on time, she would have to be gone in the next ten minutes. She made the executive decision to spend that time powdering her glazed donut of a face and locking up the deli. She pulled out a smudged compact and couldn't help but notice the gleaming deli slicer behind her. She was supposed to wipe that down, but that, along with the buttery floor, sounded like a *tomorrow* problem. She patted her nose with her makeup sponge, now caked with powder, sebum, and ham-sweat, creating more chunky white chocolate that caked on the sponge with every pass. Her final pat was cut short by the slamming of the back door.

The heel clicks let her know that the intruder wasn't Dad. It couldn't be Mom, not after they took three of her toes last year. Xtra was even more confused than usual since she didn't have time to text her bestie, Mulva Vagenstein, to come get her. She closed her compact and grabbed her purse as the swinging door swung open.

Xtra's eyes scanned the masked figure, from her sickening boots to her skintight catsuit, to her corset, to her opera gloves, and that stunning pink rhinestone ski mask. Her breath caught in her throat. Either she was gagged or her asthma was coming back.

"The CUNT.[1] The CUNT!" wheezed Xtra as the Queen eyed her adoring prey, like a lioness sizing up a wildebeest on the Serengeti. The Queen smirked and stuck a pin in her murderous rage, her cakes *were* sitting pretty high in this ensemble. As Xtra continued to gush over her outfit, the Queen glanced at her surroundings. She noted cleaning supplies, knives, and a sinister-looking bagel slicer. Xtra gasped, "Hold on, girl, let me get my keys. Hey, how did you know the back door was open?"

The Queen blocked out the insipid mouth-breathing mumbles of the moist-looking queen, still eying the space. The floor appeared to be . . . covered in mayonnaise and . . . napkins? The Queen gave Xtra a disgusted look that said, "Bitch, you live like this?"

Xtra, oblivious to anything not trending on TikTok or Flamin' Hot, yammered on, "That mask is everything, bitch!" The enamored li'l drag queen stepped closer to look at the rhinestones on the Queen's mask. "Somebody got a BeDazzler for Christmas!"

Xtra's unique scent of expired lunch meat, Victoria Secretions Vanilla Lace, and earring back invaded the Queen's already upturned nose as the words came out of Xtra's mouth.

One of Xtra's few remaining brain cells flickered to life. *Mulva Vagenstein has brown eyes, and Mulva is Jewish, and Jewish people don't celebrate Christm—.*

The Queen threw her delicate elbow, hitting Xtra square in the jaw, sending her and her loosened teeth sprawling to the mayonnaise-slicked floor.

Cue the cartoon stars encircling Xtra's culturally-appropriated braids. Xtra floundered a little, trying to get a grip on the greasy floor. The Queen's boot hit a patch of the gunk, making her knee strike the tile. The Queen let out a pained yelp, gripping her throbbing knee before pulling back a mayonnaise-slicked hand.

Rage filled her eyes as Xtra's widened while trying to crawl backward on her elbows toward the swinging door. The Queen pulled herself up by the counter, feeling the handle for the under-counter fridge and unfurled the lightweight door with all her might. Xtra winced, preparing for the damaging blow, and screamed, "NOO!" as the door lightly bounced off her shoulder. The slam would have barely left a bruise. Xtra unclenched one eye, then the other, and gave the Queen an

---

1. Charisma, Uniqueness, Nerve, and Talent, of course

apologetic frumpy-frown shrug, which only incensed the Queen even more.

The Queen's gaze moved above Xtra's head as she launched toward the counter. Xtra rolled to her side, scampering up the drawer handles as the Queen grabbed a panini press off the counter and pulled its cord free with one swipe. Xtra finally made it to her feet, inching her way closer to the door as she heard the Queen's angry battle cry behind her.

The Queen swung the panini press wide, catching the back of Xtra's head. The blow sent the sound of crunching skull and metal through the deli. Blood trickled from her crown, flowing like little rivers through her blonde cornrows. Xtra let out a groan and clung to the counter. The only thing between her and the door was the grimy deli slicer.

Out of breath and patience, the Queen slammed the panini press down on the nape of Xtra's neck. While the thick hump of flesh seemed protected by internal padding, the blow caused Xtra's vision to blur and needles to run down her arms and legs. The Queen dropped the mangled panini press as she grabbed Xtra's tight braids. The Queen's eyes lit up as they followed the cord from the slicer to the wall plug, seeing the slicer was still connected.

The Queen traversed the back of Xtra's quivering body, still holding her head in place as she clicked the deli slicer back to life. Xtra gasped and let out a bloody gurgle as the Queen started to crank the blade to max *thiccness*.

Xtra's arms and legs felt numb, her breathing now erratic. She fought to choke out her final words, "Girl . . . not . . . dis," as the Queen slammed her lumpy head onto the sliding food sled. Letting out a maniacal cackle, the Queen heaved the spiky food guard up and over the distended back of her head. Xtra's face pressed against the salty-ham-brine-stained cold metal leaving behind smears of blood and tears. Her final attempts to beg for her life were drowned out by the whirring blade only inches from her face. The spikes from the food guard punched holes into her perspiring scalp as the Queen tightened her grip and drove the sled forward.

The first swipe of the spinning blade melted through Xtra's nose and cartilage like hot piss through snow. Xtra let out a howling, gurgled scream before the Queen pulled the sled back. Blood splattered and smeared the matte metal surfaces. The majority of her cute button nose detached and sitting in a pool of blood.

The Queen grunted and pushed the sled again. The blade continued to slice the thick hide of Xtra's once cherubic face. More blood puddled, pooled, and started to drip down the counter. The Queen felt resistance at the remaining cartilage where Xtra's nose used to be. She thrust again until the slab of flesh slapped the blood-slick counter.

The Queen braced herself for one more swipe, summoning all her strength for this final push. Letting out an exasperated Valkyrie scream as she slammed the sled with all the strength she could muster. The blade whined as it sliced, then came to a screeching, abrupt stop.

The Queen stopped and attempted to see what caused the blood-soaked machine to malfunction. She released her grip on the waning queen to peer closer. The blade had caught and jammed itself into Xtra's princess pink skull. The hum of the blade still vibrated the machine as the queen looked around for something to pry the bone free.

All Xtra could do was whimper as her body started to buckle. The Queen reached for a large bread knife as she heard the slicer start to slide. The Queen pulled back against the opposite counter just as Xtra's body slumped and slipped to the floor when her sneakers hit a lone mayo-berg.

The slicer toppled down on top of her crumpled body with her skull still wedged inside, snapping her neck. Her body slid down with her limbs outstretched, contorted into a mayonnaise angel. A sight the Queen observed with stunned disbelief. She traversed the greasy floor once more, wiping any leftover mayonnaise off of her with paper towels.

Once she had collected herself, she collected her sopping-wet pig jowl, still resting where the slicer had sat. Of all the girls, this was the oddest chapter she was most excited to see come to a greasy end. Ten girls and one sow down, only one girl left. She saved the best for last. Then the true Queen would finally be crowned.

Gamble Donna Phart

Chapter 21

Gamble took a deep breath. She was prepared to hold it in as if her life depended on it. The footsteps she heard approaching made her baby hairs prickle. She hadn't planned on being trapped in a closet. Oh no, child, never again. Yet here she was, trying her damndest to stay undetected.

Gamble watched through the slats as the shadowy figure crept past her. First looking in her bedroom, then the bathroom, with no luck. Hopefully they wouldn't think to check the little linen closet in the hallway. Only a fool would try to hide in there. Gamble's lungs felt like they were about to burst. She knew it was now or never. She charged out of the closet and threw all of her weight onto Evayda before she had the time to retaliate.

"Putaaaa!" Gamble yelled as she swung her arms around Evayda's neck, both their shrieks billowing through the small apartment. Gamble let her body go slack like a sack of potatoes and Evayda toppled under their combined weight. They hit the carpet, still yelling as Evayda rolled out from under Gamble's grasp. Evayda used her long legs to keep Gamble away as she sat against the hallway wall.

"You bitch," Evayda choked out between gulps. "You know who plays like that?" She showed Gamble her pale palm and tapped on it. She took another gulp of air. "You know who don't play like that?" Evayda flashed the back of her melanated hand and tapped on it.

"Ashy people?" Gamble choked out a laugh between exasperated gasps.

"Ya mama ashy." Evayda nearly choked. "Whoops, too soon?" Gamble gasped and covered her mouth.

Evayda rolled her eyes and licked the side of her mouth. "Also, there's a fucking drag-queen-killer out there, so don't sneak up on bitches with guns in their purses." She slid down and starfish-ed on the ground. "You can tell you was an only child 'cuz me and my brothers would have kicked your little ass."

"Any of those brothers single?" Gamble asked, staring up at the ceiling.

"Nayo one of them, and they can do better, if we're being honest."

"Bitch. You say that now, wait till I snatch that crown right out from under you." They both snickered.

"I'll let you wear it once or twice in exchange for one of their numbers . . . Deal?"

"It's too early for your delusions, worstie. We gotta start getting ready. Time to get this shit show on the road."

"C'mon, girl!" Evayda said while adjusting her side mirrors.

Gamble fidgeted in the back seat before she swiftly turned and grabbed her seat belt.

"The doll babies are secured," Gamble said, glancing back at their Styrofoam wig heads strapped in with the rear seat belts.

"And away we go," said Evayda as they hit the streets.

Evayda seemed to be apprehensive about something once they got closer to the hotel. Gamble could tell by her biting her bottom lip while she drove.

Gamble broke the silence by saying, "I know you're not nervous. You've done this a million times!"

"It's not pre-show jitters. It's just a bad feeling I've got about all this," Evayda said, her voice sounding uncharacteristically shaky. "No messages from any of the girls?"

Gamble looked at her phone with a look of disapproval. "Dryer than Amanda's wig is going to be," she said, letting out a little giggle at the end.

"It's just . . . I know our girls are bad at texting, but not this bad. Not pageant weekend. I don't even know what rooms they're in," Evayda said, frowning as they pulled up to the One Billion Dollar Hotel.

Gamble's face was in awe at the hotel that dripped old Hollywood glamour.

"The Opulence! Gworl!" she said, taking pictures of the facade of the building.

"Girl, I know you're excited, but you gotta start acting like you're used to all this. This is the life of a flourishing drag queen, girl. Fancy cars, movie stars, grand hotels, bidets. All that shit," Evayda said as they pulled into the parking garage next door. "Or just a downtown hooker, but either way . . ." She pulled the ticket from the machine. "We are getting them coins, darling!"

There was an abundance of parking spots to choose from. They parked and Evayda popped the trunk. "Well you're lucky that your texts are dry because Suzee has been blowing mine UP." Evayda scrolled a few messages with cursory eyes. "Ugh, she needs to calm down, especially at her age. She used to be poppin' her prehistoric pussy onstage. She knows how chaotic this shit is." She typed a few words in response to Suzee before she pocketed her phone and helped Gamble grab their things from the trunk.

They lugged their luggage, each holding a Styrofoam head with a different color wig on each, requiring its own hand and priority, toward the elevator. Gamble said between grunts, "I thought they had those big suitcase rack things like in the movies." She pulled her stack of cases into the elevator while Evayda held the door open.

"Not when there's drag queens around, honey," Evayda said, as she scanned the elevator floor buttons. "Those girls will mop[1] anything that ain't nailed down in a room." The elevator door started to slide closed. "Can't take us nowhere."

Once inside the room, the luggage left higgledy-piggledy in the entryway. They both set their wig heads on "the cuck chair" in the corner. Then the two of them collapsed unceremoniously on their designated full-sized beds with their phones hovering above their faces. A steely silence was once again thickening the air in the otherwise well-ventilated room.

"The twins posted some Tiktok they're calling a Halloween prank but people are saying it's real," Gamble stated somberly. "It got taken down, but someone posted the screenshots and . . . it all looks pretty fucked-up." She scrolled some more. "If that's a prank, that's pretty realistic and I think I've seen every bad horror movie there is."

Evayda was quietly scrolling, contemplating her next words. "Something is

---

1. steal

going on at the Body-ody-ody Shoppe. They're saying some kind of bad accident happened."

Gamble felt her heart rate increasing. It was becoming hard to focus on the words on her screen. She locked her phone and sat up. Panic prickled the back of her eye sockets. "We don't got time for this, girl, I gotta start getting ready," she said, walking toward the bathroom, hoping some cold water on her face would calm her nerves.

Evayda snapped out of her thoughts, fighting back her own urge to panic. "Yeah, we gotta get you baking before that werewolf five o'clock shadow starts creeping in," she said, cracking a smirk and hearing Gamble in the bathroom snickering over the sound of the faucet running.

Gamble left the bathroom door open and shouted, "Watch me make you eat those words onstage, bitch!" Both of them laughing and teasing like they didn't have a care in the world.

"A ninja sword, bitch?! Is you serious?!" Gamble yelled, watching Evayda emerge from the bathroom. She placed the fabric steamer on the counter before she hit the floor, dying with laughter.

"You can't be *Kill Bill* without a ninja sword. I told you, I'm going all out for this lewk," Evayda said, pulling the Hatori Hanzo sword knockoff out of its sheath. The stainless steel glinted, creating prisms of light that danced across her tailored, bright yellow leather maxi dress. She brought the elbows of her fitted, matching yellow motorcycle jacket tight to the sides of her head. The pose allowed the blade to rest just before her line of sight and her shoulder-length platinum blonde wig. The slits in the otherwise snug dress allowed her to bend her knees. Just barely as she did her best trained assassin pose for her exceedingly impressed friend.

"Beatrix Kiddo," Gamble said through her shit-eating grin.

"Huh?" Evayda asked, turning so she could see herself in the mirror.

"Beatrix Kiddo or The Bride, you mean. Not *Kill Bill*. That's the name of the movie and the bad guy," Gamble said chuckling, knowing her worstie didn't know any of this.

"Yeah yeah yeah, I just know yellow looks good on me," Evayda said, flexing her leather-clad ass in the mirror. As she turned, she absentmindedly dropped her arm holding the sword, taking a small chunk out of the drywall.

"Bitch! That's real??" Gamble asked, her mouth a silent *O* looking at the hole in the wall.

"It was only like twenty bucks more for a real one," Evayda said, licking her thumb and trying to smooth over the drywall. "I mean, why not? You never know when you might need to cut a bitch in half. Especially since we recently became an endangered species."

Gamble picked her jaw up off the floor and reached her hand out. "Let me try it!"

Evayda was about to hand it to her enthusiastic friend until common sense and all her ancestors screamed in her head. "Hell nah, girl. I keep forgetting you played with white kids growing up. You will fuck around and lop a limb off and go about your day eating peanut butter and celery n shit. In fact,"—she slid the sword back into the sheath and fiddled with the crossbody strap—"this ain't leaving my sight with you around." She secured it to her back. "I keep that thang ON me!" she shouted into the mirror again.

Gamble stared at the fuckery playing out before her eyes and grabbed her wig before heading into the bathroom. "I can't stand you," she hissed as she walked past her friend, doing her best to hold in her laughter.

Evayda was strapping on her highlighter yellow heels and fired back, "Bad enough we got one killer out there, I don't need to be dealing with two!"

The *ding* of the elevator resonated loudly in the silence of their hotel floor, like a church bell in a black-and-white horror film. Both girls couldn't help but compare other pageants they'd done, where each hotel room door could barely contain the anticipatory noise and hysterics behind them. The silence was deafening. It took on a life of its own. It held a death grip on the secrets hiding from the decked-out damsels' impending distress.

Evayda stepped into the elevator and held the door for her friend. Gamble stepped in with hunched shoulders so her headdress wouldn't scrape the doorway. "Goddamn, bitch, did you put enough pins in this? It feels like my scalp is bleeding!" she said with pursed lips and downcast brow.

"That shit ain't coming off, though, is it?" Evayda hit the ground floor button. "You'll thank me later when they attach the runner-up crown to that thing," she said, looking up at Gamble's oversized headpiece perplexedly in the bad lighting, "…somehow."

Evayda's phone went off again. "Good lord, Suzee, I said we're on the damn elevator. Who died?!" she asked, instantly regretting it.

"This is why we are friends, bitch," Gamble said between snickers and grimaces.

"That's your Equinsu Ocha rubbing off on me, that's all," Evayda said, fumbling with her yellow purse and sword as they stepped out onto the ground floor.

A booming bellow of thousands of Valkyries greeted them, almost as fast as the hysterical harpies descended upon them.

"Gamble! Evayda! My God! You made it! I thought they got you too!" Suzee shouted, with the biggest Pink wig the two had ever seen.

"We just talked to you yesterday, girl," Evayda said slowly in disbelief, beckoning the crowd to disperse so they could get out of the hotel lobby.

"Oh, honey, if you only knew all the hullabaloo we have been going through in the last twenty-four hours! Hunnayy!" she said dramatically. Her flock of flamboyant gay pigeons behind her mimicked her almost to the note. "Huuuunay!"

Through the whirlwind of squawking and flourishing hands, the birds of *heyyy* whisked the two girls into the large auditorium while Suzee took a phone call. Her phone was in an obnoxiously large wallet case, on an obnoxiously loud speakerphone, and her obnoxiously large phone screen font read *The Fuzz* in large text. She shouted loudly into it. Sounded like she was reciting the address to the venue over the phone. It was hard to tell over the intense gasps and swoons the flock of lisping seagulls made as they took in Gamble and Evayda's pageant looks.

Suzee Ho Maker finally joined them, out of breath for some reason unbeknownst to anyone. "Gamble! My little bronze Barbie doll, you look absolutely stunning." She pulled Gamble from the voguing talons to fully take her in.

Gamble's décolletage was coiled with intricately hand-beaded necklaces. They radiated off of her neck in a rainbow of colors, leading down to a hammered bronze chest piece that matched her deep *V* belt. Wisps of white chiffon fanned out from the belt and matching arm cuffs that looked like she was swimming in the air. Her ensemble was topped off with an equally detailed bronze headdress that sparkled as much as her naturally mesmerizing eyes. Feeling the lifeblood of the innocent course through her veins, Gamble smiled with pride. She bared her fangs as her invocation of the Queen of the Damned finally reached its completion to the adulation of the growing crowd.

"Yeah, I'm here too, bitch," said Evayda huffily.

Suzee broke the thirsty stare away from Gamble's taut midsection for a split second to remark, "I like yours, too, Evayda. I thought *Charlie's Angels* was before your time."

Evayda exhaled sharply. "Bitch, I'm fuckin' *Kill Bill*! Beatrix or whatever . . ." she said, trailing off. She tucked her purse under her arm and walked off toward the stage, mumbling, "Woosahh"

Suzee called out, "Evayda! Wait! I'm sorry, come back. I'm just beside myself and trying to keep my head on straight!" Evayda reluctantly came back, walking next to Gamble, swatting the fruit flies away.

"Hold my purse, girl," she said under her breath, handing it to Gamble. "I should have left that shit upstairs," she added while they both pretended to listen to Suzee's breathy speech.

"We are in crisis mode right now, girls," Suzee said, her jaw shaking. "As of right now, you are the only two who have checked into the hotel. We know there's still time, and we know our girls are notorious for being late, but we just . . . we have to move forward." She continued, blinking away tears.

"The investors and the original coordinator are in an absolute tizzy right now trying to decide if they should just cancel everything and give people back their money. I was in a meeting with the hotel owner all morning. Due to our extremely unorthodox situation here, they said we could have the auditorium for tonight only, then we could get our deposit back. That way, we will be able to refund some of the ticket holders." Suzee fanned herself with a program. Gamble saw the glossy faces of her friends and idols, gone or MIA, flipping back and forth in front of her flickering vision.

"Now that I'm the head coordinator, a.k.a. the get shit done bitch, it's up to me to pull this off. Can you girls please, please, please, help me?" Suzee asked, the strength in her voice wavering.

"We'll do what we have to do," Evayda said, putting her arm in Gamble's. "Right, girl?" she said, looking into Gamble's unsteady eyes.

"Yeah." Gamble yielded. "Yeah . . . whatever we need to do," she said, with more vigor.

"If I had it my way, I would have shut it down, but my hands are tied. That's capitalism, ladies. But from the bottom of my heart, thank you both. I knew I could count on you two." Suzee choked, pulling a used Kleenex from her cleavage to wipe her nose. Evayda curled her lip in disgust but let Suzee finish. She blew her nose, the clown horn waking her gaggle of geese from their slumber.

"My assistant, wherever he went, is putting together a video memorial for our lost sisters." She looked around and yelled, "Brentistopher! Where the hell did you go!" The sounds of struggling exasperation came from across the room, where a tiny waif of a man was fanning an even tinier waif who seemed to have fainted.

"Oh great, just what I need today!" Suzee said frustratedly. "Chase! Tucker! Ethan! Toddathan! Help him, please!" Suzee seemed to be on her last leg, the pressure proving to be too much for her. "I just need you girls to turn it out for us. The ticket holders have been redirected to come here in an hour for a celebration of life and solidarity for our community." Suzee sniffled, the tears surfacing again. "Plus, we said open bar, so that should help things move along too."

Evayda pursed her lips and gazed up at the heavens. Gamble still seemed somewhat lost in her head. One of Suzee's Tinker Bells began showing her videos to approve. She nodded and cut back to Gamble and Evayda. "Oh, and one of the detectives finally got back to me—that's who I was on the phone with earlier—they said they're going to come keep an eye on things, but I told them we already beefed up our security." Suzee gestured with her thumb behind her.

A few feet away, two very large, very boxy men in suits stood with their hands tucked behind them in an intimidating pose. The veneer was only marred by their matching Shirley Temple wigs and *Betty* and *Veronica* name tags. Gamble and

Evayda looked at each other in pained confusion. "I have so much more to do, but you girls sit tight." With that, the little Suzee that could trudged along with her "security" in tow.

Evayda shook her head and looked at her forlorn friend. "Well this is a first, that's for sure." Gamble looked like a gentle breeze could knock her over at that moment. "C'mon, girl. Let's go have a kiki over here." Evayda put her arm around Gamble and led her toward the tables and chairs situated across from the bar/set-up area. Suzee could be heard hyperventilating from across the carpeted event space. Gamble clunked down into her seat, but that headdress stayed put. Evayda beamed with pride. "This ain't nothing, girl, this is a cakewalk. We can do this in our sleep!" Evayda said, as she pulled a chair closer to Gamble and sat down.

Gamble tucked her knuckles under her chin to support the headdress and take some stress off her neck, "That's the problem. It's nothing, girl. All this work. All this time. All that money that I scrimped and saved for. It's all gone to shit," she said, with venom more than sorrow.

Evayda glanced down and sighed. "I know, babygirl, I'm in the same boat as you. Hell, it's only us two in this motherfuckin' boat right now," she said, trying to crack a joke.

Gamble gritted her teeth, willing her tears to stay at bay. "I've dreamed of this pageant for almost a whole year now. I dreamed about my outfit, my hair, my makeup. Every single detail, I had the dream so many times I even knew what the stage would look like." Evayda reached behind her to grab a cocktail napkin. Gamble stared at the stage but shakily added, "Every time, it ended horribly and I never knew why or how, but it was always my fault somehow."

Evayda handed her the cocktail napkin to blot her makeup. "Well tell your brain she's a lying-ass bitch, 'cuz it was dead-ass wrong. Look on the bright side," she said, looking around before saying in a hushed tone, "at least we lived to see another pageant." Evayda swung her legs around the chair and leaned back, resting her elbow on the table. "And after this, what else can go wrong?"

Gamble looked longingly at her friend. "I honestly don't want to find out. I just want to get this over with already."

Evayda looked at the sets of doors behind them. "Well, we got an hour to kill, let's go get some air," she said, standing up a bit disjointedly. The strap on her sword caught the back of the chair, sending it clattering to the carpet. She looked back and down. "Fuck!" she said, picking it up, the strap torn out of its place. "That's what I get for sorting from lowest price to highest."

"Story of my life, sister. My neck hurts, though. Let me sit my ass down for a bit before my shit starts cramping," Gamble said, her head still in her hands.

Evayda was about to lay the sword on the table before remembering who would be left to babysit it. Her eyes met her friend's as Gamble flashed her a knowing smile. "Nah, man, I've already seen *this* movie." She pushed her chair in, held the sword vertically, and tucked it under her arm. "You good with my purse?"

Gamble nodded. "Maybe you can find someone with a sewing kit or something."

Evayda blew her a kiss. Her famous last words, "I'll be right back" floated through the air as she hit the double doors with her hip.

Evayda Subpoena
Chapter 22

OCTOBER 28, 2022, FRIDAY

The slam and *click* of the door behind Evayda sent an abrupt shock wave down the long hallway. She looked left and right, trying to decide which way would lead her outside or at least to a bathroom. To her left, a dark and ominous hall with flickering lightbulbs. To her right, a well-lit hallway with clear signage and a few vending machines.

"Mmmm-hmmm," she said to herself, opting for the safer bet of the two in this liminal space. Her heels clicked on the linoleum as she passed the vending machines, pondering if she should go back for her purse. The clicks that echoed up ahead had her head swiveling toward the signs saying *Backstage* and *Utilities*.

She continued down the hall, hearing the clicking again and what sounded like whirring. She glanced behind her cautiously before she entered the utility room door. She pulled it and was immediately greeted with a curious noise. A noise she knew, genetically speaking, she had no reason to investigate. As much as she wanted to avoid the taps, they were coming from the same direction as the bright green *EXIT* sign. She braced herself and walked down the new set of thin hallways. Huffing toward the exit, a figure appeared crouched in the entryway.

"Oooh, bitch!" Evayda yelled, as she grabbed her chest, sending her cumbersome sword down to the ground. The stagehand squatting down in the doorway almost toppled over herself.

The mousy girl with her ponytail sticking out of her ball cap caught her breath and laughed. "Shit, I didn't even hear you!" She tried to push herself up, but her legs seemed to have fallen asleep, so Evayda offered her hand. She was raised right, after all. "Are people here already? They were supposed to walkie me," she said, testing the lock on the exit door. Daylight was sliding in through the small gap where her foot held the door open.

"Not yet. They said we still got an hour or so. I just wanted to catch a breather." Evayda attempted to kneel down to grab her sword. "It's stuffy as hell in that auditorium."

The stagehand stared at the sword in Evayda's hand. "Just a prop, luv," she said sweetly with a forced smile.

"You had me worried there for a second!" The saccharin-sweet stagehand (who Evayda named Sally) laughed. "Okay, good. Yeah, I just fixed it. The lock wasn't catching for some reason. Just be careful if you go out; it'll lock on you and they need me up front, so you'll be on your own."

"I'm good, baby, go ahead," Evayda said, letting her pass as she held the door open. The cool air on the nape of her neck was all she wanted. "Remind me not to wear double layers of leather to a pageant again." They both laughed.

"You look amazing, though!" Stagehand Sally offered, not seeming interested in heading back so fast. "*Kill Bill*, right?"

"You know it!" Evayda beamed.

Stagehand Sally's radio went off. It was a blend of mumbles and static. "Yup, I'll be right there," she said into the mic before grabbing the bucket of tools she had by her feet. "Well good luck, or break a leg, I should say."

Evayda was shaking the back of her leather jacket in order to get some air circulation up there. "Thank you, doll!" They parted. Evayda watched Stagehand Sally get halfway down the hallway before she asked, "Oh, and which way is the little girls' room?"

"Down this hallway, back the way you came. Just to the right." Stagehand Sally pointed. "If you get to sheets of drywall, you went too far. They're still renovating part of the basement, so be careful."

"Thanks again, luv!" Evayda yelled back, shaking her wig back in place in the breeze.

Alone again, Evayda got an uneasy feeling in the pit of her stomach. Being in the drag scene as long as she had, you don't get many moments of silence. This silence felt different, though. This silence felt weighted and ominous. She let the door close softly and heard it *click* as she followed Sally's directions to wherever the bathroom was. She took a right and walked into a pretty large space that looked like it was some kind of old-fashioned reception area. Vintage painted windows in a basement seemed odd, but so did counters and unplugged vending machines. This hotel was over one hundred years old, what else did they have to do back then?

Past one of the dim vending machines, she saw doors marked *Ladies* and *Gentlemen*. The pungent stink of moldy basement hit her nostrils, making her crinkle her nose and hold her breath. The smell instantly flashed her to her grandma's house when the basement flooded one summer. Evayda got stuck holding the aerator tool against the wall while her brothers took turns trying not to kill her with the mallet in an effort to get rid of the mold behind the basement walls.

That explains all of the drywall pieces lining the hallway just past the bathrooms. She noted the holes where the trim molding should be as she passed them and the aerator tool/mallet that was in the corner with the other dusty-looking tools. She pushed the bathroom door open with her elbow, appreciative that she never had to go through that shit again. Not her gay ass.

She set her sword on the sink in the musty bathroom and daintily shuffled toward the only urinal without a garbage bag on it. The commotion going on in the auditorium was the last thing on her mind, she was busy trying her damndest to figure out how to roll her pantyhose down with acrylics on.

Gamble's anxiety was ramping up the longer she sat in the buzzing auditorium. Suzee's shrill voice was carving new channels into Gamble's brain. The cacophony of hisses and nuh-uhs was salt in the open wound. Her neck felt less strained as she rolled her shoulders and looked around for Evayda. She stood to stretch her legs and grabbed Evayda's purse. As she walked toward the double doors she was sure Evayda had disappeared into, a disturbance arose from the auditorium entrance area. Gamble was halfway through the door, unsure if this was the right time to be nosy.

Seeing a uniformed cop corralling Suzee sent her stumbling into the ominous corridor. Gamble grabbed the handle of the door, allowing it to close softly and hopefully not attract any attention. Her headdress obstructed her from placing her ear directly against the door, but she would be able to hear if anyone was following her.

As she continued to listen, bits of the shouted hysterics registered in her frazzled brain. A commotion of disembodied gay voices. *Again*. In less than a twenty-four hour period. *How droll.*

"Bitch, move! Bitch, I'm recording all this! Fucking pigs!"

"Don't worry, Miss Suzee, we won't let them hurt you."

"Oh, honey, I'm going to be on your asses like hot pants!"

"She's an event coordinator, of course she would be wherever all the victims were!"

Gamble wanted to know more but also didn't want to get involved with the police whatsoever. Of all the scenarios she had played out in her head, police were never in the picture. Her mind flooded with guilt and shame, but what else was new? She continued to listen, eyeballing her surroundings.

Suzee's crying voice sliced through all the others as she wailed, "Call my lawyer! Find Evayda, we are going to sue the fuck out of the entire precinct!"

"This is bullshit! She didn't do anything!"

The commotion quieted and Gamble seemed to be safe for the moment. She stared down the hallway and took a deep breath. She had to get Evayda and run before things escalated any further.

Evayda washed her hands at the other sink and grabbed a handful of paper towels to dab her forehead and cleavage. She retrieved her phone from the jacket pocket to check the time. It sounded like people were starting to show up out there, so it was time to sparkle and get this over with. She grabbed her sword off the sink and fiddled with the strap, to no avail. The noise outside made her jump, almost dropping her phone as she tucked it back into her jacket's interior pocket. She sighed and tucked her sword. Looks like it was finally showtime.

She stepped out of the bathroom into the musty hallway, discombobulated by the view of the open space from this angle. The sound of metal scraping and movement out of the corner of her left eye caught her attention. She turned to see a figure with their back to her; a long-ass black trench coat and big-ass high-heeled boots were all she could make out.

The mystery figure seemed to be hunched over and digging through the dusty drywall tools. Evayda wasn't sure if she should be polite and say, "Hey, girl," or mind her business and keep moving. The sound and vibration of the sledgehammer thumping the linoleum didn't help her indecision. Evayda's arched eyebrows raised and her mouth went agape as the stranger stood. The rhinestones on her bright pink ski mask irradiated the dour space with dancing points of light.

"Okay, Miss Gurl." Evayda chuckled nervously, unsure what exactly the fuck was going on here, at this moment, on this day. The Queen let the sledgehammer drag behind her, visually sizing up her opponent.

"What you about to do, girl? You got you a weapon to match my samurai sword?" Evayda laughed as she saw those vibrant green eyes behind the gauche ski mask as the Queen drew nearer. "Babygirl, you know how I feel about rhinestones. You look like a damn fool. People are going to think you got a damned BeDazzler for Christmas."

Those trademark green eyes ignited and the Queen gritted her teeth as she rushed toward Evayda, who shook her head, grinned, and nonchalantly said, "If you wanna mess up your makeup, that's on y—"

The Queen stopped just short of her target, using the momentum to swing the sledgehammer in an upward strike. The hit just missed Evayda's nose; it would have made contact if she hadn't reflexively avoided the hit by leaning backwards. "Bitch!" Evayda yelled, startled by the movement of her bangs due to the close proximity of the attempted assault.

Instinctually, she shoved the Queen away from her by her overextended shoulder after the failed swing. The Queen fumbled the sledgehammer, almost toppling over before just barely catching her balance in the middle of the open space.

Evayda was already slipping her heels and jacket off in anticipation. She had time today. "Antonio, I don't know what bullshit you're on, girl, but this is some next- level shit. I don't know why you . . . changed outfits but . . . either way . . . " She unsheathed the sword and adjusted her double-handed grip on the hilt. Staring intently at the Queen, she added, "I'm going to cut you long, deep, and wide."

The Queen almost mouthed a response, but instead lunged at Evayda with her shoulder forward. Evayda responded in time, lifted the sword just enough to slice down the Queen's lower back and the bottom of her tacky trench coat. *Mama was going to have to spank her.*

To her surprise, the Queen reeled back in a tight arc, burying the head of the sledgehammer into Evayda's stunned abdomen. If Evayda's rib cage had been a xylophone, the Queen would have hit all the keys at once. The blow sent a shock wave through Evayda's body, one that cracked every rib it collided with. Her diaphragm spasmed and sucked all the air from her lungs just as the jagged edges of snapped ribs dug into the tender flesh.

Evayda let out a ghostly howl, shock and anger contorting her face as pain coursed through her body. She crumpled onto her hands and knees, surprised her gasps for air were coming up empty. The sword rattled next to her as it hit the ground. Her vision was going spotty, unable to focus on her attacker adjusting her grip on the bulky sledgehammer. Evayda's lungs finally responded to her pleas and sucked in air. The sensation caused her both immediate relief and mind-shattering pain, compounding her threatened situation.

The Queen seemed pleased with herself, this final battle going in her favor. She with the upper, gloved hand and her victim already gasping for air on the ground. The sledgehammer proved to be worth its weight in gold, but once it took flight it was a crapshoot where it would land and where it would throw the Queen if she wasn't careful after.

Barely gathering her wits and her balance, the Queen approached her downed victim once again. The Queen noted Evayda was moving closer and closer to the hallway entrance door. However, she was determined to get that troublesome sword away from Evayda so she could finish the job and claim her final prize. The sledgehammer still trailing behind her, the Queen made a beeline to the sword lying next to Evayda.

She slid in, trying to kick the sword away, but the jostling sledgehammer caused her to miss her footing and drop to one knee in order to compensate. The toppled Evayda responded immediately. Her battered lung be damned. Evayda, on hands and knees, threw her arm back and clotheslined the Queen. So hard that the sound of gristle snapping was drowned out by the Queen's gurgled yelp.

The Queen instantly dropped the sledgehammer. She wrapped her gloved hands around her neck as if the act would miraculously bring her breath back. The wooden handle reverberated on the cold linoleum as Evayda stood up and assessed her options.

Her left side was a searing stitch that had her breathing through pursed lips every time she tried to stand up straight. To go for that sledgehammer would do her ribs in if she tried to. She had no choice but to put this bitch to sleep. Her brothers had taught her how to do a mean rear naked choke that they grew to regret. Evayda cautiously stepped closer to the wheezing Queen on her knees with one hand to her neck.

Evayda's side felt like it was on fire. "Gamble, I think you've finally cracked." She wheezed. Evayda vigilantly circled the Queen with her hand out, her eyes never leaving her attacker's hands. The Queen's hacks sounded less strained as Evayda maneuvered her back toward the exit. She had to decide whether to make a run for the door or to put the Queen down once and for all.

She instinctively took one step back toward the exit, sending the Queen scrambling forward as Evayda had expected, so she switched directions and threw herself at the Queen. She swung her arm on her good side down and around the Queen's perfumed neck. The Queen tried to jerk free but was powerless to stop Evayda as she stuck to her like a prized bullfighter.

Evayda's arm slid tighter around the Queen's chin. It finally snaked around her neck, allowing her to choke the Queen out and end this once and for all. She tried to loop her other arm to the side of the Queen's head but the more she extended that arm, the more her ribs felt like they were tearing into her.

She winced in pain and gritted her teeth as she was able to hook her other arm and pull. The Queen writhed and bucked harder, but Evayda's grip stayed locked tight even though she was seeing stars in her eyes. The Queen's arms were going wobbly beneath her as the lack of oxygen was hitting her again. In a last-ditch effort, the Queen rocked to the left and thrust her elbow back into Evayda's bad side.

Evayda instantly flinched, causing some slack in her choke hold. This caused the Queen to pull back and throw two sharp elbows into Evayda's exposed sides. Evayda yowled in pain and released the Queen, pulling her arms to her sides. The Queen took advantage of the shift in weight and rolled to the left again, leaving Evayda to drop onto the floor in frustrated pain. She took whatever strength wasn't being sapped by the blinding pain and turned away from her attacker.

With Evayda on her level, the Queen crawled back toward her injured prey, throwing her leg over Evayda's hips. Evayda screamed in agitation, inching away while holding her side. She clawed at the Queen's neck and face with her other hand in order to deter her from another attack. Evayda's nails caught more mask than flesh on the Queen's taxed but piqued face, determined to achieve her final goal.

The Queen pulled her body upright, properly mounting the prostrate Evayda triumphantly. Evayda continued to bat the Queen off her, at least keeping her away from her injured ribs. The Queen's knees straddled Evayda's torso, blocking her injury for the moment. This gave Evayda the green light to gain reach and start taking shots at the Queen's face and torso.

The Queen unsuccessfully blocked most of them, taking a few body shots and growing more enraged with every hit. Her hands flew to Evayda's exposed neck, hell-bent on watching her last target's eyes go lifeless in real time. Evayda's hands climbed the Queen's arms but already felt her windpipe being clamped while she fought and bucked her hips.

The Queen continued to tighten her grip, staring into the enraged eyes of Evayda as she squeezed. The Queen's crazed glare and predacious smile promised to be her last vision if Evayda couldn't get this bitch off of her. The taste of victory was on the tip of the Queen's tongue. She salivated in anticipation watching Evayda's eyes flickering into oblivion as her grip solidified.

Evayda's heel caught traction on the slick linoleum below her writhing legs and she threw her hips up with her last bit of strength. The Queen almost flew ass over teakettle, losing her grip on Evayda's windpipe.

Evayda sucked in gasps of air, her head swimming in a turbulent ocean. The Queen repositioned on top of her, catching herself with her hands on Evayda's stupefied shoulders.

With a roar, the Queen gripped Evayda's leather-clad shoulders and pulled her close enough to smell the adrenaline pumping through her body. The Queen dug her knuckles in and slammed Evayda's body onto the linoleum. Her head rocked and whipped before cracking down on the floor. Evayda's eyes rattled in her skull, blurring her vision. The linoleum felt like shards of broken glass perforating her head and slicing down the backs of her ears. It sounded like her head was underwater. The pink sparkly face of the Queen swam closer to her blurred vision once more as Evayda's body was raised in the Queen's fists for another slam.

The hollow thud and sickening *crack* of Evayda's head striking the floor was accompanied by the sound of the interior door to the hallway bolting open. The swish and *bang* of the door echoed through the open space, interrupting the Queen's final slam. The Queen's head shot up and toward the door. A stunned look and her suffering victim still in her grips.

The sound of heels and rage escaped her lips as Gamble bolted toward the Queen in a roaring rampage. The Queen stared in shock as Gamble got close enough to *This Is Sparta* kick the Queen off her worstie in peril. The kick rocketed the Queen off Evayda and sent her careening across the slick floor.

Gamble knelt down, trying to gauge Evayda's injuries. She laid Evayda's purse down next to her. Evayda was conscious but groggy, her eyes rolling around in her head. Gamble tried to ease her up but Evayda's hand flew to her injured side instinctually. The surge of pain caused Evayda to swim back to the surface. Her eyes bugged out as she took in a deep breath. Gamble grinned and grabbed her other arm. "Can you stand up, babygirl?"

Evayda responded weakly, "Yeah, I think so but . . ." Evayda's eyes widened again as she looked around the room. "Where'd that bitch go?" Her eyes landed on the Queen, still on the ground but slowly rousing. Gamble looked in the Queen's direction, noting where she was but still trying to get Evayda on her feet. Evayda wrapped her good arm around Gamble's shoulder and attempted to stand. Gamble helped her to an upright position and looked her up and down.

"I got you. Where are you hurt?" Gamble asked, unconsciously tucking Evayda's purse under her arm.

"My ribs," Evayda hissed and squeezed her eyes tight. "And my fuckin' head, damn," she said, opening her eyes again only to notice the Queen beginning to sit up. Evayda's nostrils flared. She attempted to move toward her attacker but Gamble stood in her way. Gamble turned but kept close to her friend, shielding her from the Queen. Evayda was still holding her side and Gamble's shoulder as the Queen stood up shakily. Evayda clenched her teeth and seethed. "Watch her bitch ass, she a muthafucka."

Gamble's eyes trained on the Queen as their eyes met for the first time. Gamble blinked and her jaw quivered. "I knew it . . . No one wears Vera Wang *Princess* anymore," Gamble said, her voice and body in a state of bafflement. "I fucking knew it, but I didn't want to believe it."

"Believe what?" Evayda asked in a breathy, hoarse tone.

The Queen couldn't take her eyes off Gamble, and they continued to stay on her as she reached for her ski mask. "It's about time," the Queen said in a gravelly voice, pulling the mask up and off of her head. "This thing was really starting to stink."

Angelica coughed and tried to clear her throat. Gamble's mother stared adoringly at her son/daughter, in awe at how beautiful she looked up close.

Gamble stared at this impossible vision before her. From her boots to her bodysuit, she had not aged a day, but Gamble's stare changed once she reached her neck and face. A spattering of dull scar tissue ran from her neck up and around one side of her head. Her right ear was merely a lump of melted flesh in a desert of bald patches where her luxurious black curls once lay. Angelica's lips remained pouty and intact but on her pinched cheek was a map of shiny, splotchy white scars. Gamble's eyes watered, more confused than she'd ever been in her adult life.

"Looking at you makes me forget." Angelica sighed dryly. "You're so beautiful, baby. You always were, but now you just . . . you look so much like me."

Evayda shifted behind Gamble, finally able to stand on her own, breathing normally. Gamble kept her hand in front of her, holding her friend back until she got answers. Gamble stared at her mother intently, choked with emotion. "All these years. Nothing. I thought you were dead." Anger rose in her. "I WATCHED YOU BURN TO DEATH."

The Queen cleared her throat, keeping an eye on Evayda as she spoke, "I might as well have died . . . Look at me!" she snarled.

Gamble shook her head, true sorrow in her eyes. "But I would have at least known the truth. I wouldn't have blamed myself all these years!" she yelled. "I could have had a normal life and been . . . normal."

Angelica took a step closer to them, causing Gamble to flinch and Evayda to raise her fists, admonishing her back. "You're not normal, baby, you never have been."

Evayda lurched from behind Gamble. "You burnt bitch! Who the fuck does Freddy Krueger think she's talking to?"

Gamble snorted, but tried to pass it off as a choked cry. *She wasn't lying.*

Angelica gnashed her teeth at Evayda, telepathically reminding her she could have ripped her throat out moments earlier.

"Let me finish, Big Bird," she said before her face softened, looking at Gamble again. "You were born to shine, baby. Why would you ever want to blend into a world you were born to stand out in?" She sniffled. "I realize that now. I was wrong, baby. I've watched you grow into the queen I see before me."

Gamble's face was a wash of tear-streaked makeup. Even Evayda sniffled through her stifled anger.

Angelica continued. "That's why we're going to win, baby. I made sure of it."

The blood drained from Gamble's face. The anger was gurgling in her throat again. "What are you talking about?" she asked, preparing herself for the answer.

Angelica smiled, her eyes became green pools of bubbling venom. "I did what any mother would do to make sure the rightful Queen was crowned." She beamed. "I got rid of the competition."

Evayda pushed against Gamble. "What in the *Friday the Thirteenth*?!"

Gamble inhaled, feeling her head start to swim. "You didn't, you couldn't have . . ."

Evayda pushed past Gamble's arm and screamed, "YOU CRAZY BITCH! YOU FUCKING PSYCHO!"

Angelica backed up, crouching down in a fighting position and kept her eyes trained on Evayda. "All but one," she spat. She pulled her hand out from her boot and flicked the straight razor open.

Gamble looked at the blade in horror, holding Evayda back by her jacket. "You are a monster! You always have been!"

Angelica screamed, "I did it for you! I did it for us! I did what needed to be done!" The mangled side of her face jerked, making her grit her teeth. "I deserve this. That crown is mine!" She took a step closer, the razor demanding more blood.

"Wait, Evayda, STOP," Gamble said, pulling her friend back. "The cops are here already! They grabbed Suzee but I know they're still out there." Gamble motioned for Angelica to stop. "It's all over, Mom. There is no pageant. We need to just go to the cops."

Evayda wasn't backing down, alternating her stare between her sword still on the ground and the crazed bitch with the razor. Gamble felt her lungs start to seize as her mind reeled. Her body started to shake as she watched Evayda inching closer to her sword. Gamble turned and bolted for the hall door, praying Evayda would follow her.

Her hand grabbed the handle just as Evayda dove for her sword and Angelica screamed. Gamble pushed the door open and looked back as Angelica ran at Evayda, still grabbing for her sword on the ground. Angelica leapt with her razor cocked back and ready to slice. Evayda slid on her side with her leg kicked out as she grasped the sword and swung it back toward Angelica.

At the last minute, Angelica pulled back and placed all of her weight on her elbow dropping onto Evayda's exposed knee. The crunching sound of Evayda's joint exploding inwards toward the floor was only blocked out by her screams when Angelica landed on it. Tendons hyperextended, tore, and snapped as the Queen's full weight dislocated Evayda's bones from their intended alignment.

Evayda thrashed and yelled, trying to push Angelica off her and pull her mangled leg to safety. Evayda's sword slashed a sizable chunk out of Angelica's arm, which sent the sword flying after her devastating landing. Gamble ran back in toward Evayda, not focusing on her mother. Just as Gamble was within range to grab her friend, Angelica had already swung around Evayda's back and brought her razor to her neck.

Gamble stopped in her tracks and placed her hands forward, almost dropping Evayda's purse but mindlessly catching it at the last moment.

Angelica turned Evayda's body toward Gamble and rested the razor on her throat. "No one's going anywhere," she croaked, out of breath and glancing at the blood trickling down her other arm and onto the floor.

Evayda caught her breath and groaned as the blade let a trickle of blood bead down her neck. She stared at Gamble and the door behind her but kept her hands to her sides through the pain and confusion.

"LET HER GO!" Gamble screamed. "DON'T DO THIS!"

Angelica looked glassy-eyed at Gamble, a mix of longing and anger on her disfigured face. She seemed to sway in place as her face paled. A sob and her breath caught in her throat.

Evayda sniffled and tried to momentarily calm her breathing before saying, "Antonio." She sniffled. "Gamble." Angelica jerked Evayda back and tried to readjust her grip on the blade, allowing Evayda to bellow, "Check your breath." Evayda closed her eyes and let her tears flow. Her chin quivered, knocking against Angelica's wrist.

Gamble's mind erupted as Evayda's words cut through her tormented thoughts. She dropped to her knees, shoved her hand in Evayda's purse, and screamed, "NOOOOO!"

A calm rage returned to Angelica's face as she stared at Gamble and licked her upper lip. She steadied her breathing and with her tired, weary voice, whispered into Evayda's ear, "There can only be one Queen," then shakily smiled at Gamble. She swiftly jerked her arm back, spraying Evayda's blood in a shower that coated Gamble and the floor surrounding them. A look of fulfilled satisfaction graced Angelica's crazed, disfigured face.

Gamble screamed and pulled the gun out of Evayda's purse. The first shot left a small dot in the wall between mother and son/daughter. The second shot whizzed past Angelica's stunned expression, her eyes never leaving Gamble's snarling, all-too-familiar face. The third shot flew cleanly through Angelica's shoulder and collarbone. The hole added a mist of blood to the already rusty air just before it burped globs of dark blood. The razor in her hand and Evayda dropped as she released them both.

Angelica's face never changed and her eyes never left their shared face. The only difference was the single tear that rolled down Angelica's cheek as the fourth shot rang out in the room. The intensity in Angelica's green eyes surged and immediately faltered as the hole between them tunneled into her skull. The bullet wound bloomed outwards, causing Gamble to blink as flecks of blood hit her face from the impact. Angelica wobbled and slumped back, landing with a slap as she dropped to the ground.

Gamble Donna Phart

Chapter 23

October 28, 2022 Friday

"Coming to the stage, everyone, *Miss* Gamble Donna Phart!"

The audience cheered. A few feeble boos wafted from the ugly section.

"Ohhhh, be nice!" a lone, shrill voice rang out above the turmoil.

It was the fishy drag queen's time to shine, but the recalled screams ricocheted through her pulsating skull. A flash of the pools of gore she sloshed through to get onstage shook her reserve. The bottoms of her platform heels were still slick with blood, leaving a ruby red procession behind her. Reliving the final body landing in the pile disoriented her, causing her to stumble into the spotlight.

Like a newborn fawn, her green eyes seemed equally lost in the proverbial headlights. Stage lights gleamed off the ornate details of her bronze headdress and chest piece, creating galaxies in her vision. The lighting, combined with camera phone flashes, blinded her to anything beyond the bright, elevated stage.

Gamble's fractured mind begged the up-and-coming drag queen to peer behind her to make sure no one had followed her onstage. She willed the ruminating thoughts away, instead tightening her smile, lifting her chin, and pulling her shoulders back. She steeled her nerves and sashayed down the catwalk. The flowy white fabric from her dress and sleeves undulating around her as if she hired wind fans to blow on her at all times.

"Miss Thang is giving us Akasha realness tonight, y'all!" piped the MC. "Queen of the Daaaamned!" Gamble could feel the echo and reverb ripple through the auditorium through her blindingly white teeth.

The MC hyped, "Shots fired!"

The bronze and white on her gown looked stunning against the skin of the golden goddess. The doll babies gushed when they noticed the intricate red beaded embellishment that resembled an arterial spray on the otherwise immaculately white fabric. Those lucky enough to be nearest to the stage noticed the "beads" on her skirt began to trickle farther down the impeccably styled garment. Gamble eyed her mark at the end of the catwalk, noting the specks of blood and brain matter that flecked the stage.

She somehow maintains her smile. The little focus she has left is dissipating. She fights the urge to scan the crowd for the active threat. Try as she might, she can no longer mask the trepidation bleeding onto her captivating face. She turns to face the crowd once more and her eyes align with those of the killer. The plague behind it all, smiling back at her with that sharp, devilish grin. The scourge intent on ruining her big chance, shattering her life, sabotaging her entire drag career. Everything Gamble worked so hard for, dashed away by the one true Queen. Her entombed fury exhumed, her visage cracking into mirrored shards. Gamble's vision blurred as her neurons flickered like the stage lights above her. Her knees felt like melted wax held them in place. She crumbled, staring incredulously as the killer's grin dissolved into hysterical laughter, their hands dripping blood and impunity.

All her good Judies were dead. Gamble, forsaken, as the Queen willed it so. She watched her world dissolve as her vision skewed and her weary body crumpled to the floor. The blood collected on her shoes skidded onto the stage. Her final thought was, *You can't return scuffed shoes.* The spectators-turned-witnesses gay-gasped in horror at the realization that this wasn't part of the show. A shriek resonated backstage. The stage lights all unceremoniously flickered into darkness. The show was over. That's all, folks.

The last words Gamble heard was the MC howling, "Hes, Shes, and Theys! We've got a death drop! Death Drop!

Camera shutter *click*.

"Death Drop!"

"Hands above your head!"

Camera shutter *click*.

"Death Drop!"

"Hands above your head!"

Camera shutter *click*.

Click.

Click.

Click.

"DROP YOUR WEAPON AND PUT YOUR HANDS ABOVE YOUR HEAD NOW!" roared the burly police officer.

Gamble stared catatonically as her finger continued to mechanically click the trigger from the long-emptied clip. Her tear-streaked face awash with dried blood and bits of flesh. She remains unresponsive as the cop sidles up to her and cautiously grapples the gun away from her jerking hands.

The other officer swept the room, checked the restrooms, and stared at the bodies collapsed on top of each other. He looked away and radioed in, "Two DBs. Start an ambulance. Life Flight on standby. One female in custody in my unit. Scene secure."

The cop slid in front of Gamble, wrenching her arm down, dropping her gun on the ground, and kicked it across the room. He pulled his handcuffs out and clamped them on her wrist, staring intently into her eyes and seeing blank nothingness staring back. He steps behind her while pulling her other wrist back before cuffing it. The other officer finished radioing in the situation and stood guard in front of the murder scene.

The arresting officer led Gamble through the backstage doors. With a deadpan expression on her plasma-speckled face, Gamble shuffled forward, ahead of the cop. They trudged across the stage and headed toward the half staircase. The officer about-faced and guided Gamble down into the auditorium.

The scattering of people on their phones and workers collecting the pageant decorations gasped as they saw the procession from backstage. Phones flew out, livestreams started, and flashes from camera phones began to light up Gamble's face. Each flash stirred Gamble from her suspended consciousness. Horrified onlookers and crying pageant volunteers watched as the officer screamed at the relentless content creators intent on getting the best shot possible of this ordeal.

Gamble continued to march forward, blinking from the explosion of lights stinging her eyes. The aforementioned gaggle of gays, turned lookie-Mary-Lous were dismantling the concessions as the cop attempted to get Gamble through the lobby doors. Speaking into his walkie, the officer motioned for Gamble to pass him.

She blinked. Her sleepy emerald pupils darted to the glass case. She froze in her zombified tracks. Her body convulsed as her mind vivified while staring at the pageant crown and scepter.

Her mouth froze in a perpetual scream. Her body jerked toward the case, breaking the grip the officer had on her. She screamed and dived forward, falling roughly to her knees. She stared into her haggard reflection in the glass case. She screamed in anguish and rage. The officer tried to gain control of her again but Gamble continued to howl and cackle as she pulled the officer forward.

Gamble's mouth opened to scream, "MINE! IT'S MINE! THERE'S ONLY ONE QUEEEEN!" Her eyes crazed and mouth foaming.

One brave little poofter swooped in. He pulled the case to the other side of the table, to the relief of the other pheasants. The cop pulled Gamble up and strong-armed her toward the lobby. Gamble rocked and rolled in his grip, staring back at the monster in the reflection before finally being pushed out of the building.

"Oh my GOD!" shrieked the *final* disembodied voice as the room fell into a hushed lull. "That chiffon is ruined!"

Fade to Black

End Credits

Lights come on

MIDDLE CREDITS

IMPATIENT PEOPLE LEAVE

JUUUST A FEW
MORE CREDITS

Cue post-credit scene

Channel click.

A chipper thirtysomething bottle-blonde with helmet hair and a streaky spray tan holds a coffee cup in front of her face. *"Good Day, LA!"* The chyron below her read *Habberdashleigh McKenna - Weather*. She shows her best dead-behind-the-eyes smile, amping up the flair.

"It's a frosty seventy-three degrees out! *Brrrr*!" she said hackily, shivering and rubbing her upper arms. "Hope you brought your gloves, Beccalynntiffaneigh!"

The TV camera pans to a completely Cheez-It orange woman in a parka. The chyron below her read *Beccalynntiffaneigh Jenkins - News*. Her severe A-line haircut appeared parched, sparse with breakage, screaming for moisture. Her paper-thin lips had a 1/1200th of an inch of cherry red Wet n Wild lipstick. They scraped her glowing white veneers like steel wool on a porcelain commode.

"Oh my garsh, Hab!" she gasped, "I wish I would have put my long johns on! And speaking of long johns . . . Today in news: we have an update to the shocking drag queen pageant massacre that took place over Halloween weekend. The final missing queens' bodies have been found, bringing the official death count to twelve. One surviving sweet transvestite who was initially confirmed dead on arrival is now miraculously listed as in critical care."

She snickered and stifled herself before adding, "God just be saving anybody, I guess!"

"Bitch." Channel click.

"Today on *50/50 with Deberbrah Falters*." A campy saxophone tune plays over cheaply made Adobe graphics of a wine glass and a cat. The camera pans in on the extremely large, pulled face of the personification of the moon . . . with purple eyeshadow. Her leopard print blouse is snug in all the wrong places and damp in even worse ones.

"Drag queens: Are they all killers? Or just the ugly ones? Stay tuned while we talk to two drag queens captured in the wild and only mildly sedated."

Channel click.

"Hear ye, hear ye, m'ladies! Do you think you've got what it takes to be on the next season *of Shauntall's Slaying Dragazons*? I'm Shauntall and I'm looking for the top and bottom drag queens who want to strut their stuff on my stage in harsh lighting and even harsher HD cameras! Can you beat me at my own game? Think you can replace me? The Irreplaceable? Only those with a death wish need apply. Abandon all hope ye who enter, 'cuz this is going to be the fight of your life!

Also, stream/watch all my reality shows and buy all my things! Now available on iChoons and all other major music platforms."

The hidden character glared at the TV suspended across from her hospital bed. Wondering why it was on, who was watching it, and why she was being subjected to more torture after her extreme degree of injury.

The antiseptic smell of the hospital room stung her nostrils, almost distracting her from the immense pain that her meds barely masked. She summoned whatever strength she had and thrust her arm toward her guest sitting off to the side of her. She willed her jerking ligaments to open her hand while forcefully uttering the word "REMOTE."

An elderly hand shakily placed the remote in the former beauty's palm. The octogenarian hand needed a manicure, but the purple polish went well with her liver spots.

The figure strained in her hospital bed and clamped her fingers around the remote, willing her body to listen to her. The crackling of plastic became a sharp explosion of black shards and buttons as the pieces dropped through her pumping hand.

Suzee Ho Maker gasped, "Oh, honey,"—she turned toward her sweetie on the mend—"you coulda just asked me to cut it off."

OK NOW THE FOR
REAL-REAL CREDITS

BYEEEE

Acknowledgements

Patrick- The only healthy obsession that Dr. Phrique prescribes more of & the only editor I would ever sleep with.

My parents-

Yes, this is all your fault.

My Queen's Court-

Krustyna Klown, Frankie Doom, Scarlett Crypt, Abominatia, and Jodie Smiles (SoCal), I promise I will never kill you in future seasons!

My Beta Team (ranked by leaderboard score)-

Patrick , Paige, Jayson, Chris, and Jeff, thank you for the constructive criticism that I will totally never hold against you at a later date and for generally putting up with my shenanigans.

Thank you to everyone else who got random DMs from me at two a.m. containing screenshots of a scene, asking if they get the reference.

Thank you for all of your direction and help with my newbie questions Judith Sonnet, Rowland J. Bercy Jr., John Lynch, & A.W. Mason.

To the readers-

Thanks for taking a chance on my weird li'l bewk!

About the author

Phrique

Phrique is not a drag queen, but he could be someday. Maybe when he grows up.
I mean, have you see that jawline? Don't test him or give him any ideas because
he's actively searching for a new obsession at the moment. Especially since this
book was his debut and now he's not sure what to do with his life. Probably more
writing. Writing proved very cathartic for him, so we all win here. You, the reader,
who stopped reading a few pages back and the author, healing while maliciously
slandering kitten heels. Good news, everyone, he has more fucked-up book ideas
in his head, so stay tuned. He will need something shiny and new to hyperfixate
on before the fires start again.

He can be found escaping his responsibilities here:
@books.by.phrique on Instagram
@phrique on Twitter
Phrique on Goodreads

<u>Trigger Warnings</u>

Amputation
Blood
Bones
Bullying
Car Accident
Conversion Therapy
Death
Emesis
Emotional Abuse
Fatphobia
Fire
Gore
Gun Violence
Hallucinations
Homomisia
Homophobia
Hospitalization
Kidnapping
Mayophobia
Misgendering
Misogyny
Murder
Needles
Poisoning
Profanity
PTSD
Religious Abuse
Sexism
Slut Shaming
Stalking
Torture
Violence